HE HAS RISEN.
HE WANTS YOUR DAUGHTER.

Her mother's haunted voice echoed in Kate's mind. She tried to push the words away and listen to Will Barrett.

"Some fabulously valuable Aztec artifacts were stolen from the Science Building," he said. "A ceremonial knife, an obsidian mirror, and an ancient scroll."

"But what has this to do with my daughter?" Kate asked.

"She's a virgin," Will replied softly. "A blonde virgin. The most prized of all Aztec sacrificial victims."

Secrets, said her mother's voice. *He has powerful, evil secrets*. The words rebounded in Kate's mind. *He wants your daughter*. Finally her mind closed down, snapping like an overloaded circuit-breaker. Kate fell off the couch to the carpet, her dress rustling softly like the sound of a whispered, evil secret.

"FRANK COFFEY HAS TURNED OUT A DANDY CHILLER WITH AN ENDING THAT HAUNTED ME LONG AFTER I HAD FINISHED THE BOOK."
—Gary Brandner, author of THE HOWLING

THE
SHAMAN
FRANK COFFEY

PLAYBOY
PAPERBACKS

THE SHAMAN

Published simultaneously in the United States and Canada by Playboy Paperbacks, New York, New York. Printed in the United States of America. Library of Congress Catalog Card Number: 81-83257. Reprinted by arrangement with St. Martin's Press.

ISBN: 0-872-16947-2

First Playboy Paperbacks printing March 1982.

This book is for Allison and Wayne

This [Aztec society] is the only *example of the violent, sudden* death *of a culture. This culture did not wither away; it was not suppressed or inhibited. It was murdered in the full glory of its flowering, demolished like a sunflower wantonly beheaded by a passerby.*

OSWALD SPENGLER

Be not deceived;
God is not mocked
for whatsoever a man soweth,
that shall he also reap.

THE BIBLE
I CORINTHIANS

There are approximately 1,800,000 Aztecs *living in Mexico today. They exist in a cultural and historical vacuum; their civilization long since destroyed they are adrift and homeless, an angry, embittered people without a country.*

EVAN CHANDLER

Whatever comes around . . .
Goes around.

ANONYMOUS

Prologue

The evil is sown, but the destruction thereof is not yet come.
APOCRYPHA II

The Plain of Mexico
November, 1982

HE STOOD BEFORE the mountain called El Trono del Diablo and knew he had finally arrived. All his life had merely been preparation for what would soon begin.

For two weeks the huge Indian had walked, like a tireless machine, from Guadelero, the village in the province of Michoacán where he had spent his entire life, north to the central Mexican plain. He lived off the land as had his ancestors: sucking the meat of the cactus for moisture, eating plump white snails found beneath the bark of the stunted trees, and catching rattlesnakes and blacksnakes he surprised during their languid midday siestas. He chewed the holy datura root for endurance and clarity. Rather than diminished by his six-hundred-mile ordeal, he felt stronger and more vital than at any time in his life—invulnerable—confirmation that the voice which beckoned him possessed true power.

The Indian, who had taken the Aztec name Xipe, stared in rapture at the great mountain towering before him into the Mexican night. A primitive, powerful instinct told him his entire life had been irrevocably leading to this lonely, fearsome place.

His one eye gleamed as he gazed at El Diablo's sheer rock walls rising six thousand feet to end in a gnarled, bare summit thrust angrily at the heavens like a clenched fist.

El Diablo stood alone, hiding its secrets, shunned by the jagged range of peaks which uneasily surrounded it. Xipe too had always stood alone.

Now, at last, he would be part of something with a great purpose. A force descended from the ancients was alive, burning with a perfect hatred. The voices of his ancestors seemed to boom from El Diablo's granite rock, urging him on, promising to reveal the mysterious strength of their long dead civilization.

Under a full, blood-red moon Xipe began clambering up the great mountain. As he climbed he felt his spirit surge, slowly transforming him into something more than a mortal man.

All the loneliness he had experienced, all the anger, he now saw as a test of will. And he had passed that test. Even in his earliest years he had never needed anyone. His own mother had sensed something terrible, perhaps something evil, in her strapping son. She had never loved him. When he was a child the other village children avoided him. He'd always been different, his immense physical size and grotesque, congenital deformity setting him irrevocably apart.

The giant head had two faces: one side immobile, dominated by a deeply set greenish yellow eye that never blinked, the other hideously marred, eyeless, the skin twisted and melted like plastic exposed to flame. His mouth was crudely wide, with thick lips covering small teeth which were widely spaced and sharp like the incisors of a canine. Long, hugely muscular arms, covered with black, thick hair, dangled apishly from his massive shoulders.

A barely suppressed rage served as Xipe's emotional armament against the world. Only once had he erupted. An Anglo tourist had somehow found Guadelero and had taken his photograph. That night the Anglo was found in an arroyo, brutally beaten to death. When the Federales arrived the villagers had said nothing.

Xipe climbed steadily through the clear, windless, utterly still night. Far below on the stark, arid plain the lonely howl of a jackal sounded, then echoed against El Diablo. Xipe's excitement grew. The Dark Warrior awaited him. Quickly, surely, he climbed the remaining one hundred yards to the summit.

When he pulled himself over a last outcrop of rock he was surprised to find below him a shelf, cut perfectly into El Diablo. Three tents sat on the shelf. For all the mountain's foreboding desolation, man still had found its secrets. Shadowed boulders and scraggly sage surrounded the natural amphitheater like ancient spectators waiting with infinite patience for a new drama to unfold.

The last, a tragedy, had been played out nearly five centuries before, when seven Spanish conquistadors and their two priests had perished on the mountain whose name the Aztecs dared not speak aloud. The ignorant Spanish Christians, who at first were not afraid, later named it "The Throne of the Devil."

For Xipe it was a sacred place.

Like a pious parishioner he found a seat in the amphitheater. He was no longer impatient.

He waited, motionless, as the night passed. When the sky seeped a mauve dawn light, a storm began with the unnerving roar of a jaguar howling over freshly slaughtered prey. Xipe knew the ritual had begun. Only his part remained.

He rose like an automaton and moved through the storm. The wind screamed, whipping the tent flaps wildly and setting the camp dogs barking plaintively. Eight terrified burros, straining against their tethers, brayed into the wind. Then above the clamor a single cry rent the turbulent air, the sound so inhuman, so obscenely triumphant that even nature fell silent before its power.

Xipe crossed to a huge boulder that had hidden the tomb for five hundred years. Now thrown aside like a pebble, it revealed a black hole yawning into the earth. He lit a straw torch which flamed wildly against the gaping entrance to the tomb, then descended the steep, narrow stone stairs.

Ten minutes later he was deep in the bowels of El Diablo. At the bottom of the stairs he followed a horizontal tunnel fifty yards to a rectangular threshold, from which a flickering yellow light shone. Around the threshold, discarded like worthless refuse, lay the pieces of three ancient golden crosses which the Spanish had used to contain the evil spirits within the tomb for five centuries. Their guardianship over, they lay powerless in the sand. Xipe stepped over the pieces and through the threshold.

Damp, oily air filled the low-ceilinged chamber he entered, making it difficult to breathe. An unmistakable stench—that of burning flesh—hung thickly in the air. He took a step forward and saw a dark stain on the rough stone floor. Xipe followed the trail of blood to the body of an Indian girl, perhaps fifteen years old, lying discarded, a jagged hole cut into her once perfect chest.

Xipe's eye moved from her body to that of his Master. He lay naked on a stone pedestal dotted with spots of fresh blood. A small piece of charred flesh smouldered in a pit next to him. His body was covered with bizarre painted designs: grotesque birds and snakes wound around his chest, arms and legs; his face was painted black with a white circle around the mouth; across his torso and pubis ran thick, horizontal bands of yellow and red pigment. Beside him, like the accoutrements of a communion service, were an ancient folded parchment covered with hieroglyphics, a black obsidian mirror, and an Aztec stone dagger.

Xipe knelt in the dust beside the altar.

"Master, I have come as you commanded. Receive me as thy servant."

Xipe rose and picked up the stone dagger whose honed blade gleamed in the dancing yellow candle light like something alive. The chamber was filled with the palpable power of the ancient shamans; their power surged through him and gave him strength.

Xipe raised the dagger above his head. "I give you, O Tezcatlipoca, thy messenger," he chanted in the long dead language of his ancestors. "Return him to this earth with thy ancient power."

In one swift, extraordinarily powerful stroke Xipe drove the dagger into the center of his Master's broad chest.

The body heaved once, then was still.

BOOK ONE

Kate—and the Beginning

No matter how closely you look into the world there will always be a day side and a night side.

GOETHE

Chapter One

New York City
December, 1982

THE RINGING TELEPHONE broke brusquely into Kate Whitworth's consciousness. Her eyes snapped opened and her heart began a rapid, uncomfortable fluttering.

It rang again and Kate groaned. On the bedside table a digital clock radio announced in red numbers that it was 3:44 A.M. Ever since the terrible incident with Allison, phone calls in the middle of the night had had a terribly unnerving effect on her.

The phone rang again and Kate got up and headed for the living room. She felt a thin line of sweat slide from her armpit down her left side. The fear swimming through her made her feel awkward and slow. She bumped painfully into the corner of the piano.

The phone rang again. It seemed shrill and alarming. She reached for the phone.

"Hello."

The line was dead.

Kate felt like sobbing. She hung up, her heart beating quickly, uncomfortably. She stood very still next to the wall phone and remembered another middle-of-the-night phone call, six months ago, which carried the most frightening news of her life.

It had been from Jennifer Ley, whose daughter had invited Kate's daughter Allison to sleep over that night.

"Come over here right away," Jennifer's voice was high with fear. "Allison's taken some pills."

Kate had thrown on clothes, run six flights to the street and raced the four Village blocks to Jennifer's. She arrived with the ambulance.

She burst into Jennifer's apartment with the ambulance attendants immediately behind her. Allison was lying on her side on the tile floor of the bathroom, her head in Jennifer's lap. Kate spotted a pill bottle, cap off, on the sink.

The rest was a blurred nightmare. Desperately trying to arouse her daughter . . . a feeble fluttering of eyelids . . . the screaming ambulance ride to St. Vincent's Hospital on 11th Street . . . Allison being wheeled quickly away from her down a dim hall. Then the waiting, interminable waiting, her head pounding with whirling, incoherent thoughts.

Finally a perspiring, fatigued young intern stood before her. "She's going to be okay." . . . and then a torrent of relieved tears.

Kate held Allison's hand through the long, dismal night, searching her daughter's blank eyes for a clue to why it had happened, wiping her feverish brow, keeping her awake—dimly awake—until morning when she'd be allowed to sleep. Allison silent, still as death.

A nightmare.

The next day a psychiatrist had begun the long process of understanding which Kate and Allison both had to experience. Twelve-year-olds—like adults, Kate learned—often felt an intense sense of powerlessness over their lives; a feeling that was all too accurate in Allison's case. She wanted Mommy and Daddy back together again; and that was impossible. The result had been a suicide attempt. Such depression could, the psychiatrist warned, be a long and frustrating illness.

Six months later, and here was Kate alone again—Allison was visiting her father for a week—once more awakened by a phone call. Kate fought her immediate reaction to call Jack. Allison had been better lately, not her old self, but better.

There was no reason to assume the worst. She did not want Allison to hear the phone ring, then later find out it was her "hysterical" mother, worrying again. She did not want to embarrass herself in front of Jack. She did not want to be an alarmist.

But she knew she would call.

Then the phone rang again. Kate snatched at it, grateful that, at least, her ambivalence would be resolved.

"Kate," came an immediately familiar voice, "it's Will."

Relief flooded through her. She'd overreacted. Again. She exhaled slowly and loosened her fierce grip on the telephone receiver.

"Kate, are you there?" Will's voice was anxious.

"Yes," she said, "I'm sorry, you startled me."

"You okay?"

"Yes."

"I thought I'd better call you right away. Your stepfather's dead. He committed suicide in Mexico two days ago. I just heard."

Kate sighed. "It seems impossible," she said.

"For me, too. But he's gone. Apparently he found out he had cancer and decided not to wait for the bitter end."

"I can't even pretend to be sorry," Kate said evenly.

"That's not surprising. I can't either."

"He was a cruel man."

"Heartless, I guess one would have to say. He caused a lot of people a lot of pain." There was a pause at the end of the line and Kate heard a match struck, then a moment later a soft inhalation. "How are you?" Will's voice sounded weak and tired—old—and Kate was startled. She had known the dean of Harding College her entire life; he's always seemed eternal, immune to time.

"Okay. I've been better." She'd never been able to be anything but totally frank with Will. It was a privilege she cherished.

"How's Allison?"

"Improving. Slowly."

"Good. Give her my love. I assume you'll be up."
"Yes, I guess so."
"We'll talk then, okay?"
"Of course." Kate paused a moment. "Will?"
"Yes."
"Thanks. For everything. I'll see you soon."
"Nothing would please me more. Now go back to sleep. Old men like beautiful women hanging around them. That means plenty of beauty sleep. Got it?"
"Absolutely. It's a promise."
"Good night, Kate."
"Night." Kate hung up the phone and walked back to her bedroom. She lay down on top of the covers. He was dead. It seemed unbelievable. She closed her eyes briefly, but it was no good. A thousand memories of the man Austin Zellmer had been, and the hurt he had inflicted, kept her wide awake. Twenty minutes later she flicked on the reading light over the bed and picked up the draft of her third novel. Might as well get something productive done. There'd be no more sleep, of that she was certain.

Chapter Two

TWO DAYS AFTER hearing about her stepfather's suicide, Kate's mind was made up. She was taking Allison and going back home. Ironically, Kate realized, Austin Zellmer still exercised control over her even from the grave. If he had not killed himself, she and Allison would not be going back to Kirkton, the upstate village where she had grown up. But now, instead of despair, Kirkton represented hope. Returning was the right move, she was sure.

Joel Weltman, her literary agent, could not have disagreed more. Kate sat in his office, preparing for what promised to be a bombastic lecture.

"Are you sure about this?" Joel asked softly.

Kate was surprised at Joel's tone. Usually he was flinty, almost truculent; today he was concerned, subdued.

"As sure as I can be. Allison needs to get out of the city. I do too."

"But the city has always been what you've written about. And written about extraordinarily well." Joel held up a newspaper column encased in lucite which normally hung behind his desk. "Remember this?"

Kate smiled. Joel was going to try after all, it was just the subtle, quiet approach. "Of course."

Joel's gravelly voice began to read from *The New York Times*' review of her first novel, *Silver City*. "'A gritty, clear-eyed portrait of men and women.'" Kate tried to interrupt but Joel kept on reading. "'The freshest, most lucid voice of urban America in ten years. *Silver City* is an exhilarating work of fiction.'"

A triumphant silence followed the last sentence. The squat, short agent slouched back in his overstuffed chair and folded his arms across his chest.

Kate stifled a giggle. God but he could be a little weasel sometimes. Still, her affection for Joel could not be diminished. He had stuck by her in lean times—always grousing but always willing to advance another thousand dollars out of his pocket when things got tough. She wanted him to understand the importance of this move—for Allison especially, but for herself as well.

"Joel, I've got an excellent memory, I won't forget what the city's like. But you know perfectly well that the main reason I'm leaving is Allison. She's got to slow down, relax. The city's too demanding. The pressure's always on. I want her to move out of herself, meet people, enjoy kids her own age. I'm afraid if we stay she'll improve in some superficial ways, but that she'll retreat into herself at the same time. Internalize things. In the country people aren't so intimidating. They're warmer, more trusting. That's what she needs."

"But what about New York's culture?" Joel was probing for a soft spot. "She's gonna miss the theatre, the ballet, you know."

Kate suppressed a smile. Joel, as far as she knew, had never been to either the theatre or the ballet—an amazing accomplishment for a lifelong New Yorker. Yankee Stadium was the extent of his interest in the performing arts. "I think she'll be okay."

"But, Katie," Joel's voice was suddenly guileless, "what about the bad memories up there? Your mother still in that institution. The same house where you experienced so much unhappiness. I mean, can it be a good idea to go back into all of that?" Joel's concern for her was apparent and Kate was touched.

She chose her words carefully.

"Mother's been sick a long time. And before my father died and Mother remarried it was a wonderful place to grow up. I remember the good times. After all, Joel, I'm a grown woman. I don't believe in bad vibes. Kirkton is a beautiful, peaceful town with a college that can provide plenty of intellectual stimulation for both of us. And that's why we're going to live there."

"You're sure, right Katie?"

"As sure as I can be."

After she had promised to work hard and call in her progress each week, Joel took Kate's hand and walked her to the door of his office.

"Thanks for understanding," Kate said quietly as they waited in the hall for the elevator.

"You can thank me by delivering a blockbuster manuscript," Joel said with mock gruffness.

"Can't let your tough guy image down for a second, huh?"

"Ruin my rep," Joel said, speaking out of the side of his mouth in Cagney-gangster style. "Bad for business."

"Well, you and I both know you're lovable. We'll keep it our secret." Kate put her arms around Joel and hugged him tightly. To her surprise, he hugged her back. Kate stepped away from him as the elevator arrived and thought she saw moisture in his eyes.

"I'll talk to you soon," she said softly.

"Miss you," he said simply.

"Me too," Kate answered.

Joel smiled at that, then held up his hand. "Until that time, Katie," he said.

She stepped in the elevator. When the door slid closed tears came to her eyes, too.

That night—her last in the city that had been her home for ten years—she could not help thinking of all the changes New York had witnessed in Katherine MacRury Whitworth. Love, marriage, motherhood, professional success . . . divorce.

Manhattan had turned sour for her since the breakup. The pressure of Allison's problems. Writing had become painfully, wrenchingly difficult. Her loneliness was constant, a small insistent ache deep in her heart that even good friends could not make her forget. The city was harder and colder under such strain, more insistent in its emotional demands.

Why hadn't it worked with Jack? It was still—after almost a year—a question that haunted her constantly.

The facts were clear. The petty disagreements so frequently escalating into pitched battles. The array of hurts slowly, steadily accumulating. Then the intimacy which she'd always counted on, even in the most difficult times, beginning to dissipate, like heat escaping through a thinly cracked window. At first it was only a trickle, a trickle they both tried to ignore. Then it increased, carrying away, in small cruel gusts, all that had been right about "Kate and Jack," all the love, all the trust, from their lives. It had taken a year for Kate to realize the relationship was empty, running only on habit. Perhaps perpetuating itself, in fear of a new world of "me alone, by myself." Finally, she'd faced the inevitable: divorce; that ugly word; the American disease of the seventies.

She would carry always a vivid mental picture of the tragic divorce proceeding. The stern, dried up, old judge who unnecessarily required her to recount three specific instances—time, date, dialogue—of mental cruelty she'd suffered. She remembered answering these most intimate questions before a roomful of strangers; remembered Jack twisting in his chair, eyes darting from side to side, visibly diminishing before her eyes. It was horrible. Worse than anyone who hasn't experienced it could possibly imagine.

Their trouble had started with the publication of her first novel. Before that glorious day when Kate had breathlessly raced up to Brentano's on Fifth Avenue and had first seen *Silver City* on the shelf—realizing for the first time that she was truly a "novelist," not a typist with dreams—Jack had been supportive and patient about the demands the book made on both her time and her emotions. (Later she'd found out his patience was made easier by plenty of company.) But after publication he grew resentful, as though the favorable reviews, and, most particularly, the TV and radio interviews, were an affront to his masculine sense of self worth. It seemed to Kate now that he had *needed* her to be dependent. When she no longer was, he rejected her.

As the attention of the media waned and *Silver City* settled down to an unspectacular but quiet success, the appearance of normality returned to their relationship. But a dry rot had inexorably set in. Jack steadfastly refused to acknowledge that anything fundamental was wrong; disagreements were always glossed over, caused by "tiredness," "a bad day at the office," or "too much to drink."

Jack's resentment toward Kate found a subtle path of expression—a lavish, almost consciously manipulative amount of attention toward Allison, who reached toward this "new" Daddy as any twelve-year-old might—with an outpouring of affection. The more Jack pulled away from Kate, the more assiduously he wooed his daughter.

The divorce had been a terrible blow for Allison. Jack's sexual alliances—openly admitted—gave Kate sole custody. For Allison the next two months had been a horror of accumulating confusion, anger, and depression which culminated in the suicide attempt.

All of a sudden Kate felt very unsure about going back upstate. Back to live in a house which had such bad memories for her. Back where she was once so unwanted. She fought her anxiety. It *was* a good idea. Her stepfather was dead now. Her mother's house could once again be home.

But most important was Allison. Starting fresh—in peaceful Kirkton—could bring them together, renew their affection and love. It was a chance for both of them to be happy at long last.

Chapter Three

"Beautiful, isn't it?"

"Yeah, it is," Allison answered quietly.

Sunshine burst from a bright blue winter sky above them, glistening spectacularly off the snow-covered landscape. The road blurred under the wheels of the old red Saab, the white dividing lines flashing beneath them mesmerizingly. It was a perfect December day.

Kate glanced at Allison. Being uprooted so quickly was difficult for her. Abandoning friends, school, and the only place she'd ever lived, the apartment on Grove Street in the Village, all had been a strain. She'd been very quiet all day. But leaving the daily, hectic pressure of the city was going to be good for her. Today, though, would not be easy.

Even Ralph, their short-haired dachshund, normally tirelessly ebullient, was silent, sleeping soundly on the back seat. He'd like the country too. Manhattan was no place for a dog.

Route 17 wove gracefully through the ancient, eroded Catskills, rising and dipping in wide, smooth curves that made driving pure pleasure. Kate noted familiar towns whose names had always amused her: Roscoe, Deposit, Fishes Eddy, Downsville. When the sign announcing "Florida" came up Kate smiled instinctively, then caught herself uncomfortably.

Jack had never missed the sign. "Florida? Florida?" he would ask, his voice rising in surprise. "I knew we shouldn't have taken that left." And Kate could never help laughing. Pure silliness. How many private, silly jokes had they shared in thirteen years? Hundreds? Thousands?

It seemed a million years ago that she and Jack had shared this road as they had shared everything in life. The thought jumped into her mind, pushing aside the beauty of the rolling countryside and the steady, comfortable hum of the Saab's engine.

"What do you say about some traveling music?" Kate suggested. "Brighten us up a little." She smiled encouragingly.

Allison hesitated at first as though she might demur, then straightened her shoulders as if deciding to do something about her mood. "Okay. I've got one." The voice full of forced brightness.

Allison snapped a cassette into place, jacked the volume up and a teenaged Stevie Wonder belted through the car.

"Shoo Be-Doo-Be-Doo-Da-Day. . . . I'm Stevie Wonder, Hey-Hey-Hey."

The relentlessly upbeat rhythm set Kate's fingers tapping on the steering wheel, Allison's feet bouncing on the floorboards, and Ralph's high-pitched bark howling from the back seat.

They laughed simultaneously and the day became a little brighter.

By one P.M. they were both ravenous. The Lum's Kate remembered outside Binghamton was still there, and they gave in enthusiastically to a desire for hot dogs steamed in beer and iced mugs of root beer.

After lunch Kate picked up a scruffy couple proudly wearing the youthful uniform of backpacks, ski parkas, and patched blue jeans. They declared themselves "into" macrobiotics and meditation and acted as if they alone had discovered both. Kate was treated condescendingly, as though someone her age, someone decadent enough to own a gas-guzzling, polluting automobile, could not possibly understand what their generation as "into." With Allison, however, they spoke solemnly, as equals—which was ridiculous, she was only thirteen.

Kate suddenly felt middle-aged, and resented it. She wanted to tell her super-serious passengers that it hadn't been too long ago, just ten years in fact, that she had also been a card-carrying enemy of the government—advocating all sorts of dope-induced heretical ideas. That she, too, had eaten plenty of brown rice and bean sprouts—still did—but God, that food could get awfully boring. That's when she would decide to head for the junkiest Mexican restaurant she could find and stuff herself with tamales and enchiladas. The recollection amused her and she giggled out loud. The scruffy couple peered suspiciously at her—as though levity were no way to respond to a world full of flesh eaters and Republicans. A mile later they asked to be dropped off and Kate was relieved. She didn't need any further heaviness today, thank you.

"Why did you laugh at them?" Allison demanded. "I think you're intolerant."

"Al, don't be silly," Kate responded. Immediately she felt the fragile good feelings between them dissipate. "They were just so serious, and I had a funny thought. That's all."

"I didn't think it was very nice." Allison stared out the side window, arms folded in front of her.

"I wasn't laughing at them," Kate said trying to explain. "Just sort of remembering myself at their age. Can you understand that?"

Allison did not respond and Kate decided not to push her. Jesus, it was so easy to make a mistake.

Chapter Four

OUTSIDE OF Binghamton they exited onto Route 81, then continued north to Route 12 which led northeast to Kirkton, and to Harding College which dominated the life of the sleepy village.

Three miles outside of Kirkton, Kate caught a flash of sun reflecting off a three-hundred-foot-high water tower which rose from a complex of buildings just off the road. The "Hop Head Tower" they had called it as kids. Serving Kirkton's only industry: The Oriskany Brewery, makers of Oriskany beer—OB to all who drank it.

With a smile Kate saw that the old slogan painted in huge letters on the side of the tower still proclaimed the same message: RISK IT: ORISKANY BEER.

Kate looked more carefully at the sign. Yep, it seemed freshly painted, meaning that some traditions hadn't changed. It was still the responsibility of Kirkton High's senior class to deface that sign each year. The Brewery's chore to grumpily repaint it.

Her mind bounced back in time to a cool spring night, thirteen years gone, when she had scaled that tower with Downs Palmer, leaving a more timorous group of friends far below. They went up rung by precarious rung, climbing into the night sky, until they reached a narrow catwalk. Kate had been the only girl ever to make the dangerous climb. She still felt real pride in the accomplishment.

She and Downs had changed the sign, cleverly she thought, to read: RISK IT: A HORNY LEER.

Afterwards they had petted a little, and had watched stars beam out of a perfect black sky over the lovely Mohawk River Valley. Later, classmates had hailed them as brazen pranksters and bold lovers. (Rumor was they'd done more than pet, that they'd done IT, and she and Downs enjoyed allowing the rumor life by refusing to deny it.)

A million years ago.

They passed the Horseshoe Bar & Grill and her memory bounced back again. The "Shoe" was a gray, ramshackle frame house surrounded by dirt and muddy ruts from years of cars and pickup trucks parked haphazardly around its grounds. It had long been a hang-out for hard-drinking locals and "degenerate" college students; the two groups sharing an intense interest in cheap draft beer, kielbasa, and eight-ball pool. Kate had wheedled her way in one night at the tender age of sixteen and had ended up being sick all over the floor of the "gals" room. Downs Palmer had been along on that adventure too. He was back in Kirkton she'd heard—teaching English at Harding. She looked forward to seeing him again. What would he be like after all these years?

Past the "Shoe" it was a straight quarter mile into town. They passed the neatly tended Kirkton Presbyterian Church (where as an enthralled teenager Kate had heard William Sloane Coffin preach passionately against the Vietnam War), Blair's Funeral Home, featuring a "convenient" monuments shop right next door, and a forever nameless, dilapidated gas station, still sagging dangerously at one corner, proclaiming yet another Tire Special: Two 4 $49.95. Retreads—$14.50—no guarantee!

The village green, a lovely square filled with elms, towering oaks, and graceful spruces, was unchanged.

"Nice, huh?" Kate ventured.

"Yeah, I guess so," Allison responded sullenly.

Around the village square, across a wide cobble-stone street, were grouped most of Kirkton's stores. The clapboard shops included two bakeries, two liquor stores, a couple of decent, inexpensive restaurants catering to students and local people, and one outrageously expensive one for visiting parents—The Inn. Tobin's, an old-fashioned soda fountain, featuring the world's greatest chocolate brownies, was still alive and well, now joined on either side by a pizza parlor and a dairy store. Two massive, stone banks stood at opposite ends of the square, facing one another in dignified competition. Kirkton's police headquarters and post office shared the only other non-clapboard building, a squat two-story brick structure, now adorned with a thirty-foot blue spruce Christmas tree blinking beatifically over the snowy square.

Kirkton's sense of stability suddenly struck Kate as a painful reminder of her own instability. The thought brought her back to Allison's problems, and her own too, and a vague, undefined nervousness edged into her consciousness.

Finally, they reached the base of College Street—an extraordinarily steep, cobbled road which twisted sharply back and forth, like a boat tacking into the wind, to the top of the hill where the college sat perched like a lonely muse, surveying the Mohawk Valley for miles in all directions.

At the hill's first sharp bend, Kate shifted down into third, then quickly into second, and lugged the car up the steep incline. College Street was tricky to navigate in normal weather, dangerous on rainy days, treacherous with snow. (Kate remembered Professor Mattingly of the Greek Department—a brilliant, eccentric scholar—who claimed never to have driven up or down that "damnable hill," choosing instead to descend the back way, a leisurely incline which added a full ten miles to the two-mile journey into the village. She smiled, picturing a big, black, Lincoln Continental creeping slowly through campus, Professor Mattingly hunched over the wheel in a posture of quivering alertness as though he were Mario Andretti driving a particularly perilous Grand Prix course.)

Churning slowly up the hill, they passed eight fraternity houses, huge old structures of clapboard and stone, which bore an everpresent look of conscientious neglect. During holidays and summer vacations the frat houses' solitude had always seemed sinister, as though the empty structures, angry at being abandoned, wanted to reach out and seize strollers who dared walk by. As a girl Kate always tried to walk calmly by the fearful, empty houses—and always failed: racing breathlessly past them instead, her thin legs flashing beneath her skirt, her heart pounding with a child's horrific dread of the unknown.

Their occupants gone for the Christmas holidays, the fraternities were empty now too, and Kate's old fear tingled at the edge of her consciousness. The frats oozed the ominous silence that seems to possess all large, empty houses.

Kate's mind bounced to King House, a huge, deserted mansion outside Kirkton which had been, in her childhood, the town's haunted house. On a dare she had once entered it. Its acrid, dead smells immediately revolted her and a sharp noise from upstairs had sent her fleeing home to her father's arms. She'd never gone anywhere near the King house again.

Goose bumps broke out on her arms as she remembered the incident and Kate chided herself silently. (Oh, *come on!*)

Just below the crest of the hill the campus began, its buildings all constructed of the same Oneida dolomite, a pale, tan stone laced with lines of pink feldspar and opaque quartz. The dormitories, classrooms, library, theatre, even the gym, were all made of the stone—done in the same style: a neo-classic design emphasizing pillars, heavy, solid walls, wide, old fashioned windows, and slate roofs steeply sloped to reject mountains of snow which fell each winter. It was a picture-perfect campus, every dreamy-eyed high school student's conception of what a "college" ought to look like.

After her father died her mother had quickly remarried, and the house where she lived had ceased being a real home. But the campus was a place of warmth: as a kid she had no trouble finding playmates, either other campus brats, or the students themselves, who were willing either to play catch, or hide and seek, or build a snowman; later, as she got older, they were willing to indulge a teenager with "serious" talk, or maybe allow her to stretch her wings and flirt a little. It was a perfect place to grow up. Except for that final year.

Her mother's precipitous decline began with periods of inexplicable silence, followed by melancholy, tears, and inevitably alcohol. Always her stepfather was at her mother's side, solicitous, displaying a patience that Kate later realized was merely coldness. It had been him, Kate was sure, somehow it had been him. He caused the breakdown, though how Kate would never know.

A week after her mother had the final breakdown and disappeared into a sanitarium, Kate left home, fleeing to New York City, not knowing what to do, only knowing she could not stay and live with a stepfather who so obviously cared nothing for her.

Now she was coming back home. To a home that for sixteen years had been a place of warmth and happiness, and then had become a nightmare.

Chapter Five

KATE PULLED THE Saab into a driveway marked with a sign declaring: A.H. Zellmer. The house hadn't changed, not on the outside anyway.

The colonial stone house was built in 1825. Three stories at its highest point, additions grew from the original center as owners grew wealthier or more numerous or both. It was painted a plain flat white, with black shutters, and had been well preserved throughout the years. Much of the work had been done by Kate's father, Ernie, who loved to putter around on weekends, never quite finishing the restoration; it was the process he enjoyed.

There were fireplaces on every floor, wide-planked hardwood floors throughout, beamed ceilings in the living room and kitchen, and beautiful oriental carpets everywhere. It was a unique and lovely home which Kate had always loved.

She hesitated in the car. It was four o'clock and long shadows lay on the white-covered ground as winter cast its last pitiless light. The setting sun caught the top of a big blue spruce in the front yard which flared briefly like a torch in the gloom, then quickly died out. Suddenly the crisp, cool December day had become a frigid, winter night. Kate shivered reflexively. She felt apprehensive about going inside, as though despite her stepfather's death, she was still unwelcome in the house. That was foolish, of course. Still she hesitated, gazing warily at the house as though she expected it to make a sudden, angry grab for her.

"Mom?" Allison's voice broke her thoughts. "What are we waiting for?" Her daughter's voice was tentative, reflecting her mother's apprehension.

"It's been a long time since I've been here," Kate said, "and I guess I feel a little sentimental." She forced a cheerful tone. "Come on, let's explore."

Their footsteps echoed hollowly as they walked down the freshly shoveled front walk to the dark, silent house.

Will Barrett said he'd have a key left in the mailbox and would have someone come over to turn on the electricity, shut off when Professor Zellmer had left six months ago for yet another extended trip to Mexico.

Kate found an envelope in the mailbox with a key and a note.

> Hi. Welcome back. I've arranged
> for electricity and heat to be ready.
> Give me a call when you get settled.
> love,
> WB

She tried the door before inserting the key and to her surprise found it open. "The man who turned on the electricity must have left the door open," Kate said to Allison, who was looking warily down the hallway. "Don't forget this isn't New York. We won't have to double lock the door. Country people are more trusting, you'll like that." She patted her daughter's shoulder, as much to remind herself that she wasn't alone as to reassure Allison. It was quite simple: the house made her uneasy.

Kate stepped into a slate-floored foyer, Allison behind her. She tried a light switch which didn't work, and sent Allison back to the car for a flashlight. Kate walked carefully down the dark, almost unfamiliar hallway and tried another switch which also did not work. Alone in the black, empty house the unease which had troubled her since last night began again, and she felt her pulse quicken uncomfortably. She couldn't shake the feeling that the house resented her intrusion.

Automatically she called out, "Is anyone here?" There was no answer. Kate walked further down the long front hall into the house. As her eyes began to adjust to the darkness she saw a huge, immobile human shape which seemed to be hiding at the end of the hall. Kate gasped, and stepped back. At that instant the hallway flooded with light.

"Ugh!" Allison exclaimed loudly from the foyer where she was aiming the flashlight. "Mom, what is *that?*"

Kate stared at a hideous stone face sitting atop a pedestal, staring back at her from eye level. She sighed, expelling her breath in a slow, long movement. The bust's thick lips were twisted in a gruesome smile as though witnessing some perverse, evil act. God, it had frightened her for a moment. Kate placed a smile on her face and turned around toward Allison.

"It must be some kind of Aztec sculpture Professor Zellmer brought back from Mexico. Why anyone would want it in their house is beyond me."

"Me too," Allison said. "Yuck."

"This thing wasn't here when I was a kid. I wouldn't have slept a wink."

"It's disgusting."

"We'll get it out of here tomorrow."

The light outside was most completely gone now. Kate found the idea of checking the main switch and circuit breakers in the basement extremely unappealing. She knew it would be even darker down there than it was upstairs. Their voices, though unconsciously lowered, seemed to violate the silence of the house, rudely jarring its permanent solitude. A storm window somewhere deep within the house rattled faintly, stopped, then rattled again. Suddenly the house was alive with lonely sounds: the dripping of a faucet, a banging shutter, finally a creaking stair.

What next, Kate thought, rattling chains and blood curdling moans? Undaunted, her imagination jumped at each sound, embracing the house's lonely noises with frightened attention.

The stairs creaked again, more loudly.

A sickening thought embedded itself into Kate's imagination: my mind isn't playing scary tricks. We aren't alone.

Another, still louder, creak echoed from the basement.

"Mom, what's *that?*" Allison's voice vibrated with alarm.

Kate stood stock-still in the hallway, her heart beating erratically in her chest. Could someone be coming up the stairs? Someone trying to be very quiet. Or was she just being silly? Her mind playing these tricks?

The silence extended for a long time and Kate, who should have been relieved, grew more fearful. Whoever made the noises had heard them speak. Now they were trying to go undetected. Waiting until their suspicions waned. Waiting until she no longer stared with horrified fascination at the basement doorknob, hoping against hope that it would not move. Waiting until she and Allison were off guard. Vulnerable.

The doorknob slowly began to rotate.

"Run!" Kate screamed, shoving Allison toward the front door.

The basement door burst open, slamming against the wall behind it with a crack.

Kate spun and ran down the hallway. She stumbled in the dark, veered toward one side and fell over the leg of a table onto the floor. She twisted toward the basement door.

A figure of a man stood before Kate, close enough to be upon her in three steps. She pushed her legs, rubbery with fear, against the floor, futilely trying to slide down the hall.

"I warned you!" an angry voice shouted.

Kate's heart jumped at her throat, and a soft whimper escaped her lips.

Then the dark figure was upon her, grasping. The terrible moment froze for Kate into a fearful tableau of a mad man reaching for a helpless victim. Her wild pulse suddenly seemed to cease, her breathing stop. Enmeshed in an appalling limbo, she waited for the awful second when everything would begin moving again.

"Please," she cried out.

"Who's that?" The dark figure's voice was abruptly soft. He moved his arm and the hallway flooded with light.

Downs Palmer gasped. Kate MacRury was jammed deep into the far corner of the hallway. He had damn near scared her half to death. Jesus, he'd lost his temper again. Kids had gotten into the house twice during the past week, dragging mud and snow all over the place. They'd taken nothing but booze. But he had to clean up the mess just when he'd gotten the house in good shape for Kate's return. When he heard somebody above him he'd just assumed it was the kids again and had decided to creep up the stairs and throw the fear of God into the little asswipes. Jesus, when was he ever gonna learn. That temper was gonna be the end of him yet.

"Kate, it's Downs." He reached out and helped her to her feet.

The last few minutes suddenly struck Kate as totally hilarious. She started to giggle in relief and quickly was roaring with laughter. Sheepish, he hesitated, then joined in. Their laughter burst exuberantly into the night.

Outside the front door Allison's head appeared. She was holding a thoroughly cowed Ralph who was whining nervously. "Mom?" she said hesitantly.

Kate laughed even harder. Between gasps she managed to get out that it was okay, perfectly okay, that the slim, handsome man now giggling beside her was her old friend Downs . . . it was all just a misunderstanding.

Allison stared at the man who so casually had his arm around her mother's shoulder. She did not smile.

Chapter Six

FOR THE FIRST TIME in years Kate was attracted to a man again. She'd had a few dates since the divorce, but nothing close to a romance. Intellectually she'd been ready, but emotionally not at all. Thirteen years of marriage was a lot to forget.

Tonight she felt like a sixteen-year-old waiting for her first date to show up at the door.

Downs, whose unfashionably long hair, trim physique, and unlined face made him seem ten years younger than thirty-three, had gone home to shower and change. He was bringing back some food—hot Szechuan—a switch from his youth when he had considered the MacRury family refrigerator as his personal treasure chest to plunder. It had been impossible, even for her slightly formal mother, to get annoyed with him. He was too much fun to have around.

Kate was apprehensive about the evening as well as excited. They'd known each other so well, had been so close, and though just kids when they'd been friends, it would be such a disappointment if that special feeling were gone.

Three hours later Kate knew she'd had no reason to worry. Everything was so natural between them. Hardly any awkwardness. And Downs could still talk; his stories of the last ten years had kept her smiling all evening.

But Allison had reacted badly, sitting very quietly through dinner, excusing herself immediately afterwards and going straight to bed. It had been a difficult day for her, Kate knew. She'd be okay after she got more used to things.

Downs had lost none of his bright-eyed inquisitiveness. He

was intrigued by things, his curiosity unencumbered by pretentiousness. And he still had an infectious enthusiasm, a what's-in-store-for-me-today attitude which was easy to pick up on. Simply, he was fun to be around.

Downs had gone through four colleges during a span of seven years before finally getting his degree. He'd been bounced from nearby Hamilton College for violation of social probation; the incident, a naked stroll through the school's library ("I wasn't entirely naked, I had a washcloth"), had resulted in a wild campus chase involving two overweight security guards and one "unfortunately" fast state trooper.

From Hamilton he'd bounced through two other schools before finally alighting at Redlands, in California. There he had launched a wildly successful—and thoroughly illegitimate—college debating career. His secret of success was simple: he created the quotes necessary to support his position, rather than doing the "tedious, time consuming work" of researching real ones. His senior year he'd won debate after debate and reached the California State Championships. From a "well-situated spy" he found out that his opponent, convinced he'd discovered the secret of Palmer's remarkable string of successes, had decided to challenge every one of his perfectly apt quotes. For the debate Downs had "worked his ass off," thoroughly researching every quote he needed. That night a confused and chastised opponent went home with second place honors while Downs led a celebration at the college pub, drinking numerous beers to assuage his conscience.

Before finally taking a "real" job—as a reporter on a now defunct Manhattan daily newspaper—Downs had wandered the country, working as a bartender, assistant funeral director, and circus clown, among other jobs. He claimed he got the clown job by walking into the circus manager's office and performing a pratfall so realistic that he broke both a floor lamp and his right arm. The manager had laughed until tears came to his eyes, then hired him.

Downs reminded Kate of the first time either of them had gotten drunk. It was a Saturday night, and a disheveled sixteen-year-old Kate returned home, plopped into a living room chair, and in a valiant effort to hide the all too obvious effects of a six-pack of OB attempted to read the Utica Press—upside down. Her father had taken one look and barked: "What the hell have you been doing?" At that point her charade ended and an unsuccessful run for the bathroom began. At approximately the same time Downs was getting sick at his house. Her parents had called the Palmers, a big, terribly serious powwow had taken place—and they had both been grounded for a month.

Now, by ten o'clock, Kate had a warm glow on, a result of good food, good beer, good company. Especially good company. She was as relaxed and comfortable as she'd been in a long time. With Downs, Kate didn't feel guarded or wary about anything; their affection was immediate and natural.

Downs Palmer watched Kate as she tilted the bottle back and emptied the last drops of her fourth bottle of Kirin. The spicy shrimp was sweating-hot tonight, so it took lots of cold beer to kill the fire.

He grimaced as he watched her pick a curly, dark red pepper from the sauce on her plate and pop it into her mouth. Though he craved hot food, the thought of eating the little Szechuan cooking peppers was beyond his comprehension. It was like putting a dab of Ben Gay on your tongue.

Kate had eaten at least ten of the things, picking his, Allison's and her own plate clean. Her stomach must be indestructible. Or dead.

His own was very much alive. And clamoring.

"What's for dessert?" Downs took another pull on his beer.

It was Kate's turn to be incredulous. "You're kidding," she groaned. "Where do you put it all?" She looked at Downs' tight waist.

"Metabolism of a humming bird. Got any ice cream? Don't get up." Kate hadn't moved a muscle. "I know exactly where the refrigerator is."

"But you just opened a beer."

"Good with ice cream."
"God."

Downs finished a heaping bowl of Haagen-Dazs chocolate ice cream, then put a record on the stereo. The clear, soft notes of George Benson's guitar filled the room with raindrops of sound. A roaring fire cast the room in a warm, orange glow. Sporadically, eruptions of sparks shot from the dry, fragrant cedar logs to die quickly against the blackened fire screen.

Downs picked up his beer, took a swallow, and looked at Kate staring into the fire. She was slim but her body was still soft and rounded, feminine in a sort of old-fashioned way, not angular like so many women's these days. Downs discovered himself staring at the modest rise of her breasts beneath her purple turtleneck sweater. He had always been attracted to small women.

And he'd always been attracted to Kate. He'd only one affair of any importance in his life and that had ended badly over four years ago. Something beautiful was happening to him now, and he sensed Kate felt the same way. Suddenly his world seemed brighter and more optimistic than it had in years. She was a fantastic woman, just as she'd been a fantastic girl. Attractive, sensitive, opinionated, funny. In three hours Downs had fallen in love with her all over again.

Kate snuggled deeper into the overstuffed chair which had always been her father's favorite. Her feelings were moving too quickly. She couldn't help it. She was attracted to Downs in such a powerful, yet totally natural way. Exactly what was going to happen, she had no idea.

Unexpectedly, Kate felt done in by the events of the past few days. The trip full of memories of Jack. Worrying about Allison. The stupid scare in the house. She looked at Downs smiling at her. She needed some emotional support. The hell with caution.

"You know what?" she said. "I could use some hugs." It came out very naturally. As though she regularly hugged

Downs Palmer in front of a fire on cold winter nights.

His reaction seemed natural too.

"Good. So could I."

Kate's eyes filled with tears, which she blinked back unsuccessfully. "It's the marriage more than anything, Downs. Sometimes I thought I'd never be able to feel anything again. But I do."

He beckoned to her as he slid from the couch onto the rug in front of the fire.

Then she was next to him, leaning lightly against his chest. She felt his arm around her shoulders, and the shaking of her body as she cried. She tugged at him and then they were lying facing each other. He put both arms around her and she returned the embrace. Downs swung his right leg over both of hers so that they were loosely entwined. His arms went around her back and she could feel the heat of his palms through her blouse.

Then she relaxed completely, letting her body fall loose in his arms.

Occasionally he gently stroked her hair. He said nothing—for which she was grateful. The closeness was all she needed.

The silence stretched out and Kate felt suddenly uncomfortable, as if she ought to say something.

"Downs, I want to. . . ."

"Shhhh. Later. There's no hurry about anything. Let's just stay right here like this."

She smiled up at him, then closed her eyes. A moment later Kate was sound asleep.

Chapter Seven

OUTSIDE, at the edge of the woods, he stood still and silent in the lightly falling snow and watched the Zellmer house. Winter starlings, normally curious, fled from his presence, leaving the frigid night deathly quiet.

He noticed neither the night's silence nor the cold. He did

not feel the loneliness of the interminable night. He paid no heed to the thick gray-black clouds scuttling in from the north, promising still more snow by morning.

Like a godless machine he waited in perfect, unstinting, unthinking vigilance throughout the pregnant winter's night.

Chapter Eight

THE BRAND-NEW, two-story brick buildings surrounding the rolling grounds gave the appearance of a college campus. Only the bars on the windows gave its identity away. The place always unnerved Kate.

She walked through a large antiseptic waiting room to a reception desk manned by a bored girl of perhaps nineteen, who was loudly and unselfconsciously snapping her gum as she read a movie magazine.

"Excuse me," Kate said, "I'm here to visit a Mrs. Zellmer. Am I in the right building?"

The girl looked up slowly, looked down once more at John Travolta, sighed, then reluctantly closed her magazine.

"Patient's name." No pretense of manners.

"Joan Zellmer."

The girl seemed surprised to hear the name. She looked at Kate quizzically, like a cow at a vaguely annoying fly.

"Is something the matter?" Kate asked, an edge in her voice.

The gum chewing stopped and a glint of displeasure flashed in the girl's small hard eyes. "No. She don't get many visitors, that's all." The girl was obviously pleased to be delivering what she hoped would be bad news.

"I'd like to see her now." You little jerk.

The girl picked up the phone without responding and dialed. "Dr. Johann. There's a woman here to see Zellmer." The girl waited a moment, listening. "All right." She dropped the phone back in its cradle with a bang. "The doctor will be right out," she said opening the fan magazine again.

A minute later a bald heavy man with a neat mustache, sallow skin and an old-fashioned three-piece tweed suit appeared. With the curiously precise steps often used by men who are very overweight he guided Kate past the reception desk and down a long, white hall into an office whose door plate announced: Dr. Frederic Johann, Director.

"Your mother is completely and most probably permanently schizophrenic. She is still totally disassociated." He paused to light a pipe. "Sometimes the awful finality of cases such as your mother's is difficult for family members to accept. I feel it's my responsibility to warn you."

"Thank you Doctor, but this is not a new situation for me. I know quite well the seriousness of schizophrenia in adults. My mother has been sick for a long time."

Kate thought back to a time when her mother had been another person entirely. Joan MacRury had been an ideal mother, married to an ideal father. She was an extraordinarily cheerful, bright person, rarely "down" or discouraged, always available when her only child needed support or advice.

Their relationship had been a special one, unique in its honesty and mutual respect. Her mother had worked very hard at being open and frank. In many ways, they'd been like sisters.

Until Austin Zellmer began courting Joan MacRury.

It was as though Joan MacRury were somehow under his power. He was so unlike Kate's father, Ernie. Like a moth to light, Joan MacRury was fatally attracted to Professor Zellmer, and two months after Ernest MacRury died, they married.

During the courtship Professor Zellmer had treated Kate well, though something about him had always bothered her. Something cold. After the marriage, his attitude changed dramatically. He no longer attempted to show concern or tenderness; he treated Kate like an annoyance he was loathe to suffer.

A short time later an ugly problem arose for the first time. Joan MacRury, now Zellmer, started to drink. The dimensions of the problem slowly began to grow more and more serious. Soon she was drinking heavily and often. And when Joan Zellmer drank she was often angry. From a person whose lighthearted humor had been over the years a consistently wonderful trait, it was so unexpected. And so terribly painful.

Especially for Kate, who more and more became the target, the "enemy" during her mother's drinking sprees. Just how much Austin Zellmer had been behind those attacks, Kate could never be sure. That didn't stop her from hating him. Somehow, it had been him. It had to be.

The indelible memory of her last trip with her mother to Westmoreland Psychiatric Hospital flashed painfully before Kate's eyes. Her stepfather had talked to Joan the entire half-hour, his voice low, lulling and cruelly pedantic; repeating over and over that she would have to "work on her problems," to "bear down," to "stop feeling sorry for herself," if she ever wanted to get better.

Her mother's response had been a quiet flood of tears which would not stop. Tears which to this day—fifteen years later—Kate knew must still be flowing unabated deep inside her.

When Kate had gotten back into the car with her stepfather after leaving her mother she simply said: "I'm leaving."

And Austin Zellmer had smiled.

"Mrs. Whitworth?" The voice floated softly into her consciousness and Kate snapped back to Dr. Johann's office. "Would you like to see your mother now?"

"Yes, thanks." Now the anxiety struck her. It had been two years since her last visit when her mother had sat totally unresponsive to her questions, talking in half-sentences to herself, completely wrapped up in a nether world of madness. It had been an awful experience. She was not merely ignored, but completely unrecognized. Now the hurtful memory of that last visit was with her again.

At the open door to her mother's room Kate stopped. She looked in. It was pathetic, really. Her mother looked so thin and haggard, much older than fifty-six. She wore a faded pink gown which hung loosely on her body, and an old pair of slippers which only half held her feet. Kate watched her pick up a comb and with a shaky hand begin combing her thin, frizzy hair, each strand stubbornly resistant to the pathetic attempt at order. Her mother ran the comb through her hair twice, then with a gesture that could have been a shrug, gave up her half-hearted grooming efforts. Kate wanted to cry.

"Mrs. Zellmer," Dr. Johann said loudly, "you have a visitor."

The expression on her mother's face remained blank and uncomprehending. Then the expression seemed to change. Her jaw began to work, and her brow furrowed, as if struggling to remember.

Kate looked over at Dr. Johann. His face registered surprise.

Then Joan Zellmer stood up and faced the doctor. The war of emotions across her face abated, and a look of understanding appeared. In a clear, unslurred voice, a voice familiar from a thousand years ago, Joan Zellmer asked: "Who's there? Please, who's there?"

Kate was confused, Dr. Johann stunned.

Kate stepped through the doorway, not knowing what to expect. "It's me, Mother. It's Kate." It was probably futile. There was no reason to hope. Still. . . .

Her mother's hands began clenching and unclenching, as though a struggle was going on somewhere deep within her. Her thin body twitched. Then her face began to recompose itself again, this time the features magically realigning to form what seemed like an expression of recognition.

(My God, it can't be!)

"It's Kate, Mother." Hope sneaked into her mind, and her voice broke with emotion.

(Please know me. Please.)

"Kate." Her mother spoke *to* her for the first time in fifteen interminable years. "Kate," she repeated slowly, as though testing the word's reality. Her mother's eyes filled with tears, which slowly fell down her face.

Kate ran to her mother, enveloping her frail body in her arms, hugging her tightly, trying to obliterate the years of blackness with an outpouring of love.

"Oh God. Mother. Thank God you know me." The words poured out from a reservoir of hope long denied. Crying, Kate gently stroked her mother's thin hair. She could feel sobs rack her mother's body. Kate found it almost impossible to speak again, as though verbalizing her feelings would break the magic spell, puncturing this wondrous bubble of new-found life.

Joan Zellmer spoke first.

"A nightmare. . . . I've been sick for so. . . . I can't begin to describe what. . . ."

"It's all right now."

"The last few days a light seemed to come into my mind." The words came out haltingly. "Something's happened." Her mother suddenly gripped Kate's arm tightly. "Something's happened. Tell me."

Kate was confused. What did she mean? "Mother, you've got to go slowly because. . . ."

"Tell me!" The grip intensified and Kate saw a flash of anger in her mother's eyes. "What's happened?"

Kate looked at Dr. Johann who nodded.

"Professor Zellmer is dead."

"I knew it," her mother responded in a flat, unsurprised voice. "I knew. How?"

Kate was terribly worried, intensely aware that the conversation was skirting an area that had to be dangerous for her mother. But she had no choice.

"He committed suicide."

"Three days ago."

Kate nodded her head dumbly. (What's going on?)

"It was him all these years. Always watching me. Knowing what I was thinking. I couldn't get away from him." The words poured from her mother in a torrent. "All these years he knew what I was thinking. I couldn't fight him. He has secrets, powerful, evil secrets. I couldn't fight him."

"Mrs. Zellmer, wouldn't it be better if . . ." Dr. Johann's authoritative voice was ignored.

"I've been waiting all these years. And I don't have to wait any longer." Suddenly a look of terrific fear crossed her face. "Do I?" she asked, her voice breaking. "He can't ever scare me again, can he?" She gripped Kate's arm tightly, desperately.

Joan Zellmer seemed to need Kate to confirm that some terrible, mysterious, crazy ordeal was over. That there was cause for hope again.

"No, he can't. Never again," Kate said quickly. She held her mother again, but doubt and fear filled her mind. What in God's name was she talking about? Was this a beginning? Or just a different kind of madness?

An hour later Kate sat in Johann's office, still shaken, confused, and desperately in need of answers. They had been joined by a bearded young clinical psychologist, Dr. Wayne Ryerson, who had been responsible for Joan Zellmer since he had arrived at the hospital a year ago. Her mother was asleep now, after receiving a mild sedative. She had asked about the funeral, and after being told it was planned for the next day had made a strenuous plea to be allowed to attend. "So I'll know," she said.

Kate was thoroughly confused. Dr. Johann was strongly opposed to the idea, describing it as "dangerous" and "unnecessarily risky." They'd seen a remarkable, almost unprecedented occurrence, there could be no denying it, but they had to go slowly, or chance a relapse.

Dr. Ryerson thought it was indeed "risky," but that it was a risk they couldn't afford not to take.

Kate was impressed by the young psychologist's sincerity, and even more impressed by his obvious compassion. There was genuine concern in his voice for her mother.

"After all," he said brushing a stubborn strand of long, dark hair from his forehead, "this is the first time she's wanted to do anything, the first thing she's ever expressed any interest in whatsoever. I don't think we ought to ignore it."

Johann winced as he listened to his young colleague, as though his compassion was an embarrassing and unprofessional display of emotion. He turned to Kate. "Of course this decision is up to you. Your mother has the right to a pass providing we do not think she would be dangerous to others, which we of course do not. However, I disagree with Dr. Ryerson. I think it would be a serious mistake."

Wayne Ryerson turned to Kate. "Mrs. Whitworth, we've got a shot now. It might not be a great shot, but it's all we've got." He stopped and looked unwaveringly into Kate's eyes, then added in a slightly softer tone, "I think we ought to take it. I know this is a horribly difficult decision. But let's face it, the profession still doesn't know very much about schizophrenia. We may not get another chance."

Kate could see little choice. "Dr. Johann, I appreciate your advice, but I think she should go to the funeral. She wants to, and that seems like the most important thing of all."

"I think this is a mistake," Johann said gently. "I hope I'm wrong."

Chapter Nine

"YOU WILL HAVE a visitor. An Indian. He is my messenger. Obey him as you would me."

Ingrid Fox reread the letter for at least the fiftieth time. She listened for a sound from the hall. He was out there. Waiting, watching, listening. Never sleeping. Never tired. Every time she met his unblinking eye she shuddered. But her lover's instructions had been plain. "Obey him as you would me." She had no choice.

Ingrid sat on the edge of her bed, his last letter in her hand. It was two A.M. For all her belief in him she feared what this night would bring.

She stood up and pulled her black nightgown over her head. She was tall, angular, with tight muscles and small firm breasts. No one had ever called Ingrid Fox pretty. Her face was dark, her eyes recessed under heavy eyebrows, her lips thin. She wore her hair pulled severely back and never applied makeup, except for a dark red lipstick which served only to make her appearance all the more forbidding.

For her entire life she had been a woman who loved other women. Until she had met him. He had saved her, given her purpose and strength. He was unbelievably powerful, unstinting in his absolute belief in himself. No self-doubts. No ambivalence. From his cold grey eyes poured a sexual magnetism which she had found irresistible. Within an hour after meeting they were in his bed. They had not made love; he had fucked her to the point of insensibility. And for five years, she had never left his side. Until his last trip, a trip he made alone.

Now they would be rejoined.

Ingrid quickly put on her heavy winter clothes and left the bedroom. She did not have to look back for the Indian. His heavy, shuffling gait told of his presence.

The old car pulled off the road to a stop two houses down from the funeral home. A flickering blue light—a television set she immediately realized—shone from a third floor window. She hadn't expected anyone to be up. It would be more difficult.

She got out of the car, waited for the Indian to come around next to her, then led the way down the snow-covered road to the funeral home's driveway. They turned in the driveway and disappeared into the shadow of the big old

Victorian house. They reappeared behind the building underneath a bright outdoor light. Steps led from a parking lot to a double-door first floor entrance. Like a black sentinel a long hearse stood in front of the entrance.

They walked around the hearse and climbed the salted steps, bright artificial light cascading garishly upon them. Her companion yanked on the door and its cheap lock snapped. They moved into the funeral home's utter stillness, found the stairs which led to the basement, then descended into a room of dank air fouled by formaldehyde and death.

Her flashlight panned the room. A long stainless steel sink lined the left wall. Floor-to-ceiling metal shelves containing cardboard boxes, plastic trays, and glass bottles of clear, blue, and yellow chemicals, filled the right wall. Aprons and towels, some blotchy with dark stains, hung from hooks on the back wall. She moved the flashlight and its beam found the naked, emaciated body of an old woman lying on a metal table. Her legs were blotchy and varicose. Two jagged incisions, closed with wide, crude stitches, crisscrossed between her limp breasts. From behind her neck, a tube led to a quart jar half full of colorless liquid hanging from a rack above.

They moved into an adjoining room. Immediately she saw his bronze coffin gleaming dully in the flashlight's beam. She noticed the padlock, and the still intact customs seal.

Her companion approached the coffin, broke the seal, then inserted a key and turned it. He seized the handles of the bronze lid, heaved, and the coffin silently opened. The woman moved next to the open coffin and with a deep breath looked down. What she saw was impossible, as if some narrow line between imagination and reality had finally been crossed.

The skin of her lover's face was now unwrinkled. The gray hair brown and full. His chest, where there should have been a terrible scar, was unmarked. Instinctively she reached out a shaking hand and touched his shoulder, then quickly pulled her hand away. His skin was cold and damp: the skin of the dead.

The Indian grunted behind her as if urging her to hurry. At that moment a loud click sounded behind them. She turned and saw a small flash of light. An instant later her mind made the connection: the furnace.

It was too late. From the Indian's twisted lips came a low inhuman snarl. He stared angrily across the room. She followed his gaze and realized it was not the flash of light which was bothering him. A large cross-shaped floral display rested on a coffin directly across the room from them. The Indian snarled again, then sprung across the room like an animal attacking a natural enemy.

"No" she cried out.

The Indian's hand smashed the cross apart and its wooden support skeleton crashed loudly to the floor.

Somewhere above them a chair scraped.

BOOK TWO
The Awakening

The boundaries which divide Life from Death are at best shadowy and vague. Who shall say where the one ends, and where the other begins?

EDGAR ALLEN POE
The Premature Burial

If a man die, shall he live again?
JOB XIV

Chapter Ten

THE LATE SHOW theme faded into a tinny rendition of the "Star-Spangled Banner," but Timmy O'Roarke didn't budge from his comfortable overstuffed chair. When a test pattern appeared on the screen he still did not move.

Feet up, eyes half closed, Timmy sat and savored the warm feeling in his ample gut that had nothing to do with the OB he was sipping. At fifty-seven years of age he had finally fallen in love. For the first time in his otherwise lousy life. Now it seemed like everything he did reminded him what a lucky man he was.

Take this movie, for example, *The African Queen*. Channel Eight must have shown it just for him. Bogart was a tough little guy, just like Timmy, rough around the edges but at heart trustworthy and true. And that classy Kate Hepburn had enough sense to realize she needed a real man like Bogart—even though he couldn't throw around a lot of fifty cent words. Last Sunday, Sally had shown him some snapshots of her wedding, and, goddamn, but she was so beautiful it took your breath away. Like a young Katharine Hepburn. He'd practically floated home that night.

Life had always dealt Timmy low cards, and though he wasn't a complaining kind of man, down deep he resented his misfortune. Now, after all those years of misery, Sally coming into his life seemed like a dream come true. After the war he'd come home so sick and tired of being lonely and scared that he up and married the first girl who smiled at him twice. That was Lillian. Hell, he'd been young and strong and the whole world was in front of him. But Lillian had turned sour. He used to tell the boys down at the "Shoe" that she had the disposition of a constipated nun. That was always good for a few laughs.

But it hadn't been much fun. Lillian gained fifty pounds in two years. She was always angry at him though he supposed she was probably really angry at herself. Some nights her hollering got so bad the neighbors would have to shut their windows in self-defense. For thirty years Timmy's life settled into a dreary routine: up and out of the house by five; breakfast at the Friendly Diner; work at the Brewery 'til 3:30 P.M.; a coupla beers at the "Shoe"; then home to face the firing squad. Course he coulda got loaded every night—and shit he wasn't no saint, he did that plenty of times—but that wouldna been any more right than Lillian's bitchin' at him. She was his wife.

Then one evening four years ago, he'd come home to find her sprawled on the floor, stone dead, a melted Hershey bar oozing out of her pudgy hand. He was surprised when he missed her at first. Rattling around alone in the big house made him feel a mite funny.

Then young Al Cranston, the funeral director, had gotten married and moved to a new house; he offered Timmy a job caretaking and generally helping out, plus Timmy could move into the apartment on the third floor of the parlor. So Timmy took early retirement from the Oriskany Brewery and was getting along just fine. Even saved a little bit; and now for the first time in his life he could stay up as late as he wanted.

The funny thing was that the funeral business seemed to suit him. Dressed in a brand-new black suit, he attended all the wakes and funerals, lending an ear or a hand or a shoulder when the time was right. More than once Al Cranston told him he did more for business than the new carpeting and the shiny new hearse combined.

Then came the icing on the cake. Chester Hults, manager of the bookstore up on the hill, died of a heart attack. His widow, Sally, was consumed with grief, and so helpless that Timmy's heart went out to her. He ran some errands for her, picked up her younger sister at the airport in Utica before the funeral, made sure someone came in to clean her house, then got some food together for folks stopping in after the service. A month after Chester had been buried, Sally invited Timmy up to tea to thank him for his help. Somehow they'd hit it off so well he stayed right on through dinner.

One thing had led to another during the last year, and now they were talking about setting a date. When Hepburn and Bogart had finally kissed there at the end of the picture, Timmy saw him and Sally doing the same—at the altar—and his heart seemed to thump like a schoolboy's.

The buzzing of the test pattern finally broke into Timmy's reverie. Time to hit the sack. What with Professor Zellmer's funeral tomorrow, he had to get up early.

Timmy hoisted himself to his feet and padded over to the TV in his slippers. He hit the knob, then was startled by a crashing noise from somewhere down stairs.

Damn, not again. Two weeks ago Opal, the funeral home's black cat, had somehow gotten into the basement and knocked over an embalming fluid stand. When Timmy arrived Opal was taking a tentative nibble at Mrs. Holcomb's toe. He'd been royally pissed off, not so much about the mess, but by bein' startled in the middle of the night so bad. The funeral home got awful quiet at night and what with the basement chuck-a-buck full of corpses sometimes even Timmy got to feelin' a little weird.

This time, of course, wasn't so bad. He was prepared. Last thing he wanted to do was lace up his shoes and go downstairs. But that's what Cranston paid him for. Opal had better skedaddle though.

A minute later, in an undershirt and green chinos with suspenders, Timmy was downstairs. He flicked on the overhead light in the hall on the first floor. Everything was in order. Had to be in the basement, just as he suspected.

Timmy paused at the bottom of the basement steps. A

strange, kind of uneasy feeling came over him. He scolded himself. God damn, but I'm getting antsy in my old age. Must have been that movie, with all those crocodiles and such. He shook his head to get Africa out of it, and turned on the fluorescent lights.

Everything looked okay. Old Mrs. Dietz's fluid was upright and dripping slowly, he was grateful to see. Christ, when Opal had tipped Mrs. Holcomb's fluid over he'd a like to died, the smell just God-awful. Timmy walked forward feeling more confident. Must have been a noise from outside.

Then he saw Professor Zellmer's casket—with the lock hanging open. That shouldn't be. His heart suddenly felt too heavy for his body. He had the urge to turn around and run up the stairs. Al could take care of the problem in the morning.

He even took a step toward the stairs before the guilt strayed across his mind. It was his job, not Al's, that's what he got paid for. He oughta check the problem out. Sally would expect that from him, too.

Timmy walked over to Professor Zellmer's coffin. For a moment he stared at the bier as though he expected it to explain the situation itself. Then he grabbed the casket's bronze handle and pulled open the half lid.

When he saw the body his heart leapt to his throat and he thought he might lose his dinner. The professor's eyes were open, staring, it seemed, directly at him. In a corner of his mind, a rational voice told him it was just the gum on the eyelids coming loose. But the eyes weren't the clouded eyes of death. They were more like death itself. Dark and compelling like a fathomless pool, they seemed to draw him.

"Get out of here," a voice inside him said. He struggled to move away from the casket, away from the power of those eyes, but his muscles were suddenly limp with terror, as heavy as lead. With enormous effort he managed to turn his head away.

For the flicker of an instant his unbelieving brain registered a huge shadow moving swiftly at him. Timmy knew something terrible was about to happen. Still he could not move.

Then a giant arm rose in front of his glazed eyes and a slow-motion, endless moment later a shattering blow crashed into the side of Timmy O'Roarke's skull.

Chapter Eleven

ALBERT CRANSTON was standing in front of the hall mirror punctiliously reknotting his tie for the third time when Hasty Malone stuck his head in the door.

"Hey Al," his burly employee said, "can ya give me a hand with the Zellmer coffin? I can't find Timmy nowhere."

"That's not like him." Cranston was surprised. "You check upstairs?"

"Yep. Maybe he's out shacking up with Sally." Hasty laughed pleasantly.

"If he is, more power to him," Cranston said as he put on his black topcoat. "But if he isn't back by noon I'm gonna wring his skinny Mick neck. There's a viewing of Mrs. Dietz this afternoon and Timmy's a wonder with those old ladies."

"Timmy'll be back," Hasty said as they walked down the stairs to the basement. "He takes to mourning like a hen takes to layin'." Hasty laughed again. Timmy was his best friend in the world. Even when he wasn't around Hasty liked to kid him.

"He's got a gift for comforting the bereaved," Cranston said as he and Hasty slid the heavy bronze coffin onto a metal car. "Guess living with that wife of his he had to learn how to comfort himself. Man who could survive that could live through anything."

"Ain't it the truth," answered Hasty, "Timmy's got the patience of a saint."

The two men wheeled the coffin into the next room, then up a ramp to the funeral home's back entrance.

In Timmy's mind he was a child, rocking in his Grandma's arms on the front porch of her old house. He could hear her high, thin voice singing, "tura lura lura, tura lura li." It was warm and safe in her arms, the gentle back and forth motion lulling him to sleep.

But when he opened his eyes the total blackness remained. It was hard to breathe. Where was he? What had happened? He remembered the huge shadow moving at him, nothing more—but the pain.

His hands and legs were bound; even with the greatest effort he could only move them slightly. His mind drifted toward some horrible truth. He tried to call out, but his mouth wouldn't open.

He felt more movement, and he knew he was being lifted. The upward motion continued for a few seconds, then stopped. Then his encapsulated world dropped sickeningly, like an elevator plummeting down a dark shaft. The landing was a hard jolt. A jagged pain flashed through his mind like lightning through a black sky and unconsciousness grabbed him again.

Chapter Twelve

The Plain of Mexico

THE TALL, lean man could not shake a nagging feeling of nervousness. Though it was past midnight, and he had put in a full day at the dig, still he could not sleep.

At seventy-two, he found sleep an elusive pleasure. Tonight he did not feel like reading, so instead he walked the flat, sandy plain stretching interminably in all directions.

Occasionally a coyote would howl in the night, but otherwise he was deep in the deathly stillness of the Mexican night. The plain he walked had once been described—charitably, he thought with a humorless smile—as inhospitable. Even that description was an understatement.

Why the Aztecs had chosen such a place to build and live was a question he did not think he would ever satisfactorily answer. Perhaps because their astrological beliefs governed so much of their lives they felt it necessary to live high on the plain, as close to the gleaming vault of the night sky as possible. But even that was not close enough.

Belkonsky stared at the huge pyramid whose steep steps seemed to climb endlessly into the dark heavens. Twenty full stories they rose; a height which defied all logic. The Aztecs had neither iron, nor the wheel, nor even the plow. Compared to the ancient Egyptians they were technological primitives. But in 200 B.C. they began this temple and completed it seven hundred years later; how they managed such an enormous and majestic feat baffled modern science. It seemed, simply, impossible. Yet it had been done.

Belkonsky's eyes caught the gleaming obsidian teeth of the massive, grinning serpent heads which flanked the pyramid's steep granite steps. He shuddered slightly at the macabre smiles, but continued to stare, like a moviegoer watching a gruesome horror film from which he cannot tear his eyes. Past those awful heads, and up steps now marred with mesquite and sagebrush, hundreds of thousands of young men had climbed complacently to their deaths. They had waited patiently for hours under the torturous Mexican sun, lined up in neat rows on the broad plaza called the Avenue of the Dead; captives of war serenely ready for the final journey of their lives up the steps of the Temple of the Sun. Once on top of the Temple, two hundred feet high, they would lie on narrow sacrificial tables without restraints; fearless in the belief that they would now ascend to a kingdom of greater splendor; a kingdom where they would be forever honored by the dreaded Tezcatlipoca, the Lord of Darkness. The

Aztec Devil. A priest would howl incantations to the awful god, then seize a stone dagger, stained black with the blood of thousands, raise it high above his unquivering victim and plunge it downward. . . .

Belkonsky caught himself. Morbid. But tonight he could not help himself. The older he grew the more closely he felt tied to the societies he had spent so much time studying; societies—particularly the Aztec—which were arguably the most unrelievedly gruesome in the entire horrid record of human history. As a Christian he felt that being so close to such monstrous evil made his own faith stronger, deeper. But tonight, for the first time, his flights of imagination into the ancient culture had truly scared him.

Something was wrong, he could feel it.

A strange sense of regression took hold, as though he were thrown back in time; now he was a primitive man in whom a sudden cold, dark, inexplicable fear was growing. Unreasoning, unconsidered—just alive. From some subconscious, vestigial mental cave, long sealed by training and education and logic, he felt a sense of doom slowly crawling into his consciousness. He stood mesmerized by his own dread in front of the huge serpent heads, unsuccessfully fighting off the relentless thought that the impending tragedy he felt in the air would somehow seek him out—and destroy him.

Later, near dawn, he fell to his knees and prayed to his Christian God that the prophecy of tragedy which had haunted him throughout this sleepless night would not come to pass.

He was too old to feel such fear.

Chapter Thirteen

DEAN WILL BARRETT stood in the snow, his gloved hands thrust deep in the pockets of his greatcoat. His face was a deeper red than usual from the bitter December day.

"Jesus H. Christ," he mumbled under his breath as he shifted his weight from one foot to the other in a futile attempt to keep his toes from freezing. He hoped to hell that the hearse arrived soon, so the service would end before the leaden sky began delivering the twelve new inches of snow that prissy TV weatherman had so gleefully predicted.

Will looked around at the couple dozen people who had congregated in the two-hundred-year-old graveyard. He'd stood here before with most of them, mourning colleagues and friends. But it wasn't grief he read in their faces today, but thinly veiled relief. A strange maliciousness had hung around Austin Zellmer like a stubborn odor. Instinctively he was shunned. Now that he was dead the community gathered around to see his unsettling presence lowered into the ground, finally out of their lives.

Will heard a door slam and then he saw her. Joan was on Kate's arm, walking slowly up the path, her head pivoting side to side like a turtle peeking from its shell. Kate had called him with the wonderful news last night.

For ten years Will had visited Joan MacRury regularly at Westmoreland Hospital. He had never been recognized. Her face a blank nightmare, more dead than alive.

After every visit, driving home, he would recall Joan as a girl—beautiful, high-spirited, full of life—and cry for them both. He had loved her then, but she had chosen Ernest MacRury. Later when Ernie had died, Will came back and asked for her hand. But it had been too late. Somehow Zellmer had already infected her.

So much time gone. The years had ravaged her brutally. Still her eyes were alive. She put a frail hand on his forearm, smiled briefly but said nothing. Then she was gone. Will retreated into himself. A moment later the funeral service began.

Kate held her mother's hand as Reverend Wellborn began reading from the Book of Psalms:

If thou, O Lord, shouldst mark iniquities,
Lord, who could stand?
But there is forgiveness with Thee
that Thou mayest be feared.

Forgiveness, Kate repeated to herself. How could a just God forgive Austin Zellmer?

O Israel, hope in the Lord!
For with the Lord there is steadfast love.

Kate looked at Allison who stood silent and solemn beside her. She reached down to take her daughter's mittened hand, but Allison shook her head. Kate's heart sank. Sometimes it seemed her love could never bridge the distance between them.

"And now," Reverend Wellborn intoned, "please join with me in reciting the twenty-third Psalm."

As the minister's smooth baritone began, the small crowd followed along.

The Lord is my shepherd, I shall not want
He maketh me to lie down in green pastures.
He leadeth me beside the still waters,
He restoreth my soul.

Kate heard the weak, shaky voice of her mother reciting beside her. Her face was drawn, her body slightly quivering and Kate began to worry.

Yea, though I walk through the valley
of the shadow of death,
I shall fear no evil.

Kate heard her mother's voice stop with the word "evil." Her shaking became worse, like the beginning of a fit. Kate reached out and put a hand on her mother's shoulder, and whispered, "Are you okay?" There was no response.

For Thou art with me
Thy rod and Thy staff
They comfort me

"STOP! IT'S NOT HIM. IT'S NOT HIM." The shrill scream was piercingly loud in the graveyard stillness. Kate turned in horror to see her mother's face twisted into a mask of terror.

"HE'S ALIVE. ALIVE!" The shrieking voice stabbed into Kate like a dentist's drill hitting raw nerve.

Kate hugged her mother tightly. The last scream became a sob, repeated over and over and over, like a mad incantation.

Downs was suddenly by her side. Reverend Wellborn had stopped reading. The mourners stared uncomfortably at Joan Zellmer. Most had known her in another time; to see this was tragic—and somehow embarrassing as well.

"Let's get her out of here," Downs said. Kate hesitated for a moment, and he said, "Come on." Her mother screamed again.

Downs picked Joan Zellmer up and carried her back down the hill. Her pathetic cries echoed back through the still morning to the small group around the grave.

"This service is over," announced a shaken Reverend Wellborn. He motioned impatiently to two graveyard workers who quickly emerged from behind a nearby shed.

Kate stood motionless next to the grave as the heavy sound of dirt thudded onto the bronze coffin.

What happened? What in God's name happened?

She started to cry.

Chapter Fourteen

DEEP IN THE RECESSES of his mind a single eye pierced the oppressive darkness. No matter how he twisted, he could not escape its penetrating stare. Compelling his attention, drawing him irrevocably deeper and deeper into an inky horror.

Timmy was fully conscious again. This time he remembered everything.

Walking down the steps into the basement, the open coffin, and then . . . then those terrible red eyes. Then turning . . . seeing the blow coming . . . a hideous face behind it . . . then the fist blocking everything out. Slow motion, stop action, instant replay terror.

Timmy spread his fingers as widely as possible searching for a clue about his prison. He felt something smooth . . . like silk, and with an extra effort he reached a ruffled edge.

A terrible realization thrust itself upon him. He knew where he was. A coffin. He tried to call out but his mouth was covered tightly with tape. He tried to twist, to kick out at the side of his coffin. It was no good. The air seemed viscous and each breath of the stuff stabbed painfully at his lungs.

NOT ME. NOT NOW. The cry screamed silently through his brain. SALLY. PLEASEDEARGOD. SALLY.

Then he heard a metallic, scraping noise. Clumps of dirt began falling from the edge of the hole onto the top of the coffin, resounding loud and sharp in his tomb like lead raindrops. Now a deeper, more paralyzing terror seized him.

The first monstrously loud shovel full of dirt crashed directly over his face, quickly followed by another, and another, and another. A vivid picture flashed in Timmy's mind: a stiffening body—his own—lying beneath the cold ground, six feet of earth on top of him, miles of earth on all sides; the surrounding stillness so total it defied even his inflamed imagination's capacity for horror.

Soon he'd be gasping for every breath. Then a burning pain in his lungs would begin. His face would turn blue like those of the silent corpses that passed through the funeral home basement. His body would bloat with gas, distending before bursting from the incessant rotting pressure. Then the blind worms and maggots would begin; mindlessly crawling over his body, penetrating everywhere, feeding until there was nothing left but a gray skeleton.

A thunderous clap of dirt broke through his panic.

With a tremendous act of willpower he stopped his screaming mind. No! Not yet! I'm not dead yet.

There was a last chance. He might be able to move his legs. He might be able to kick. They could hear a kick. If it was loud enough.

Fueled by the energy of his terror he managed to move his knees up a few precious inches. He could snap his knees down, and his feet up . . . his toes would hit the top of the coffin. He jerked his knees up with all his might . . . and gained another inch of leverage.

Timmy sucked in his breath, concentrating completely on his knees and feet which were tensed and ready to strike. With a short powerful jerk he snapped his knees down. The toes of his shoes hit the coffin lid.

"Al, you hear something?" Hasty Malone asked. He paused above the quarter-filled grave with a shovel full of dirt.

"Hear what?" The funeral director continued to fold up the white cloth which had covered the pile of dirt beside the grave.

"I thought I . . . heard a noise . . . like a thump." Hasty's thick eyebrows twitched nervously. "Down there," he pointed into the grave.

"Jesus Christ, give me a break willya?" Albert Cranston was still highly irritated. He'd seen a lot of bad scenes at grave sites before, but nothing remotely like what had just happened. Ruined a beautiful service. "The old lady was crazy enough, don't you start."

Hasty dropped a shovel full of dirt back on the pile beside the grave, then knelt at the edge of the hole. Nothing. He listened a moment longer, and then a thin, humorless laugh rattled nervously at the top of his throat. Jesus-to-God he thought he'd heard something.

"Hasty, get up," barked Cranston.

The gravedigger sighed heavily, then stood up.

"Hasty, you gotta lay off that grain. Stuff'll kill ya. And I'll end up throwing dirt on you." Albert Cranston laughed.

Hasty did not laugh. Ever since Timmy hadn't showed up he'd been feeling kinda nervous. Just wasn't like him not to show. "Maybe I outta drink more not less." Hasty jammed his shovel into the dirt. "And lay off that dyin' shit or you can find another fuckin' gravedigger." He rammed his long-handled shovel into the dirt viciously.

Albert Cranston was surprised. Hasty never got pissed off. He stared at the muscular figure furiously throwing shovelful after shovelful of frozen dirt into the grave.

Jesus, now what's got into him?

Chapter Fifteen

"SHE SEEMED SO GOOD," Kate took another sip of brandy and felt the warmth slide down her throat and spread comfortably. Her shaking had stopped. Now she sat with Downs before a blazing fire, troubling questions nibbling at her.

"I mean I saw that Mother was paranoid, but I also saw that she *knew* she was paranoid. She had a handle on it. I'm sure."

"It must have been a precarious hold," Downs said.

"I don't think so. It was a risk, of course. But I was confident. Maybe that was my mistake. Shouldn't have allowed her to push so early. But I can't help feeling that something happened to change the way she felt."

"What do you mean?"

"I don't know. Jesus. But her paranoia centered totally on my stepfather. When he died it receded. Like magic."

"But people don't just magically recover from schizophrenia. Especially adults. It must've been an observable, steady progress, right?"

"Wrong. Dr. Ryerson said there's been no progress. Zero. Until Zellmer died. That's what's so weird. After that there were a few glimmerings. Nothing anybody took real note of until after the breakthrough when I showed up."

"That's strange," said Downs.

"I know. It doesn't make sense to anybody. But the inescapable fact, as far as I'm concerned, is that when my stepfather died my mother started to show signs of life. For the first time in thirteen years. When I showed up I must have acted like some kind of trigger. And then she did come back to life. And she knew what was going on, and what had happened in the past too. And," Kate paused, wondering how bizarre what she was about to say next was going to sound, "she knew that Professor Zellmer was dead."

"What?"

"Well, actually I told her, but it was like I was confirming what she already knew."

"But you did tell her. So you just had the feeling that she knew, right?"

"No. Because after I told her he committed suicide, she said that she knew that, and that it had happened three days ago. How could she have known?"

"Hospital employees? Doctors?"

"Definitely not, according to Dr. Ryerson. She'd had a bad spell and had to be confined alone. Only Ryerson and one nurse saw her. Ryerson didn't tell her and the nurse had no idea that Zellmer had died. So how did she know?"

"What are you saying?" Downs felt uncomfortable with the conversation. Kate was strung tight, her mind playing dangerous games.

"I'm saying that my mother knew he was dead." *But what in the world does that mean?* "And I'm also saying that she didn't seem very crazy to me. Nervous yes. Crazy no."

Downs began gently. It had to be said. "But what about now? She had a fit at the cemetery."

"I know." Kate had been following a tenuous thread of hope, but had deliberately ignored where it led: to the cemetery. To madness. There was no way to out-think that. It happened and it was . . . the thought stuck in her mind as though struggling to stay out of her consciousness . . . insane.

(Somewhere deep within her mind an idea flickered like a

birthday candle in the breeze, sputtering, nearly dying, flaming again. *What if she wasn't insane. What if he were alive?* Then the minute flame wavered, threw off a final weak, incomprehensible shadow . . . and went out.)

Downs put his arm reassuringly around Kate's waist. She looked up at him, suddenly conscious of the concern—and of something more—that she saw in his blue eyes. She reached up and stroked the back of his head, a gentle massage through his prematurely graying hair. Almost immediately his drawn features softened.

His arms tightened around her small back and he moved her to him, their bodies touching at the thigh and waist and chest. They pressed against one another more warmly. Kate leaned back from him, her head thrown slightly back, her dark, thick curly hair falling in a vertical line, the movement pressing them tightly together where heat was building most pleasurably.

Her lips parted slightly and Downs thought he'd never seen a more desirable woman; her thin, delicate neck exposed, the muscles standing tautly out, a vulnerable, accessible portrait of beauty.

As he leaned down to her, Kate realized how much she'd missed being desired. Missed the look of a man who loved and wanted her. Then they kissed and her thoughts quieted, and finally ceased altogether.

They sank to the floor wordlessly. Kate dropped her hands to his hips and caressed him, then moved around in front.

As he undressed her she whispered, "Let's be good." They made love before the fire, shyly at first, then gently building an exquisite pleasure for each other.

And it was good.

Chapter Sixteen

"YOU DUMB CUNTS," Harold Hogan said to his TV set. He pushed his heavy body out of his favorite chair in the custodian's office of Harding's science building and switched *Charlie's Angels* to the Boston Bruins hockey game on the cable.

Harold was nervous. And whenever he was nervous he sweated profusely; always had. That's why in high school everyone had called him the Pink Hippo. God, he hated that shitty nickname.

He took another pull of a Genny Cream Ale. There wasn't much longer to wait. Then everything would be different; wouldn't be any reason to be nervous anymore.

For the longest time Harold couldn't understand why when he was growing up, the other kids picked on him so mercilessly. Or why in his one year of community college he'd been a campus joke; his ponderous, rolling gait openly parodied by men and women alike. He couldn't get any dates; was never invited to parties. He just never understood it.

Now he understood. She had helped him to understand.

The world was filled with a bunch of stupid shitheads, that's why. Shitheads who had nothing better to do with their miserable, putrid, fucking lives than to be as rotten as possible to anybody they felt superior to.

Harold W. Hogan Jr. had had enough. He'd always played by the rules. Held doors open for the girls in high school who'd invariably titter as they went past him without a glance. Volunteered to be the football team's manager (he'd been cut on the very first day of practice) only to suffer endless indignities ranging from being "goosed" every time he bent down to pick up a towel, to being loudly called "Hippo" anytime the cheerleaders were within hearing distance. Gone to college only to have his professors fail him in three out of four courses he took—just 'cause they didn't like him.

All that playing by the rules had ever gotten Harold was a kick in the ass and a slap in the face. He quite simply decided that he wasn't taking any shit anymore. The final straw was being passed over for the head custodian's job—that shitfuck Stonesifer, who was the superintendent of buildings and grounds at Harding, had chosen a guy with four years less seniority. Harold coulda killed Stonesifer the day he heard.

No, he'd take none of it anymore, that was his decision.

After he'd decided that, everything was easier. He just sat back and waited. He was smart, he knew. There'd come a time, and he'd be ready. While he waited for his opportunity, Harold continued to do his job capably, drink his beer, shoot pool with the boys down at the "Shoe," call his mother once a week—and go quietly, stark raving bonkers.

Meeting her had been the opportunity he'd been waiting for. A lucky coincidence, looking back on it. (Anyway, he was pretty sure it was a coincidence, her drinking at the same bar over at New Hartford). And the drunker she got—which was pretty drunk he recalled, though he couldn't be absolutely positive since he'd had a real snootful himself—the madder she got about that fucker Zellmer and how shitty he'd treated her.

Later they'd stumbled out of the bar together and before he knew it, she was holding on to him, and then kissing him. She was older, but good looking anyway. And he wasn't in any position to be choosy. She'd pressed into him so tightly in the car he thought he'd come right in his pants, just like a kid. That woulda been awful embarrasing; luckily he calmed down. She said she was too drunk to drive and would he please drive her home. And come on in too.

Which, of course, he did. That night, with a loud groan, Harold Hogan, age thirty-two, became an ex-virgin. They'd done it two more times that night and once in the morning and he was damn happy with himself and she wasn't doing any complaining either.

The next morning, when he was devouring a huge pile of eggs, bacon, and sausage that Ingrid served him in bed, she'd come up with the idea that would allow them both to get even—and then some. It sounded a little crazy at first, but after he'd thought about it—and she'd gone down on him for the first time—it seemed really possible.

That had been the start of it; when Harold Hogan decided

to become an accomplice to a theft, a big theft, and finally make a killing. Finally show everybody what he's made of.

Now, a month later, he was ready. The sex had stopped, but he didn't really care 'cause he'd soon have enough goddamn money to buy and sell women ten times as pretty as her. Fuck it, he wasn't bitter or mad at her; if it hadn't been for her this rich new life he was about to begin wouldna been possible.

Harold opened another Genny—his fifth but that was okay, he could always hold his beer—and waited anxiously for a prearranged signal. The quiet, normally so familiar, tonight was unfamiliar, a little threatening.

A flutter of regret crossed his mind. He dismissed the thought. This one, small chance would mean a brand new life.

At precisely eleven P.M. the knock came. And Harold immediately lost his nerve. Woodenly he moved out of the custodians' room and headed toward the rear door, each heavy step requiring an act of willpower. The dim night lights made the hallways of the science building seem like eerie ancient tunnels. Finally he reached the proper door and pushed hesitantly on the horizontal lock bar. The door inched open a fraction, then suddenly was yanked open from outside. Harold, who'd been leaning forward, stumbled out into the snow.

As he fell forward a hand grabbed him at the shoulder, stopped his motion, then pushed him roughly backwards through the open door.

Harold looked up and saw a hideously ugly face inches from his own. One yellow eye stared at him as though he were an insect about to be crushed under a boot heel. The thing's nostrils flared wide like a wild, enraged animal's. The eye glared at him for a terrible moment longer, then looked away. The huge body seemed to follow the eye as though it were a leader. The giant stepped behind Ingrid as she walked in the open door.

Harold tried to swallow but couldn't. He coughed instead,

then sucked in a gulp of air like a drowning man unexpectedly bobbing back to the surface. He'd never seen anything as frightening as the terrible creature before him.

"It's all right, he won't hurt you."

Harold couldn't take his eyes from the giant who stared unwaveringly at him, fixing him to the hallway like a piece of statuary.

"I don't understand. Who is . . ." Harold pointed.

"It doesn't matter. You just listen to me and he won't hurt you." It was a new Ingrid, he now saw. Tough and decisive. Commanding.

"But . . ."

"You don't have any choice," Ingrid interrupted, "just follow my instructions and nothing will happen. Take us to the room."

Harold hesitated.

"Now," she hissed menacingly.

Harold turned and headed down the long corridor, his heavy workman's boots squeaking on the marble. As he walked he kept glancing over his shoulder. The yellow eye never left him.

Harold switched off the silent weight-sensitive laser alarm system. He unlocked the huge metal door's three locks, each bolt snapping loudly as it withdrew.

"Close the door and wait outside. We won't be long," Ingrid said.

Harold did as he was told, then leaned wearily against the metal door. He felt nothing but the oppressive stillness of the big building around him.

Fifteen minutes later a soft tap sounded. He swung open the door and they came out. Ingrid's face was tight and triumphant. The giant's single eye seemed to glow with an almost religious intensity. Harold quickly averted his gaze. He couldn't stand to look. Ingrid swung a leather bag over her shoulder. "You have done well. You will be rewarded."

"What did you take?" Harold asked.
"That's none of your business."
"When can I expect . . ."
"I told you already," Ingrid said impatiently. "You'll be called."
Ingrid turned and walked briskly down the shadowy corridor. The giant followed. When they reached an overhead light the giant turned and stared at Harold, the fixture above him surrounding his huge figure with a strange, purple light. For a long, awful moment he stared at Harold, then rounded the corner and was gone.
Harold pulled a pint of Jim Beam from his back pocket and took a long pull. The liquor hit his stomach but did nothing to stop his shaking hands. He took another pull. Oh, God, what have I done?
Harold walked toward the outside door. The fear inside him was like something alive, feeding on his guts, growing larger by the minute.

Chapter Seventeen

HE CAREFULLY LIFTED the ancient parchment and placed it beside the still body lying on the table. The room was dark save for the flickering light of a yellow candle. An obsidian mirror beside the body's head picked up the light and reflected it crazily against the rough concrete walls.
He could feel the calling within him growing more and more powerful. The sacred implements were obtained last night. The ritual was prescribed; now only the living flesh was necessary, the blood that would empower his master.
They were ready to begin.

Chapter Eighteen

PALE WINTER SUN greeted Allison when she woke. It was still early but Ralph, the fearless watchdog, would soon be clamoring for breakfast. For a second she thought it odd that Ralph hadn't already been whining at her door.

Probably developing some manners in his old age. Yeah, sure.

Manners weren't his strong suit. He was a ferocious protector of his helpless mistress. Allison giggled at the thought. Ralph was about as ferocious as the Pillsbury Dough Boy.

Her daddy had once said that if "violence is the last resort of the incompetent, Ralph must be the most competent dog that ever walked the earth." She giggled again, then stopped abruptly. Thinking about her father always made her feel bad. Like she was gonna cry. It wasn't fair. It just wasn't.

Sometimes when she thought about Ralph she remembered the day her dad had surprised her with the puppy. The day he'd moved out of the house. She'd cried and cried that day, and promised to love Ralph better than any dog was ever loved.

"That's my dream boat," her dad had said. "I know you'll love him. But you're going to have to protect him a little bit too. Dachshunds aren't fighters."

It was funny about that. Since they'd been in the country (which Allison hated . . . it was so cold and she didn't know anybody and there wasn't *anything* to do at all) Ralph had upped his growling dramatically. Maybe Dad was going to be proved wrong about Ralph. The fresh air probably brought out the hunter instinct in him.

Their first night he had growled and yipped at the back window constantly. And last night he was doing the same thing—so Allison let him out. Let him explore, get the wits scared out of him by a few swaying bushes and dark shadows, that'd cure him. But Allison had to give him credit, the mighty hunter had been out almost an hour by the time she went to bed. New bravery.

Allison yawned, stretched luxuriously, briefly considered falling back to sleep, then popped out of bed. She danced her way across the room, toes pointed, arms extended gracefully above her, spinning to a perfectly balanced stop in front of the window. She looked out and was unpleasantly surprised to see an old Mercedes in the driveway. First irritation, then anger welled inside her.

What was that car doing there? A disturbing realization imbedded itself in her mind. That was *his* car, Mr. Palmer's. She hated what she was thinking.

She dressed quickly, ripped open her bedroom door, and marched down the creaky old stairs. The guest rooms upstairs were empty and Mr. Palmer wasn't on the couch. Her mother's bedroom door was still closed.

Anger descended, engulfing her. It wasn't right. Her mother couldn't do this to her. It was unfair. Suddenly, Allison realized why her mother had come back to Kirkton—and dragged her along—using the pretense of it being "more relaxing." That was a big, shitty lie.

One angry thought begat another and another until a towering, irrational rage, like a fanned fire, seared through her. Her mother was upstairs with a man.

She tried briefly to grapple with the complexities of her mother's situation, but it was impossible. She was too upset, too threatened to think clearly. She just couldn't understand why. Her confusion and anger built, sweeping her along in a powerful emotional current. Suddenly everything seemed hopeless. Everything in her life stupid and worthless.

She thought of Ralph. At this moment it seemed like he was her only friend. The stillness of the house suddenly struck her. Where was Ralph? Without fail he joyfully greeted her—if he hadn't spent the night on the foot of her bed—when she came down for breakfast.

Allison checked the old rocking chair which Ralph had

adopted as his own. Empty. Was he still outside? Allison had reminded her mother right before she went to bed to let him in.

But of course her mother was probably *occupied* last night.

If Ralph didn't come in he could've frozen to death.

(OH NO. OH NO.)

How could her mother forget? What an awful thing to do.

Allison threw on her yellow ski parka, slipped her feet into a pair of heavy boots and headed for the garage.

Ralph would be there, she was sure, a plaintive look on his face; a quiet protest at his shabby treatment. Allison was really gonna let her mother have it this time.

But Ralph wasn't in the garage though the door was open. And there weren't any dog prints in the fresh snow.

"Ralph! Here Ralph!" Desperation raised her voice unnaturally high. "Ralph!" Her frightened cry echoed loudly in the early morning quiet.

Allison was scared.

She walked around to the back of the house. As she rounded the corner she cupped her hands to her mouth to call again.

Then she saw him.

Her call became a scream of horror.

Downs heard Allison's first call for Ralph without registering its desperate tone. He stretched and looked over at Kate whose eyes flickered open, then closed again.

She was lying on her back, her bare shoulders enticingly exposed. Her dark hair was spread out on the pillow like a halo framing her pretty, delicate features. With a smile he stared at her, then leaned down to softly kiss her shoulder. Kate murmured and a sleepy smile crossed her face.

Downs thought he noticed something odd about Allison's second call. But he was sleepy, he couldn't be sure.

He got out of bed carefully so as not to disturb Kate, then walked naked across the big bedroom to the window overlooking he backyard. He spotted Allison with her hands to her mouth. Then her hands fell to her sides, limply, without muscular control.

An instant before she screamed Downs knew something was wrong. His mouth went cottony dry like it did after a night of too much beer. His pulse quickened.

Then Allison's scream riddled the air.

Downs scanned the back yard, his eyes moving slowly as though instinctively avoiding for as long as possible the grisly sight that awaited them.

But it was unavoidable.

The small dachshund, coated with dark, frozen blood, hung from a crude wooden cross. (Later they found he wasn't hanging, but nailed.) Ralph's lower jaw was dropped open and Downs could see blackened blood and gobs of thick, frozen saliva glinting in the morning sun. His lifeless eyes, clouded with death, drooped dramatically as if in somber contemplation of some unutterably melancholy future. Around the base of the cross black drops spotted the sparkling snow like oil droplets glistening on the surface of a clear lake.

But worst of all was a hole, the size of a man's fist, dug into the dachshund's chest. Tendrils of vein and artery and muscle stuck out from the dark, empty hole. The heart to which they had been attached was gone.

Downs closed his eyes. When he opened them again everything was still there.

He snapped his eyes from the macabre body to Allison, who stood riveted in place twenty yards from the cross. Her screams had stopped. As Downs watched helplessly, she began trembling, then pitched soundlessly into the powdery new snow.

Chapter Nineteen

"I HATE YOU, I hate you, I hate you!" Allison screamed.

Downs had rushed outside and carried Allison into the

living room. By that time Kate had dressed. When Allison revived the hysterical anger had begun.

It was all Kate's fault. Downs she ignored, as though he did not exist.

"You don't care about me. You don't love me, only Daddy loves me." Allison's voice rose and fell as she gasped for air between sobs. Now it was full blast. "It's your fault Ralph's dead! How could you do it?"

"Allison, please. . . ." Kate reached out to her daughter who pulled violently away.

"Don't touch me!" she shrieked.

Downs stayed in the kitchen, afraid his presence would only provoke Allison further. What he'd just seen in the backyard seemed half real, a dim, ungraspable reality. He had no time to think about it. His one concern was Allison. She had to be calmed down. Downs picked up the phone and dialed a friend who was a doctor, quickly outlined the situation; yes, she'd come right away. Of course.

Fifteen minutes later, Dr. Healy arrived and immediately gave Allison, who was still sobbing frantically, a strong sedative. The drug took effect quickly, as usual with children; five minutes after the injection, Allison was fast asleep.

"Thanks Trisha," said Downs.

"That's okay." Dr. Healy dropped a syringe into a waste basket. "She's one very upset girl."

"With reason."

"God, that's for sure." Patricia Healy packed her bag, took a second look at the horror in the backyard, then shook her head.

"I'm so sorry Kate. If I can help don't hesitate to call."

The smile Kate attempted as a thank-you never reached her lips.

"She'll calm down and realize it's not your fault," Downs said.

"I'm not so sure." Kate's eyes were red from crying. "The psychiatrist in New York told me that sometimes in divorce cases the relationship can't ever be repaired. I'm afraid, Downs. Really afraid."

He felt helpless. And frustrated. Kate had every reason to be afraid. He wasn't going to patronize her by saying everything was going to be all right.

"What the hell is going on?" Kate said with sudden anger. Her voice was high and shaky and she was speaking rapidly.

Get it out, thought Downs.

"I brought her to the country 'cause it's peaceful. For chrissakes, I might as well let her wander around the Lower East Side on a Saturday night, for all the peace she's gotten."

Downs thought of the hopeless mess that was the Lower East Side: blaring radios . . . smashed glass . . . angry voices ringing in the night . . . ominous shadows in lonely doorways. Perhaps you couldn't get away anywhere. Perhaps America, or the dream of what America was supposed to be, was coming apart at the seams: a vulgar, titillating, dissolute havoc in the cities; a subtle, insinuating, fearful madness in the country. Both deadly: fire or ice.

No, he didn't believe that. Wouldn't believe it. He had no idea why that cross with its unholy burden was standing obscenely in the backyard. Or who in God's name would ever do such a thing. But he was going to find out.

He looked over at Kate. I love you, he thought, I really truly do.

The rush of feeling he had for Kate was sudden and overwhelming.

Kate looked up from the couch and sensed his emotion. (Amidst such ugliness he had happened. God, she was lucky.)

"I love you," Downs said.

She came into his arms and they embraced desperately. "It's going to be all right," Downs heard himself saying. "It has to be."

With all her heart Kate wanted to believe him.

Chapter Twenty

THE THOUGHT of meeting Ingrid in the graveyard flashed uncomfortably in Harold Hogan's head. He'd always been not exactly scared but sorta uneasy in cemeteries, and he wondered again why the fuck it was necessary to meet there.

Of course he couldn't admit his uneasiness to her. What was he gonna say: "I'm afraid of graveyards at night. And I'm also afraid of black cats, zombies, and sleeping without a night light?" No fucking way. He'd pick up his money, then hit the road. Start new. Not even tell his mother where he was going, at least not right away. It was gonna be the best Christmas of his life.

Still he couldn't shake his nervousness. He hated those fucking creepy graveyards.

Exactly two hours later (Harold prided himself on being punctual) he pushed his bulk out of the leatherette bucket seat of his Z-28 Camaro and began walking up the snow-covered path to the top of the cemetery hill.

It was a bitter night and Harold, who as usual had a cold, felt the moist hairs in his nostrils start to freeze together.

Above him the Milky Way was bright, alive with rhinestones of twinkling light. Like billions of electric crystals the snow around him sparkled in the moon's light. The evening's beauty could not lessen Harold's quickly accumulating dread.

With each step his boots squeaked loudly in the straw-dry snow. He wished the squeaking would stop, but that wouldn't be good either. Then it would be too quiet.

The beers he'd been drinking all day hadn't done his nerves much good, heightening his already soaring, fearful imagination. Suddenly he wanted to turn and run—and he didn't get *that* urge very often.

Get outta here!

Instead he dragged his heavy legs up the steep hill, wishing he were anywhere, anyplace but this lonely place.

RUN!

"No!" he said out loud. Immediately he was ashamed. He hoped to God Ingrid hadn't heard him. Still, his internal debate continued.

Can't you do anything right?

(Why don't you leave me alone? I've done something that took a lot of guts. Give me some credit.)

What exactly did you do? Open a door?

Harold knew the voice was right. He hadn't done anything really gutsy. Suddenly he didn't feel a bit like Edward G. Robinson. He felt scared.

"Ingrid," he called out softly, "are you here?"

There was no answer, and he called again.

A frozen tree trunk creaked in the wind and to Harold it was the cry of a frightened child. A pine cone dropped, scratching its way through the branches of its tree like a fingernail raking over a blackboard. A moment later an owl screeched hideously.

Harold wanted to cry.

They're going to get you!

NO!

His chest heaved, constricted with fear. He had trouble breathing. He felt like he'd been hit by a huge fist dead center in the solar plexus. A vein pulsed in his forehead and his stomach felt like it wanted to rid itself of all the beer.

A small sob escaped his lips. He couldn't help himself.

Ingrid, please, please get here.

"Harold." The voice was joyously familiar. Relief flooded in on him; followed quickly by shame for being so scared.

Everything would be okay.

It was Harold's last coherent thought.

Thick, enormously strong hands snapped out of the darkness behind him and seized his neck. Harold's corpulent body was yanked off the ground, his feet twitching, like a man hanging at the end of a gallows rope. The possibility of resisting such an overwhelming force never occurred to Harold. As a swift gray curtain rushed in on him, Harold Hogan gave up his life as a child discards an unwanted toy.

The Indian pulled the stone dagger from its sheath on his belt and grinned ferociously. Then the thudding noises, like a rubber mallet pounding out an automobile fender, broke the quiet. In fifteen seconds the grisly ripping sounds began.

Chapter Twenty-one

KIRKTON SHERIFF GLOVER FREDERICKS was born in Gloversville, New York, about fifty miles east of Kirkton. His mother had thought it a grand idea to name her strapping son after their home town. Glover wasn't the best name in the world but the sheriff decided early on he was pretty much happy with it. At least it wasn't boring like John or Bill.

Glover liked being different. That's why he took the job as sheriff in the first place. He was his own boss. Worked his own hours. All he had to do was occasionally appease a few big shots. Drive their kids around with the light flashing now and then. Ignore a traffic ticket or two. Collect a little money from some deadbeats for the local businessmen. No big deal. He didn't mind. A good job was worth a little trouble.

And it was a good job. Kirkton didn't have much crime. How much trouble could five thousand people cause? Oh, it was getting a little suburban, what with Syracuse and Utica, like cities all over, getting shitty. There was still some dope up the hill at Harding, but not the way it had been in the Sixties and, shit, as far as Glover was concerned, marijuana sure wasn't worth getting your dander up. There was a little breaking and entering. Not anything real serious at all. Until *this*, of course.

Kirkton had been a dull little college town when Glover had arrived in the mid-thirties. Now it was prosperous, compared to the way it used to be. The college put a lot of bucks in people's pockets. Land prices were going up and people around town liked that. Even some small apartments were being built. People now paid $295.00 a month for places with wall-to-wall carpeting and sliding glass doors that looked pretty but kept you hot in the summer and cold in the winter. Guess anything's better than the city. Some old houses had been converted into apartments, using masonite and aluminum wall supports. Made for noisy apartments, but college kids, who loved the old places, never seemed to notice nothing anyway.

Kirkton was normal the way Glover saw it. Normal was real nice in the summer—except for a few bitching hot days in August—and pretty in the fall, but cold as a witch's tit in winter.

But what was happening now wasn't normal at all. That's why Glover was so upset. First that dog being staked up outside the Zellmer house. Ugly as sin, that's for sure, and not funny, of course, but not really all that serious. Glover figured the dog thing was a sick prank, nothing more.

But then this happened. Jesus Christ. Glover stomped his feet in the snow and tried to think. A whiff of vomit glided by and he moved further away from the source of the smell. His deputy, Johnny Rumsey, who was absolutely hopeless, tossed his cookies practically the minute he saw Harold. Glover could hardly blame him though. The sheriff had seen more than his share of dead men—soldiers blown apart on Pacific beaches during W.W. Two, victims of godawful automobile head-ons, knife fight losers—but he'd never seen anyone ripped open like Harold Hogan. Not like *that*. Jesus.

Chapter Twenty-two

NOT A MILE away from Sheriff Fredericks, another person was struggling with an altogether different dread.

Ingrid Fox lay in her big four poster, her head propped up

on a pillow directly beneath the single rose painted in the middle of her mahogany headboard. She could not sleep. Alone in the bed they had shared for thousands of nights, she could control neither her loneliness nor her growing fear.

Before this night she had never regretted her decision to become Austin Zellmer's possession. Now she was confused and worried and quickly losing her nerve. Harold's death had affected her badly. The awful gurgling in his throat would not leave her mind. The pathetic eyeballs bulging in death. Worst of all the ripping sounds—and Xipe's unholy smile when he was done.

She still believed in him, it was herself she doubted. Ingrid had seen the body healing itself—younger now than she had ever known it—and that removed the last shred of her uncertainty. He would live again, she knew. But she did not know about herself; she could not trust her own strength.

The thought of Harold's death did not revolt her. His life had been a useless, whining, self-pitying existence which served no purpose. Only in death had he made a contribution. But the manner of his death she could not bear. She would not be able to confront a victim. To look into his eyes—and then kill.

And that was what she must do.

Ingrid yearned for her lover. She needed his impervious confidence. His power. His sex, so she could abandon her fears in physical delight.

Suddenly, as if on its own, Ingrid found her desire building; a purely physical sensation that seemed unconnected to her mind, outside of her control. Slowly, unconsciously, she began to rub herself, her legs twitching uncontrollably as her excitation rose. She caressed her breasts and groaned deep in her throat, and her heat began increasing to the familiar crescendo.

It was then that Xipe appeared in the doorway.

Ingrid gasped. He was naked, his penis huge and erect. The expression on his face voracious.

He watched her with a cruel, unearthly smile, his yellow

eye violating her body. Then her nightmare became insanity as she felt her betraying body respond to his nakedness. Despite his hideous face, she was drawn to him. Her mind full of self-loathing, still she reached out for him.

He was upon her like an animal. His hands were harsh and demanding, forcing her with savage strength.

Her pleasure was ungodly, a seething, febrile exhilaration as cold and empty as the soul of the devil.

Her frenzy became delirium as he penetrated her; his penis so searingly hot that she cried out in pain as he burned into her. His pace quickened impossibly and the throbbing in her loins rose in a screaming arc of unearthly delight. When the convulsive orgasms started, the air rang with her screams of exultation.

But he did not stop. And in a small corner of her mind a terrible realization burst in upon her: he would not stop.

Her storm of masochistic pleasure became a terminal horror. Her self-doubt, her weakness, a capital offense; death was her sentence. She writhed desperately beneath him, scratched at his face futilely; but his power was overbearing, implacable.

Finally the giant rode up and almost out of her, then plunged down in one final, brutal impalement. Her pain became white, hot light fusing her brain, like a torch liquifying butter.

For Ingrid Fox, in the fierce heat of hell, it ended.

Chapter Twenty-three

I BRING THEE FLESH, O TEZCATLIPOCA.

HE HELD THE blackening organ extended in his hands, offering its oozing putrescence to the shining stars painted on the ceiling above. Arching his enormous head backwards he opened a black-toothed mouth and chanted guttural, ugly sounds which seemed to momentarily dull the white stars above with their ancient, primitive malevolence.

He was naked except for a leather loincloth and an elaborate crown of black feathers atop his head. Black ash darkened all his exposed skin. Around his neck hung a gold chain with a gleaming heart-shaped obsidian pendant.

GOD OF THE SMOKING MIRROR HEAR MY PRAYER.

The man's enormous arms quivered slightly as he held the heart above his head. His eyes, staring up at some unseen point, did not blink. Blood dropped from the pitiful flesh he held, splattering on the man's bare feet, each plop loudly distinct, like the sound of a leaky faucet in the dead of a lonely night.

SURROGATE OF THE SUN, LET THERE BE WAR BETWEEN THE NIGHT AND THE DAY.

The naked body of a man, younger now than it had been just a few days before, lay on a stone pedestal near the chanting figure. Though still and cold it was chillingly lifelike; the open eyes unclouded; the musculature soft and pliant, untouched by the stiffening of rigor mortis; the skin as pink as living flesh; the unshrivelled genitals firm and full.

LET THE WEAK AND THE FEARFUL BECOME THY LEGIONS.

The Indian looked at the body as if confirming that it still continued to bear silent witness to his benedictions, then pulled his head back to his painted heaven. Again Xipe held the pitifully small heart, laden with coagulating, encrusted blood, above his head.

O TEZCATLIPOCA, LET OUR PRIEST RISE

He turned and cast the woman's organ, as he had the man's and the dog's before, on a bed of white-hot coals smouldering brightly on another stone pedestal. It crackled briefly like dry wood in the intense heat, then immediately began to shrivel. Dark, foul smoke filled the room, a stench unnoticed by the chanter.

Once more the man raised his arms to the heavens. An obscene cry filled the room.

RISE O MESSENGER OF TEZCATLIPOCA. RISE.

At first the body on the stone pedestal lay still.

Then the fingers of its right hand began to tremble.

BOOK THREE
Allison

I know this world is killing you.
ELVIS COSTELLO

Chapter Twenty-four

THE UTICA DISPATCH

TWO DEAD IN BRUTAL MURDERS

Kirkton Rocked by Hideous Deaths

by George Cornell

KIRKTON, *Dec. 24*——The village of Kirkton was shocked yesterday by the murder of two residents.

Ingrid Fox, 38, long time assistant to Dr. Austin Zellmer, former chairman of Harding College's Archeology Department, who committed suicide two weeks ago, was found murdered in her bed yesterday morning. In another incident, Harold W. Hogan, a Harding College custodian, was found murdered in the college cemetery.

The two murders are Kirkton's first in over fifty years.

It has been reported by at least one eye-witness that both bodies were similarly mutilated. The same source contends that the hearts of both victims were torn from their chests.

Sheriff Glover Fredericks refused to confirm or deny these rumors. He did say that the murders "were the ugliest things he'd ever seen," and "probably connected."

Asked if the police had any leads, Sheriff Fredericks responded by saying that the murders were "obviously the work of a psycho or psychos and that's the direction our investigation will take."

Both murders occurred sometime during the night of December 22nd. In a possibly related incident, a dachshund belonging to Mrs. Kate Whitworth was found mutilated in her backyard on the morning of the 22nd. The dog's heart was torn from its chest. Mrs. Whitworth is the step-daughter of Prof. Zellmer.

Sheriff Fredericks has warned the community to use "extreme caution" and "to report any strange person or persons seen in the Kirkton Village vicinity."

A special telephone number has been set up to take calls. The police also request that. . . .

Chapter Twenty-five

THE MORNING AFTER Ralph's death, Kate sat in the living room with her morning coffee. She couldn't bear to be in the kitchen looking out into the backyard.

Allison had slept almost the entire previous day. The light went on in her room around seven in the evening and stayed on until almost midnight. She refused to come out, saying only "leave me alone" in such a way that Kate knew it would do absolutely no good to try to talk with her.

Now Kate waited expectantly as she heard Allison's door open and then light steps descend the creaky staircase.

"Let's talk, okay?" Kate's eyes pleaded with her daughter.

"It's too late for that, don't you think?" Allison's voice was full of cold anger, her eyes flat, baleful, like an animal confronting a predator.

"Allison, I'm so sorry."

"Were you too *busy*," Allison drew out the word sarcastically, insinuatingly, "to call Ralph in from the cold? Or did you just figure since Daddy gave him to me we ought to get rid of him?"

"I did call him."

"You're lying. You always do. You lie to me so I won't get upset. So I won't try to kill myself again."

"I don't want you to be upset, that's true. But I don't lie to you." Kate kept her voice soft and unchallenging. Desperately she sought a way to make contact with her daughter, to show her that she loved her more than anything in the world. But the look in Allison's eyes seemed unalterably hostile. Kate held her emotions in. Go slow. Only reach out when Allison's ready. Don't force her.

"If you called Ralph, then why didn't he come?"

"I don't know. I called him and he didn't come. Mr. Palmer went out and opened the garage door and got a pile of army blankets for him to sleep in. He would've been fine there."

"Well he isn't fine, is he?" Allison's voice rose and then cracked. "And it's your fault!" she yelled shrilly.

"It's a terrible, ugly thing," Kate replied softly. "We're going to find the person who did it. Be sure he's punished. But it's not my fault. You must know that."

"I don't know. I don't!" Allison's voice was shriller than before. "I'm stupid, remember?"

"Don't say that."

Allison glared at her mother who sat on the couch looking, as usual, like she had all the answers. Except she couldn't talk her way out of this one. It *was* her fault. Allison couldn't understand why her mother hated her so. She pretended not to, but yesterday proved it. If she cared, Ralph would be alive.

Kate stood up and reached for her daughter. Allison spun away, ran down the front hall, got her coat, and opened the front door. She didn't need to be comforted. Not by *her*.

"Where are you going?"

The front door slammed in reply. Kate followed her daughter as far as opening the front door, then thought better of chasing her. She needed more time. Kate could see no other choice but to wait for her daughter.

She watched Allison walk quickly away across the gray campus, then noticed the dark clouds scudding low over the college hill. It seemed appropriate that it was about to snow again.

Please, dear God, please let her love me again.

Tears formed in Kate's eyes. She blinked in a futile attempt to keep them back. Kate closed the door on the diminishing figure of her daughter and turned back to the empty house.

The telephone rang, its tone loud and unnerving in the quiet. She picked it up and listened.

"Yes, of course. I'll be there immediately."

Kate hurriedly put on her coat and boots. Her face, puffy from her tears, now grim. "Come immediately," Dr. Johann had said. "What's going on?" Kate asked. "I'll tell you when you get here. You'd better hurry."

Chapter Twenty-six

AT WESTMORELAND PSYCHIATRIC HOSPITAL Kate was appalled to find her mother strait-jacketed in a padded cell.

Dr. Ryerson and Dr. Johann were both subdued, obviously despairing. Her mother's condition had deteriorated to a state of continuous babbling punctuated with violent fits of fearful screaming. Physically she seemed to have aged ten years in two days; the thin figure now emaciated; the pale blue eyes hollow and impossibly deep; the face crisscrossed not with lines but crevices which seemed to be eating their way into her flesh.

All attempts to communicate with Joan Zellmer had been utterly futile. Food was completely ignored, and IV tubes impossible to keep lodged as she kept up a constant, frenetic struggle with some ghastly unseen foe.

"She's eating herself up. Literally eating herself alive," Johann explained.

"What about sedation?" Kate asked as she tried to control her rising panic.

Johann looked nervous and uncomfortable; his eyes darted back and forth like a professor who is asked a question he cannot answer. "Well I, I just don't know. We've given her increasingly large doses, first of valium, then thorazine. The dosage now is as high as we can possibly prescribe without running a real risk of overdose."

"Why isn't she calmed down then? I don't understand." Kate looked at Dr. Ryerson who avoided her gaze. *(What's going on?)*

"We don't either," answered Johann. "In twenty-four years of practice I've never seen anything remotely like this. The drugs have had absolutely no effect. None. Even the most severe cases of manic-behavior—or hyperactivity—are controllable with thorazine." Dr. Johann stopped speaking, started again, thought better of it, and remained silent.

"What are you going to do?"

"We don't know," answered Dr. Ryerson, the sadness and turmoil plain in his voice. "We just don't know."

"Mrs. Whitworth," Johann said, "we don't think there's anything anyone could do for your mother. She is running an extraordinary temperature, 104 degrees, and her entire metabolic process is going at breakneck speed; her pulse is enormously fast. I can't even guess why the drugs aren't having any effect, but it seems that she is metabolizing them at an astronomic rate, burning them up so fast they have no chance to brake the system."

"We're doing all we can, believe me," Dr. Ryerson said. He spoke without a shred of hope.

Kate's first reaction was anger, but before a word even rose in her throat it was replaced by despair. Something monstrous was happening to her mother and it was futile to lash out at anyone for it.

"I have described the symptoms to a colleague, an old friend at Massachusetts General Hospital. He has chartered an airplane and will be arriving within the hour."

"Will he do any good?" All of a sudden, Kate knew her mother wouldn't survive; that she could not possibly fight whatever was assaulting her.

"No, I don't think he will." Johann took her hand gently. "Your mother is experiencing something we have absolutely no knowledge of. It makes no sense in terms of the way the human body is supposed to work, as far as we understand it. We're powerless to stop what's happening. I'm sorry."

"How long does she have?"

"I don't have an exact idea, but her system is under unbelievable stress. She could go anytime. An hour. Two."

"I want to see her."

Johann hesitated a moment, then replied, "Of course." They walked down a long hall at the end of which was a padded chamber.

Johann hesitated again, looking through the window. "She's capable of violence, in fact, she badly scratched a male nurse last night. Please be careful. We'll be watching from the door should you need help."

The moment the padded door closed behind Kate, her mother's awful cries stopped. She was crouched in the corner, legs free, arms pinioned behind her. A rattling whisper of shallow breaths, like dry leaves blowing down a deserted street, became the only sound in the room. Her mother's head fell on her chest and Kate, thinking it was the end, rushed across the room.

At first Joan Zellmer's voice was only a weak gust of air; the words so faint as to be indistinguishable. Then Kate realized her mother was trying to speak, and she put her ear to the cracked, parched lips. The voice creaked out like an ancient machine, unoiled and dying.

"He has risen. He wants your daughter." Her voice grew fainter still. "You must fight him. Or he will destroy you. Destroy everyone."

The voice made no sense whatever, full only of madness, and fear.

Kate shuddered.

Then it was over, though even in death, life was cruel to Joan Zellmer.

In a violent, jerking motion her mother's body was yanked from the floor, lifted high into the air, then slammed back down as if thrown by an enormous, invisible hand. The crash sounded of a hundred splintering bones.

For Kate the manner of death was too unreal, too impossible, to register in her mind. But she would never forget her mother's final scream: a harrowing, blood-chilling howl of recognition.

Chapter Twenty-seven

AS SHE WALKED, Allison's anger dissipated, changing into a forlornness which gripped her tenaciously. She wandered aimlessly about the campus, kicking at clumps of snow as she shuffled her feet, her mind occasionally focusing on the painful memory of Ralph, then quickly shifting away only to inevitably return to it once again. She passed two people on her walk, a maintenance man sanding a walkway who greeted her with a smile; and a student, laden with books, who threw out a cheerful hello. She responded to neither.

Finally she found herself on the top of a long, gentle rise, above the golf course and overlooking the entire campus.

The campus seemed absorbed in silence, preoccupied with a profound immutable quiet. But Allison sensed something else too, something that felt different, out of place, alien. As she stood motionless in the snow her feeling crystalized: I'm not alone. Someone is watching me.

Underneath the pine trees, Xipe stared at the girl standing at the top of the nearby hill. For the first time he could feel his own power, like his master's, growing stronger. Unblinking, he trained his mind at the girl, his burgeoning power aimed at her soul like a laser beam.

A drop of thick saliva sat in the corner of his mouth and his tongue was dry with expectation. She had not moved for several minutes. It was time. She could not run. Like a fisherman all he had to do now was slowly draw in his net.

His wide lips formed a smile as he rose from his haunches and stepped from behind a towering pine. He looked at her standing mesmerized in the snow, her long blonde hair hanging outside her bright yellow parka like strings of gold, her thighs, wrapped in tight jeans, those of a fully developed woman. His excitation grew.

He started from the trees.

The stillness around Allison seemed to expand as her uneasiness increased. She was cold, her body suddenly shivery and trembling. Her legs felt heavy as though they'd been pumped full of a viscous fluid. Her mind was slow, and drowsy.

Vaguely she noted it was odd that she should be scared in such a peaceful place; the city, which was really scary, hardly ever frightened her. Her eyes drifted across a snow-covered field to a stand of tall, thick pines squeezed tightly together perhaps a hundred yards away.

Something about the pines bothered her. Allison nervously wiped her lips with a gloved hand, the wool glove uncomfortably dry against her lips, and stared at the swaying trees. The wind whistled in the top branches, the sound eerie, hypnotizing in its steady cadence. When she took a deep breath, the air was harsh and raspy in her throat like smoke from a cigarette.

The green of the pines sharply contrasted with the surrounding snow, but it was the dark shadows between the trees that caught her attention. She thought she detected movement, indistinct against the shadows. She knew her mind was playing a frightening game. But it didn't help to know, didn't make the scary thoughts stop.

The wind continued to whine through the dark trees. Her vision narrowed, then browned at the edge like a sepia print, and she wasn't sure if she were even awake anymore. She stood still in the snow, like a frightened deer caught in an automobile's headlights.

Something moved again in the trees. Its shape became

more distinct, the shape of a man. The man emerged from the trees and started toward her.

"No," she whispered.

Chapter Twenty-eight

DOWNS ARRIVED at Kate's house and found a note. "I've gone to the hospital. Mother is sick. Allison out walking—very upset. Love, Kate."

Immediately Downs was uneasy. He'd just heard over the radio about the two murders. He stared out the broad front window at the college quad. Allison shouldn't be walking about alone. Evidently, Kate hadn't heard about the murders. Quickly he was out of the house and back into his Mercedes. He wasn't sure Allison would go anywhere near him but he'd deal with that when he had to. Now he just wanted to find her.

The snow, which had started slowly on his way over, was now falling heavily. There was no breeze and the big flakes fell straight down, forming a dark, ominous curtain.

He drove hunched over the wheel, straining to see through the snow, the windshield wipers beating in front of him like frantic metronomes. His eyes darted from side to side as he circled the inner quadrangle. He saw nothing.

He circled the outer quadrangle and again saw no one, then turned up College Hill. The Mercedes' rear wheels spun in the snow, the car slowed nearly to a halt, then the tires grabbed again and it laboriously crept up the road. At Reservoir Street, above the campus, Downs turned right and was again on level roadway. He drove past a line of huge old Victorian homes overlooking the college golf course. He could barely see the campus now as the snow fell ever more heavily. He passed the new campus housing development further down the street. Still he saw no one.

As he reached the end of the college golf course a border of pines rose out of the murk. Then he spotted a dim flash of yellow through the snow and hit the brakes. The Mercedes skidded sideways across the road to a stop, its shining headlights facing the pines. Downs threw the door open and jumped out into the snow. At first he saw nothing but falling white, then again picked out the faint yellow. He ran toward the color and saw her standing still in the snow, perhaps fifty yards away.

"Allison, hey!" Downs yelled.

There was no response. He called again. No response. She stood in the snow as motionless as a statue. What was wrong?

Downs plowed through the snow toward her, but still she did not move, nor acknowledge his calls.

When he reached her she remained completely unresponsive. He spoke her name softly, then reached out and touched her shoulder.

As his hand fell on her shoulder, Allison's head jerked toward him and her eyes, closed before, snapped open.

"Allison," he said softly, quizzically.

She fell into his arms.

The man, hidden again in the trees, stared with primitive hatred as the blonde virgin was carried up the hill to the automobile. When the automobile moved away down the road he followed it with his yellow eye until it disappeared in the falling snow. He stood for a long time in the pines, letting his rage dissipate.

He was a patient man. There would be another time.

Chapter Twenty-nine

WILL BARRETT was in uncharacteristic ill humor as he limped across the inner quadrangle toward his meeting. Defiantly he wore no overcoat against the cold, only a white silk scarf wrapped around his neck and a leather trooper's cap, ear flaps untied and dangling, perched cockeyed on his balding head.

His wife—God rest her soul—used to tell him the get-up made him look like a senile aviator searching for the Great War. Today he expected a war.

Frederick Waltham Collier, eighteenth president of Harding College, holder of doctorate degrees from Harvard College and the London School of Economics, wizard of the balance sheet, and possessor of the finest set of ivories ever to blind a wealthy alumna, had requested the presence of the dean for a "conference on a matter of grave importance."

Will Barrett hated people who talked like that. But he had plenty of other reasons to despise Fred Collier who was, hands-down no-contest, the most humorless asshole he had encountered in his forty-two years of academic life.

Dollars and cents. Debits and credits. "Fiscally perilous days ahead." Blah, blah, blah. The man was so totally passionless Will wondered how he'd ever gotten it up long enough to sire his two bloodless little brats. Artificial insemination, no doubt. The thought produced a smile, brightening his mood and taking his mind from yesterday's awful scene at the graveyard.

On the day after that ugly scene he had to experience one of his infrequent meetings with Collier. Jesus.

Collier's name invoked a volcanic rumble in his ample belly. Shit, here we go again. Will stopped, rummaged in the pocket of his rumpled tweed sports coat and pulled out a plastic vial half full of the odious little pink pills. After dropping two into the snow with an audible curse (bringing a giggle from a passing co-ed) he popped two probanthine into his mouth, then grimaced at their intense bitterness. Taking the stomach medicine without water was a little penance he imposed on himself. Well worth the price. He'd stuffed himself last night with blazing Bombay lamb curry and numerous Murees—a tart Pakistani beer he adored—a meal which could not have been worse for his ulcer. Will was grateful that despite emotional crisis, he had never yet lost his appetite.

Which is more than he could say for Collier . . . or the current generation of students who seemed devoid of any appetites—culinary, emotional, even sexual. Increasingly the students of the early eighties seemed to walk the campus with nervous, grim expressions pasted on their unlined faces. An entire generation suffering a case of hemorrhoids.

Rather than fully enjoying the riches of youth, today's students spent four years frantically acquiring undigested lumps of "useful" knowledge, like squirrels storing up chestnuts for a lifetime of bitter winters. Will was aware that tough economic times were very likely ahead. Modern man had squandered energy resources while ignoring his environment, placed too much confidence in dangerous technology, and ignorantly used his knowledge to perfect increasingly more lethal weaponry—obviously penance would have to be paid. Will was not blindly optimistic about the future.

But imagining potential calamities was always ten times worse than coping with present problems. Worried, nervous students, drilling themselves like troops preparing for some apocalyptic battle, were robbing themselves of the pleasures of the moment.

The man who's looking over his shoulder while screwing the farmer's wife might as well be home milking the cows. It was difficult for Will to understand why people felt the need to look over their shoulders. If you didn't live as fully in the moment as possible, life could be deadly goddamn boring.

As he laboriously walked up the steps of the administration building, he thought about Fred Collier's pert wife, Diane. She had more spirit in her little finger than her husband had in his entire body. He still considered the possibility of making a serious pass at her. Even thought he'd had some subtle encouragement. If he'd ever succeeded in getting her in his bed he wouldn't have looked over his shoulder if the College of Cardinals walked in.

The thought of screwing Diane Collier put a smile on the

dean's habitually unshaven face as he pushed open the door to Collier's outer office. A trim, attractive looking woman with half glasses perched on her nose looked up as he came in and said, "Will, you look like you've just gotten away with something."

The dean's smile broadened. "Holly, the only thing I'm trying to get away with is you. Let that behaviorist husband of yours play with his rats down at the psych lab; you come over to my place and press my bar." Will roared at his joke. "I could use the reinforcement."

Holly Carlson laughed. "You don't need any reinforcement. Not as far as I can tell."

"Well I know what I like."

"Women. Any size, any shape," Holly said with a smile.

"We all need hobbies." Will produced a comical leer. "I bet you'd be a nice craft to take up."

Holly smiled again. "I suppose because I have a broad beam."

"Yeah. And I could plank you all day." Will roared again.

"Oh brother," Holly groaned.

"That bad?"

"That bad," she said with mock sternness.

"Okay, I'll do better next time. Is Bottom Line Collier around?"

"Waiting expectantly as a matter of fact. Something's up."

Holly stood and walked in front of Will to the president's office.

As she reached the door, the dean lightly caressed the curve of her derriere. "Ah, something could be up indeed," he whispered with exaggerated lasciviousness. "You don't know what you're missing." He laughed gaily as he went through the door, the sound high and unaffected like that of a happy child.

Holly stared at the door after it had closed behind Will's wink. His touch had been light and delicate. She was amazed at the unexpected tingle she felt. God, he was twenty-five years older than she was.

And she was tempted.

What in the world am I thinking? A guilty smile arranged itself comfortably on her face as she sat down at her desk and resumed her typing.

Chapter Thirty

"How do you feel?" Downs asked Allison who had just woken up. She looked around with a bewildered expression on her face.

"What am I doing in your car? What happened?" she asked.

He decided there was no reason to tell her that he had been looking for her. "I was driving by the golf course and saw you just sort of standing in the snow. It looked kind of funny you just standing there and . . ."

"I like to walk in the snow. It's beautiful." There was an edge in her voice, but nothing like the antipathy Downs expected.

"Anyway, I stopped the car and called out to you. On account of I'm just a naturally friendly sort," he smiled at Allison who returned it tentatively. "But you didn't answer. So I ambled over and you just kind of looked at me and then fainted. I didn't think I was *that* unattractive."

She smiled full at him this time. "Thank you."

"That's okay. You're feeling all right now?"

"Yeah." Allison sensed the concern in Downs' voice—and the sincerity.

"You had a funny expression on your face. Almost like you were scared."

"I guess I just got a little tired. After everything that's happened. You know?"

"Sure." Downs turned to her as he drove slowly back to the house. "Allison, I'm very sorry about yesterday."

She returned his gaze briefly, solemnly, then dropped her

head. He sensed that she was trying to decide how to react. Fervently he hoped that Allison would be able to understand that yesterday's horrible incident hadn't been his fault and hadn't been Kate's.

He looked over at her again and saw a tear running down her cheek. Downs pulled the car to the side of the road and reached out to hold Allison's hand. She turned to him, her eyes now full of tears. "Why, why would anyone do it?" She began to cry softly.

"I don't know. I don't think anybody does. It's a terrible sickness somebody has."

"It's so awful," Allison sobbed between tears.

Downs held her hand and was silent, glad that Allison did not feel the need to pull away. He felt something important happening; a breakthrough whose suddenness both surprised and delighted him. She was trying to reach out. Had sensed that his concern was sincere. He gently put his arm around her shoulders and she turned quickly to him, throwing her arms around his back and hugging him with a fierce desperation.

Downs held her and let her cry.

After a few minutes he spoke. "Do you know your mother loves you very much?" His voice was soft and gentle.

Allison looked up and nodded.

"She's worried sick about you."

"I know that, too," Allison said.

"I want to tell you something, okay?"

"Okay."

Downs paused and took a deep breath. He wasn't sure this was the right time. But it felt right. It was so important how Allison would react to what he had to say.

"I love your mother. I want her to marry me." He stared at Allison gently. She remained silent. "I guess I've loved her ever since we were kids. I just didn't realize it. And I want that love to be good for everybody, your mother, and me, and you."

Allison wiped a tear from her eye, and managed a small smile.

Downs felt himself welling up with emotion. "I know it's hard for you. But I'm going to try very hard to be your friend."

Allison smiled a little less tentatively this time.

"Do you think you can try to be my friend?" Downs asked.

Allison paused for a long moment, then a full smile, despite the tears in her eyes, spread across her face. "Yes, I think I can."

It was Downs' turn to feel the tears roll down his cheeks. He reached out for Allison again and they embraced in silent, mutual understanding.

Chapter Thirty-one

"I APPRECIATE your coming over so promptly, Will." Frederick Collier forced a pleasant expression onto his soft face.

"You know me, Freddie. I've got the goddamn fastest feet in the country." Will smiled briefly.

Collier stopped a sour expression from arriving on his face. He hated the name Freddie. Also he was a prim, fastidious man who disliked all vulgarity, which Dean Will Barrett embodied down to the tips of his tobacco stained fingernails.

Barrett looked more like he belonged perched on the stool of a dockside gin mill than in the brocaded Italian provincial chair he was sitting in now. The man was a slob and a libertine. His appearance befitted his personality. A barrel chest covered with a wrinkled white shirt, the shirt inevitably adorned with blobs of last night's meal. He wore his pants comically low, accentuating a stomach distended like that of a woman in the last month of pregnancy. He rarely shaved it seemed; and he constantly puffed strong French cigarettes whose acrid smoke always made Collier queasy.

Only his eyes, clear and sharp, revealed the intelligence and wit that had allowed William Barrett to captivate and charm generations of Harding students. He was, quite simply, a beloved institution. And that was the worst thing of all. Because it was impossible, even for a Machiavellian of Collier's considerable skill, to ever get rid of him.

Collier still shuddered at the thought of the trustees' meeting, six months after he'd taken over the helm at Harding, when he had "tactfully" suggested kicking the dean upstairs. The room had suddenly gone silent, as though he'd just suggested turning the chapel into a cockfight pit.

Then the chairman of the trustees, who'd come to Harding from the coalfields of Pennsylvania and had risen to become president of the nation's second largest steel company, had turned to him with cold, flashing anger in his eyes: "I respect Will Barrett more than any man on the face of this earth. *He's* not going anywhere—unless *he* wants to."

The humiliation of that meeting still tugged at Collier like a persistent hangover. Today the discomfort was worse because he needed Barrett's help. Desperately.

"You know, Freddie, if I didn't know you better I'd say the expression on your face means you're not happy to see me. That couldn't be it, could it?" Will couldn't help jabbing at Collier; the man brought out the worst in him.

"Of course not, Will. Of course not."

"Well, I didn't really think so. But that expression! Jesus Christ, you're not having that constipation trouble again are you?" Control yourself, Will thought.

"Please, Will." Collier's face was suddenly white and strained. Old looking, Will thought with a start. "We've got some . . . trouble," Collier said in a shaky, nervous voice. For the first time in Barrett's experience Fred Collier was revealing something akin to human emotion. To his amazement, the dean almost felt sorry for him. Almost.

"What in the world's the matter?"

"The Aztec collection has been . . . been disturbed."

Will lit a Gaulois. "Disturbed?"

"Well, uh, robbed. Of some very valuable pieces. Very valuable." Collier looked like he wanted to cry.

Immediately Will was concerned. "When?"

"Last night."
"What did they get?"
"We're not exactly sure. But some kind of instruments used only in very rare Aztec religious ceremonies. That's why they're especially valuable."
"You mean instruments that were part of the Aztecs' sacrificial ceremonies?" Will was impatient; the Aztec artifacts were certainly valuable but not easily turned into liquid cash. His first thought was the theft sounded like a college prank. Collier's reaction should be anger rather than this childish fear.
"No, not the sacrifices. A special ceremony. Apparently a kind of priestly ascension rite. For the highest priests only. Those who were destined to become gods."
As a historian Will specialized in Asian and Oriental studies. Still he knew something of these gruesome Aztec ceremonies; and a little about this highest of ceremonies which was the most gruesome of all, involving animal and human hearts torn from the chests of living beings. Will was surprised, however, that Fred Collier had even heard of it.
"Obviously our beloved Professor Zellmer discussed some of these ceremonies with you, huh?"
Collier hesitated briefly, then replied. "Yes, that's right."
"Do you have a new-found interest in the Huactl cultures?"
"No." It was unavoidable, what he now had to say. Collier felt physically sick. "Actually some of these pieces were so . . . so unusual that there was some question whether Professor Zellmer had proprietary rights to them. And he wanted to . . ."
"Wait a minute. You don't mean unusual, heh? You mean valuable, right?"
"Ahh . . . well, yes Will, that's correct."
"Cut the crap now, Fred. What the fuck is going on?" Will was immediately angry. He loved Harding College more than anything else in his life. Instantly he had the awful feeling that this pinched asshole in front of him, along with Austin

Zellmer, had done something which might sully Harding's reputation.

"Okay." Collier took a gulp of air between tightly pursed lips. "Zellmer surreptitiously took some extremely valuable pieces out of the Cachton dig."

"How valuable?" Will interrupted.

"At least three million. Using my office's auspices we labelled the pieces incorrectly, as artifacts which by a previous agreement with the Mexican government's Historical and Cultural Preservation Commission were okay for us to take, assuming a certain prearranged price was met."

"A very low price." Will was getting angrier quickly.

"Of course. A number of those pieces Zellmer gave to the college so we could take out loans on them. That was my idea." Collier paused as though expecting congratulations for his fiscal acumen. "I explained the delicacy of the matter to John Blair down at the bank. He cooperated and we received a very large loan which the college has been using to pay its debt service on the new constructon we began back in 1975."

"You idiot." Will wanted to smash Collier. Hurt him. It was a totally alien emotion. "Let me fill in the rest of this lovely little scenario, Fred. The most valuable pieces are the ones missing."

Collier nodded his head glumly.

"If word of the theft gets out the following will happen." Will held up a thick finger. "One, exposure of a fraudulent loan—and our friend John Blair is in a world of trouble. Two, foreclosure of loan and fair Harding will be unable to make payments on a huge debt service—a debt service for buildings we never needed. Three, the eighteenth president of Harding College arrested, later indicted . . . then fucked."

Collier winced, then dropped his head. He began quietly sobbing.

"Do you think I've covered the situation fairly accurately?" Will was trying unsuccessfully to stem his rising anger.

Collier nodded and his sobbing got louder.

In a sudden motion Will rose out of his chair and with a

startlingly swift, violent swing slapped Collier out of his chair onto the floor. The crying stopped. Will Barrett hadn't hit anyone since he was practically a boy.

"Get up Fred."

Will sucked hard on his Gaulois as he watched the younger man struggle to his feet.

"It wasn't my welfare . . ."

"Bullshit. It was your ass. Don't give me any crap about Harding's well-being." Will sucked on his cigarette again, sending a hard stream of smoke toward the ceiling as he exhaled.

If that loan blows up, we're done. Bankrupt." Collier looked up with pathetic sadness. Will wanted to hit him again. "It's not just for my . . ."

"Shut up," said Will flatly. "Maybe you're not as dumb as I thought. You knew enough to call me. Knew that I'd do almost anything to save Harding. And you were right.

"I'm going to see about this theft. The artifacts aren't the kinds of things professional thieves would steal. It doesn't make sense. Maybe we'll get lucky. I mean I'll get lucky.

"I hope you never get lucky again. Have your undated resignation on my desk in an hour. Then we'll see."

Collier started sobbing again.

Will stood up. "It's about time you economists learned about what we historians call the 'natural law of action and reaction.'" He stared contemptuously at the slumped form below him. "I'll translate for you. He who fucks, gets fucked in return."

Will turned and walked from the room.

Chapter Thirty-two

THE SNOWBALL sailed upward in a high arc, then descended unerringly to smack wetly into Downs' left ear. The perfect shot practically knocked him off his skis and he howled comically.

"Retaliation!" yelled Allison. A high, teasing laugh followed, and echoed through the pine trees. "You started it!"

"Bullshit," he muttered back.

"Naughty, naughty," she sang out. "I'm a kid. You're gonna corrupt me."

"Gimme a break," he said plaintively, shaking the snow off the side of his head.

"You did *too* start it."

He didn't have a leg to stand on. It was true.

Allison laughed again, and Downs thought how nice that sounded. With her straight blonde hair shining in the bright afternoon sun, she was a picture of adolescent beauty. Her smile added a dazzling vitality to the picture. (She's gonna break some hearts.) Downs was suddenly struck by her resiliency; the strength of youth. She had experienced a terrible ugliness yesterday, and a strange, unnerving incident this morning; now three hours later she was laughing.

After talking in the car their rapport had blossomed throughout the day. They'd talked about many things, but especially about Kate, and Allison's problems about the divorce. Allison poured her heart out to him, her trust so complete, so unexpected that he still was not sure why it had happened. It was as though Downs had a key for a long sealed lock.

He found Allison to be a willing and perceptive listener; he had tried to explain the difficulties that her mother had encountered about the divorce. The shock, the pain, the wounded pride, the anger. He thought by the expression on Allison's face that perhaps for the first time she was really appreciating the enormous difficulties that her mother had had to confront. For the first time in a long time, Allison was outside of her self and her own pain. The effect was startling.

"I guess I just didn't think of Mom enough."

"Maybe. But don't be too hard on yourself, either. It wasn't easy for anybody."

"Yeah, I see that. But still I feel now like I did think too much about myself."

"We all do from time to time. We all have to watch that. And the watching makes us better people."

Allison nodded.

"That's why," Downs continued, "it's so important to have friends."

"What do you mean?" she asked.

"Well, good friends, people you're really close to, and really honest with, can tell you when you're thinking a little crooked. Like when we get, you know, a little self-absorbed sometimes. A little kick in the tail, a gentle kick, can do wonders."

"Is that what you're doing to me right now?"

"Sort of." Downs smiled a little shyly. God, this was a perceptive kid. It was almost scary.

"I think I understand what Mom went through better now. And why I reacted the way I did. You make it seem easy to understand."

Downs smiled broadly.

"Downs?"

"Yeah?"

"Are we friends?"

"I hope so."

"I guess that means I can kick your tail sometimes too, huh?"

"It would be an honor," Downs bowed gracefully. "Just don't kick too hard, I've got a tender ass."

Allison giggled and Downs' smile got still broader.

By three P.M. they'd both grown restless. Downs offered to give Allison a cross-country skiing lesson. She looked full of energy with no ill effects from the morning incident. The heavy snow had stopped around noon and now the winter sky was a perfect azure. With four inches of new snow the skiing would be perfect.

Allison asked him a barrage of questions about the ski touring: how did the bindings work, how do you stop, how do you get up when you fall. She was sure, she said, that she'd never be able to do it right. Downs reassured her, describing with clarity and accuracy, he thought immodestly, the fine points of the sport. He helped her into a pair of skis and they were ready.

With her first, perfect, gliding step it became obvious that Allison had been playing him along. She roared with laughter at his dumbfounded look, then skied off, leaving him behind, shaking his head in surprise.

As she skimmed away he quickly packed a snowball and let fly. Teach her a lesson. His snowball smacked against tree with a splat, barely missing her. The snowball fight started.

For Downs that was unfortunate. Because Allison turned out to have a powerful, accurate throwing arm (he found out later she was the shortstop on her New York school's softball team) and proceeded to pepper him with missiles which connected with various parts of his body with disturbing frequency.

A direct hit in the ear convinced him that he'd better surrender. He hadn't hit her once, and thought he'd have to stay in the battle, at grave personal risk, for a long time before he finally did.

"Okay," he yelled, "peace. I quit."

"I accept your humble surrender," Allison said with mock pomposity. "Come on, let's ski."

"Lead the way," Downs called back gratefully. "Just give an old man a chance to rest now and then."

They skied for an hour, circling the campus entirely before Allison finally called for a stop.

"Old man my eye," she said. "You're barely breathing hard." Her own face was flushed red with exertion.

Downs smiled. "If I don't keep this deteriorating body in shape, it'll just fall apart. But enough's enough. How 'bout some hot chocolate?"

"Sounds terrific."

He realized that, quickly, improbably, they had become friends.

They sat at the kitchen table, each with a second cup of hot chocolate, still flushed from the cold and the exercise. Allison sipped the steaming chocolate, then daintily picked out a marshmallow and popped it into her mouth. She thought she'd never tasted anything quite so good.

Downs was so nice. She knew he was keeping her company on account of . . . of what had happened, and that was nice. But she was also pretty sure that he really liked her too. And she sure liked him.

He was cute. She giggled silently; she liked cute boys. Well, at least she thought she did. Allison giggled out loud at herself and Downs looked up from his chocolate and smiled.

"So vat's zo vunny?" Downs' silly accent made her giggle some more. "Vat are you looking at me vor?"

Allison reddened in embarrassment. "Well, I was just thinking that you were pretty cute." There, she said it.

Downs grinned. "I think devastatingly handsome would be more accurate." He threw his head back and began lavishly patting his hair like a movie star preening before a mirror.

Allison giggled.

The sound of the Saab's tires squeaking in the snow on the driveway broke into their silliness.

Downs quickly got up from the kitchen table and walked into the living room. He watched Kate get out of the car. Her shoulders were slumped slightly forward in a position of fatigue. She seemed smaller, somehow diminished. Downs looked at Allison who returned his look quickly. She too knew something was wrong.

"Come on," he said, "let's go out."

They met her on the front porch. Allison hesitated a moment, then ran to her mother and threw her arms around her. They hugged tightly. The moment extended as mother and daughter bridged a gap that had separated them for so ong. They both cried as they held each other; the tears confirming the significance of their embrace.

Finally Kate pulled slowly away from her daughter.

"I love you so much," she said softly.

"I know Mom. And I love you too." Allison looked up at Kate's tear-streaked face. "Are you okay?"

"I guess so." Kate reached out and held her daughter again. "Grandma's dead,"she said, then stretched past Allison to tightly grip the hand which Downs quickly offered.

Allison's heart went out to her mother. Only this morning she was so angry at her she couldn't see straight. *(Thank God for Downs)*. Now her mother needed her support. And her ove. It made Allison feel needed—and important.

"I'm sorry." Allison had heard so many stories of the way Grandma used to be before she got sick. A warm, loving mother. It seemed so unfair.

Kate was touched by Allison's empathy. And exhilarated by the love she felt from her daughter. A love that had been absent for so long.

She was suddenly struck with the shocking fact that her own daughter was growing up. That soon they could be real riends. A fierce protectiveness struck her at the same time; no one was going to mistreat Allison. It would be different for them now. They could concentrate on a new life. A fresh start.

She looked at Downs and saw his pain for her—and saw his ove as well. She was so lucky to have him. A miraculous reunion had just taken place; as though Allison had been nstantly transformed to her former self—a warm, sensitive girl on the edge of becoming a woman. Downs had gotten through to her somehow. An accomplishment that all the sessions with the psychiatrist and all the explaining she herself had done had been unable to achieve.

But Kate couldn't ignore the bitter irony of the moment. Her mother's horrible death, a nightmare whose implications she had not even begun to contemplate, followed so quickly by the rekindling of the love and affection that she and

Allison had always shared. Death and life, holding hands.

"Let's go inside," said Downs, his arm around her shoulder.

Kate kissed Downs softly, sadly.

"Okay," she said. She felt his arm go tightly, reassuringly around her waist; but she also felt a sudden fear as well. A fear that everything would not be okay, a fear that would not go away.

That night as they lay side by side in bed, Kate finally talked about what had happened at the hospital.

"It was horrible. It couldn't have been worse."

She took out a cigarette and Downs watched her hand tremble as she tried to light it. He reached over and steadied the flame.

"You okay?"

"I don't know." Her face was pale and pinched, the pressure of the awful day contracting her small features. "Mom's death I can accept. I've been ready for it for years. She's been in a living hell for so long." Kate exhaled slowly. "It's almost better. At least that's what I would have said three days ago. But I saw her come out of it."

"Are you sure it wasn't just wanting her to be better so badly?"

"I've never been more sure of anything in my life." Kate saw doubt in Downs' face. "You've got to believe me," she said, "she was lucid, conscious of herself. Then it was like . . . like something just drove her crazy. Something powerful. And she just couldn't fight it."

"But that didn't happen. Right?" Downs was trying to be patient, but he was worried about what he was hearing. What was Kate talking about? It didn't make any sense.

"I don't know." Kate pulled on her cigarette nervously.

"How could it? That's crazy."

"Jesus, I know that," Kate snapped. "But I saw her acting very normally and then I saw her at the graveyard and she was scared."

"But she'd been diagnosed a paranoid," Downs said gently, "and that's what paranoids feel."

"Downs, I know that. Give me a little credit."

"Look, I'm not trying to patronize you, I'm just thinking out loud. Okay?" Downs reached out to hold Kate's hand but she pulled suddenly away.

"You know what she thought?" Kate said very softly.

"What?"

"That he was alive."

"Zellmer?" Downs asked.

"Yes. That he wanted to destroy us. And that I had to fight him." Kate sighed heavily. "That's what she told me at the hospital today."

"I'm sorry," Downs said. He shook his head. "God, it must have been terrible for her to walk around with things like that in her head. It's hard for me to even imagine."

"For me too. But she said it with such conviction, that's the weird part. Like a prophecy. Combined with seeing her die, it just got me unnerved. The whole thing's so much harder because I made contact with her again. And now she's gone." Kate began crying and Downs held her tightly. "Her life was so miserable for so long, that's the horrible part. It's so unfair."

Downs said nothing, holding Kate, letting her cry herself out. For Kate to have to hear such mad predictions from her mother's death bed must have been awful.

"Good God, what's happening to me?" Kate said suddenly through her tears.

"Nothing anymore. It's all over. Give yourself a few days."

Kate found it hard to believe the words which she knew were true. "Downs, hold me tight," she said fiercely. "I need you to hold me."

She embraced him with a desperate passion. Together it seemed better. The embrace blocked out the fear and horror which had filled her mind all day.

"Make love to me," Kate said, her voice strained with emotion.

Solemnly, slowly, he slipped off her nightgown and began

caressing her soft body. She reacted with incredible intensity, an electric response of desire.

When he entered her finally, she cried out. Then they became a single entity, a refuge of passion, separate from everything else in the world. Later, with a swift, cleansing rush, they climaxed together.

But after, too soon after, her fear came back—shadowy, and stubbornly tenacious. It was hours before she could sleep.

Chapter Thirty-three

HASTY MALONE swerved into the rutted parking lot of the "Shoe." He pulled in too fast and the old Impala let out a couple of shrieks as it bounced crazily on its worn-out shocks. Hasty cursed Danny Herman, the "Shoe's" owner, for at least the thousandth time.

Damn but that fucker was a cheap shit. A roller and a coupla loads of crushed stone and he'd have a real parking lot. But no, not old Danny, he'd rather have his regular payin' customers breaking axles than lay out a coupla hundred bucks. Fuckin' re-diculous.

The whole situation annoyed Hasty mightily. He glanced up at the ten foot sign sitting on two rusted poles overlooking the parking lot. It featured an ancient wooden horseshoe which circled a four-leaf clover and announced to the world Horseshoe Bar and Grill. It hadn't been painted in ten years. Jesus, but Danny was one hell of a cheap slob.

Hasty hitched up his chinos as he got out of the Impala. Though thoroughly irritated about the parking lot's condition, there was something else on his mind. Something other than Danny Herman's skinflint ways. He nibbled at his upper lip vacantly as he walked up the four creaking stairs and swung open the dilapidated front door.

Since Timmy hadn't shown up for the Zellmer funeral ar

unspoken dread had been building within Hasty, though he didn't associate his feeling—at least consciously—with the incident. Hasty just felt out of sorts. He figured he'd gotten some kind of bug. Some new chink flu those godless commies were sending over.

"Hasty, whatya know?" Danny cut an OB from the tap, carefully letting the beer slide down the side of the glass so there'd be only a small head the way Hasty liked it. He set the beer before his old friend, then noted with surprise the dour expression on Hasty's face. In thirteen years of sucking beers with Hasty Malone, he could count on the fingers of one hand the days his friend had acted even a little pissed off. Just wasn't like him.

"Why don't ya fix that fucking parking lot." Hasty glared at Danny angrily.

"Jesus, what's got into you?"

"You'll get your ass sued into the next county when some poor son of a bitch breaks a leg out there. Then come and ask me what the fuck's the matter." Hasty threw down his beer and slapped the glass down on the pitted, wooden bartop. "Another. Gimme a shot of schnapps too."

"You naturally happy or just full of the Christmas spirit?" Danny was about to kid Hasty some more when he caught himself. He'd forgotten for a second about Timmy. Him and Hasty were real close. He didn't want to make things tough on Hasty. "Heard anything?"

"No." Hasty downed his schnapps in a gulp and followed it quickly with half a glass of beer. Again he nibbled at his lip. He'd had very little experience with fear. Too young for the big war. Korea had come up but nobody'd asked him to go and he sure as hell hadn't volunteered.

Hasty had always taken things as they came. Easy going, always had been. Things just didn't upset him. His life had been one of calm evenness; no big highs, no big lows. A smooth, straight line continuing unquestioningly into a dependable, unsurprising future.

Now something was out of whack. And Hasty did not know

why or how. He had no experience with things going out of kilter.

He and his wife Marge had one child, Evelyn, who married a fella over in Herkimer; they had their own baby girl now. Marge took in sewing and embroidered damn well too. Hasty had worked for the college for twenty-two years. Then moved over to work for Al Cranston for a little bit more money, oh six years ago. When Hasty drank his beer and shot pool—usually right here at the "Shoe"—Marge would come along. She could hold her own and played a damn fair game of eight ball herself. They went to Florida, St. Pete usually, every coupla years. They both enjoyed TV, and wasn't that *Mork and Mindy* a corker? Neither he nor Marge ever worried much at all. No reason to.

But Hasty was scared now. Timmy O'Roarke was his best friend and Hasty knew goddamn well that he wasn't never comin' back and that somethin' Godawful had happened. He just knew it.

"Glover Fredericks thinks maybe Timmy just took off. Couldn't face getting married again." Danny didn't believe the theory for a minute.

"Fredericks couldn't find his own asshole with a map."

"Yeah, I know." Danny cut a beer for himself and another for Hasty. They were alone in the bar though it was six-thirty. What with the murders all the wives weren't about to stay home alone. "What do ya think happened to him?"

"Maybe off somewhere getting a marriage license. You know, like in Reno, someplace like that." *(He ain't anywhere like that. And you know it).*

"Yeah, that's probably it."

Hasty grunted and drained his third beer and second schnapps. The liquor was beginning to work on him and it wasn't good. He felt like talking to Marge, usually did when he wasn't feeling just right.

(Something awful's happened. Awful.)

"Danny, can I tell you something?" Hasty leaned across the bar.

"Sure, Hasty." The bartender watched his friend bite his lip again. He looked nervous, Danny realized with a start—which was odd 'cause Hasty didn't have a nervous bone in his body.

Hasty knew for sure he'd heard something in that coffin the day Timmy disappeared. He started to tell Danny, then caught himself. Weirdo stuff. Danny would probably jump on him just like Cranston had. No, there wasn't any point in it.

(You didn't hear anything.)

(Yeah, I did.)

(Well, whatja hear?)

"I don't know," Hasty said outloud.

"What you say?" Danny wasn't sure what was going on. It didn't seem like Hasty was talking to him at all.

"Huh?" Hasty looked up as though he'd been surprised.

"You said, 'I don't know'."

Hasty hesitated. "Oh . . . yeah. That's right." He hesitated again. "I meant . . . ah, you and I, we just don't know . . . ah, what's happened." Hasty quickly took another big swallow of beer.

Danny looked at him with concern. "Maybe you oughta take it a little easy, huh?"

"Yeah, maybe so."

"You said you wanted to tell me something."

"Nah, nothing, it was nothing." Hasty finished his beer and got off the bar stool. "Nothing," he muttered. His legs felt a little shaky and he sure as hell hadn't drunk *that* much. For sure it was that chink flu. He'd go home and get to bed. He was halfway out the door before he finally heard Danny's third, extra loud, "Seeya."

"Yeah, okay." Hasty slammed the door between the two words.

He wanted to get home to Marge real bad.

Chapter Thirty-four

"HEY MOM! Wanna nudda hot chocklet?"

Kate smiled when she heard Allison bellow in her best Brooklyn cab driver imitation. It had been a long time since she'd heard it.

"Sure. Plenty of whipped cream."

"Jeeeezzzzz, don't I treat ya gud? Tink I'd shawt change-ya on da cream?"

Kate groaned in mock pain. "Terrible accent. Terrible. Getting worse all the time."

Allison's head immediately appeared around the kitchen door, her face adorned with a hurt look. "It's a terrific accent," she said gravely.

"Whatever you say. It's great. Just great."

Allison stuck out her tongue.

"Listen," Kate said, "I'm doing a heavy job of work here. Let's go with the hot chocolate already."

"Don't split a gut, it's comin' up."

Kate resumed haphazardly placing tinsel on the fourteen-foot blue spruce she, Downs and Allison had picked out that morning. ("Hang 'em individually, not in clumps . . . sure, sure" . . . Kate sometimes wondered who was the mother in this relationship.)

The house was filled with the aromatic smells of the dinner she and Allison had spent the entire day working on. Kate had thrown herself into the meal—an exact replica of the Christmas Eve meal served at Thomas Jefferson's Monticello home in 1798—and the effort helped her to temporarily forget her mother's death.

The meal would be excellent, she was sure. Molasses-glazed ham with pineapple was baking in the oven, surrounded by new potatoes, small pearl onions, and mounds of raisins; soft, mild grits mixed with cheddar cheese, and sweet potatoes with brown sugar and marshmallows waited on the oven top to be reheated; broccoli and brussels sprouts were ready to be quick-steamed and would be served with hollandaise sauce. The dessert was Allison's favorite: double-fudged chocolate cake.

Kate stepped back to admire her tinselling job. Not bad. A little clumpy, perhaps, but if Allison didn't approve she could repair it herself.

"Hey," she hollered toward the kitchen, "where's my hot chocolate?"

Allison walked into the living room smiling, wiping her hands on an apron. "Wadja want?"

"That accent gets worse all the time. I want the hot chocolate you promised me."

"We gotta change-a plans."

"My work's done, I want some hot chocolate." Kate spread her hands wide in a pleading gesture. "What kind of service do we have here anyway?"

Allison shook her head gravely, staring intently at her mother. "I'm only doing this for your own good," she lectured. "Downs is coming over later, right?"

"What's that got to do with my hot chocolate?"

"Downs is my friend." Allison's eyes were twinkling and Kate thought how wonderful that was. "And I want him to have a nice time tonight." Allison couldn't stop the smile from spreading across her face. "I can't have my thirty-two-year-old mother pigging out on chocolate."

"Why not?"

"Zits. That's why. They'd ruin the whole evening and Downs would never forgive me."

Kate roared. Then Allison started. They laughed until they had to slap each other's back to stop the hiccups.

Five minutes later the doorbell rang. "Happy birthday," Downs called as Allison opened the door.

"It isn't my . . ."

Downs stepped inside and kissed her noisily on the mouth. "I'll take any excuse I can get," he said, "besides kissing's good exercise, haven't you heard?"

Allison blushed, and Kate called from upstairs, "I heard that! What's going on down there?'

"My Lolita fantasy," Downs answered. "Happens every year around this time. Merry Christmas."

"Same to you," Kate called. "Behave yourself down there."

"Right."

Allison tugged at Downs' jacket and pulled him into the living room. In an excited whisper she said, "I want to ask you what you think about the present I got for Mom."

"A present for your mother?" Downs repeated loudly.

"Ssshhhh," Allison said with a playful pout.

They walked into the kitchen. "What is it?" Downs asked.

"I got her a combination diary and notebook. It's got a leather cover and her name embossed on the front. Do you think she'll like it?"

Downs turned a beautiful leather notebook over in his hands. "She'll love it," he said. "It'll be perfect for her writing."

Allison beamed with pleasure.

"Do you by any chance happen to know what she got you?" he asked while sampling the chocolate icing with his finger.

"You think I'd spy," Allison said indignantly, "nice kid like me?"

"Of course not. Perish the thought."

"But a funny coincidence did happen today," Allison said.

"No kidding?"

"Yeah, I just happened to be strolling through the back of the attic and stumbled over a brand-new ten-speed bicycle."

Downs chortled, shaking his head. "Shameless. Absolutely shameless. How do you live with yourself?"

Allison's eyes twinkled. "I'm a good cook."

"Well, that's fortunate. I'm famished. I'm going upstairs to say howdy to your mom."

With a smile Allison listened to Downs' steps bounding up the stairs. She liked him a lot, and it happened so quickly. In some ways she was already closer to him than to her father. Sometimes when she had wanted to talk to her father about something important, his eyes would drift nervously around the room, as if the conversation were a duty he was anxious to get through. She loved her daddy, but Downs was so easy to talk to, like a friend and a parent all rolled into one.

Kate stepped back to admire the ridiculously inept wrapping job she'd just completed on the ten-speed bicycle. Tonight they were celebrating. And so what if no one wrapped bicycles?

When Downs walked into the room she took one running stride and jumped into his arms. He caught her easily and their kiss was long, and thirsty and totally lovely.

"That's the real Christmas spirit!" Kate said breaking the kiss.

"Not exactly." Downs carried Kate across the room to her bed, laid her down gently and stretched out next to her. He neatly unbuttoned the top of her blouse, and freed a breast which he began to kiss with exaggerated passion.

"Ohhh," said Kate breathlessly, "so *this* is the true spirit of Christmas. How nice."

"I was hoping you'd like it," Downs said.

"Will there be more Christmas spirit later, do you think?" Kate asked.

"There'd better be."

"And I assume the Christmas spirit is not anything you'd want to rush."

"Of course not," he replied.

"In fact it could probably take hours to properly experience."

"At least," Downs said softly into Kate's ear.

Kate lightly stroked the front of Downs' pants. She got an immediate response. "My, my, what's this?" she asked wide eyed.

"The Christmas spirit apparently likes you."

Kate caressed him again. Downs lay back, relaxing. Just as a soft sigh escaped his lips, Kate pushed him off the bed. He landed on the floor with a grunt.

"You're going to pay for that."

"I certainly hope so," she said. Kate hopped off the bed and stretched a hand down which Downs grasped and used to pull himself up. He was always surprised at the strength in Kate's small body. Surprised and delighted.

"Let's eat," she said.

They walked down the stairs holding hands, both of them wearing wide smiles.

Chapter Thirty-five

"THAT WAS STUPENDOUS!" exclaimed Downs as he tilted back on the hind legs of his chair. "That's one of the best dishes I've ever had."

Kate and Allison grinned with satisfaction.

"Of course there was that girl in Monte Carlo," Downs began with a smile, "why she had the biggest . . ."

"Seems to me," Kate interrupted, "I've heard this lie, errr, story before."

"Ancient history," Allison chimed in.

"Okay, okay," Downs said, "obviously you people don't appreciate a good story."

"But we do appreciate good presents," Kate said as she got up and put her arms around Downs' neck, "don't we Al?"

"We sure do." Allison lifted the delicate silver pendant which hung from a silver chain around her neck. "Downs, I love this, I really do."

Downs smiled.

"And Mom, I love my bike, too. It's great." Allison embraced her mother. "Thanks."

Kate kissed Allison back. Everything was perfect.

"Okay," Allison said three hours later as the clock over the fireplace chimed midnight, "Twelve o'clock. Let's go, you promised."

Kate tried a mock groan, an eyeball roll, and finally a shoulder slump. Downs sighed loudly. Nothing was going to work. Kate had promised Allison a glass of champagne to celebrate Christmas Day. And her daughter was determined to collect.

Downs popped the cork on a bottle of Dom Perignon he'd brought over and poured them each a glass. Before handing Kate a Waterford champagne goblet, he leaned forward and kissed her slightly open lips. He kissed Allison too, then raised his glass: "To us," he said.

"To us," repeated Kate.

Allison giggled as the bubbles fizzed in her mouth and snuggled up her nose. It was sort of . . . sort of tickly, but also kind of sour. Weird. She didn't think she liked it. At least not that much.

She took another sip, then another. Kate and Downs exchanged a smile. A few minutes later the giggling had picked up dramatically and Kate wondered what the hell she had started.

By 12:45 Allison had fallen asleep on the couch in front of the dying fire, her lovely girlish features softly illuminated in pale, orange light.

"She's a beauty, you know," Downs said softly.

"Thanks."

"Just like her mother."

Kate leaned back into Downs' arms with a contented smile. He stroked her hair slowly.

Downs gazed back at her and thought he'd never had a better moment in his life.

When the clock struck one, Downs drained the last champagne in his glass. He kissed Kate and tasted the wine on her lips. Quietly he said, "Let's go to bed." Kate smiled and nodded.

Allison was sleeping so soundly they decided not to wake her. Kate covered her with a comforter and fetched a raggedy stuffed dog that had been her constant sleeping companion since infancy. Then they walked up the stairs, leaving Allison to her gentle dreams.

* * *

Outside, a man waited with infinite patience in the cold night. When the lights in the house finally went off his mouth opened and his thick lips stretched tightly over his short, sharp teeth into something resembling a human smile.

He stood still for a long time staring at the house, his eye gleaming, his smile a red stain across his twisted face.

When the night at long last flickered into extinction, beat back again by a gray, blurred dawn, the man abandoned his vigil, like a vulture impatient with the slow dying of a helpless prey.

BOOK FOUR
The Inception

And what rough beast
Its hour come round at last
Slouches toward Bethlehem to be born?

YEATS
The Second Coming

There is a sore evil which I have seen under the sun . . . a sore evil.

Ecclesiastes

Chapter Thirty-six

ALLISON WOKE UP shivering in front of the fireplace, the draft from the open fireplace flue lapping at her feet sticking out from underneath the blankets. She smiled at her doggy doll. Mom must have brought it down, that was nice.

The champagne was fun. But that second glass had made her tipsy (Downs' word) and, she was sure, stupidly giggly. How did they ever stand her silliness?

She swung around to a sitting position on the couch as the clock bonged eight times. Time to get going. She wanted to surprise Mom and Downs with breakfast so she had to get over to the little grocery store she'd spotted near campus the other day and get some country sausage and English muffins. They had a big sign in the window saying they'd be open a half day on Christmas.

Allison vaguely realized that she'd promised not to go out alone. But that didn't make any sense. It was a beautiful Christmas morning, nothing was going to happen. She'd be back before they woke up.

She was up quickly, made a cup of tea, which she'd just started drinking a few months ago, and finished it in three gulps. Then she sat down and jotted a note just in case they were up before she returned.

Mom and Downs,
Merry Christmas!

I went to the store to get some
stuff for breakfast.
I'm the chef this morning!
Love,
Al

Allison zipped up her parka after carefully tying a brown scarf around her neck. She glanced at the thermometer which registered two degrees—God, the country was cold—then launched herself out the door, squinting against the diamond-bright sunshine. The ice-covered trees sparkled with a vivid, silver brilliance against a deep blue sky. The air was crisp and frosty.

It was a glorious Christmas morning.

The old Chevy idled roughly, vibrating the steering wheel which the man grasped tightly. The driver was excited, his palms perspiring despite the cold. Again he looked in the rearview mirror, down the empty snow covered road.

Just a little longer.

Allison walked quickly to stay warm, the dry snow squeaking comically beneath her fire engine red boots. Her breath formed light vapor clouds which hung like ragged balloons in the still air, and her nose tingled in the cold. There was a still tranquil beauty to this Christmas morning, as though the weather was a logical extension of the love and peacefulness Allison had felt last night. For the first time in so long she was experiencing her own world as a sanctuary, known, constant, a place where chaos did not hold a hammerlock on her fragile emotions. The relief she felt was physical, a soothing airiness of body and mind, like bouncing on white, puffy clouds.

"Merry Christmas, Allison!"

She turned to see Mrs. Cahalan, a neighbor who had brought over a plate of wonderful brownies the day after they had arrived, waving from the door of her house. Sherry, as she insisted she be called, had been really nice.

Allison waved back. "Merry Christmas."

"Can you come in for a minute? I've got some home-made eggnog."

"Thanks, but I've got to get some stuff for breakfast. Maybe later?"

"Great. Say hi to your mom for me."

"Okay. Thanks."

Allison smiled, waved, then walked on. That was nice of Mrs. Cahalan . . . Sherry . . . to ask her in. People are different in the country, friendlier. Allison wanted to be more that way herself. At the far side of the Cahalan property she came upon a perfect Christmas scene: Sherry's three kids tucking themselves together on what was obviously a shiny new toboggan.

"Come on, Shawnie," a little blonde girl who was in the middle of two boys called to an older brother, "Push us, we want to go fast!"

The boy pushed the toboggan, then hopped on as it began to slide down a short hill.

"Whhheeeeee," the kids' cries floated in the air as Allison smiled, watching them race down their little incline. At the bottom they hit a mound of snow and spilled over, giggling and laughing in the bright snow.

Allison turned to continue down the road. She noticed a beaten-up old car, backing slowly down the road toward her. It stopped beside her, and the driver, dressed in an old Santa Claus costume and hunched over the wheel with a nervous, confused expression on his face, rolled down the window.

He thrust a crumpled piece of paper out the window, then motioned for her to take it.

Allison hesitated, wondering what the old man could want.

Again he motioned, a plaintive look apparent through his beard and Santa makeup. He held up a rumpled Christmas present, then pointed to the piece of paper and shrugged his shoulders.

He's lost, Allison realized. But she didn't know the roads, herself—how could she help? But he looked so confused, she felt sorry for him.

The old man motioned again, practically pleading this time.

She could at least read the street name. Maybe that would help. Allison walked over to the car.

As she got to the window the man's hand snapped out, seized the front of her parka, and jerked her powerfully against the side of the car. His other hand slapped something wet and soft against her nose and mouth. Allison pulled frantically against the man's powerful grip, her mind a blank of terror. The wet pad was jammed against her mouth and nose and a horrid, sweet smell hit her nostrils. The man's strength was overwhelming. She gagged, then desperately held her breath for as long as she could. Finally, she was forced to inhale. As she did the world started to turn, the sky spinning above her like a blue whirlpool as her arms fell loose at her sides.

Night and fear invaded her brain as one. The spinning accelerated, throwing black and red shadows on the walls of her fading consciousness. Then tendrils of darkness flowed together to form a solid mass and Allison slipped painlessly into a black, silent sea.

"Look, look at that!" the little blonde girl shouted, pointing to the top of the hill she and her two brothers were trudging up. "They're fighting!" Joanie Cahalan said excitedly.

Her older brother, Shawn, looked casually toward where Joanie was pointing. A girl was leaning into an old car and it sorta did look like she was fighting, that is, if you didn't know anything at all about what teenagers liked to do. Which Joanie didn't, of course. Shawn was continually amazed how stupid little kids, especially sisters, could be.

Shawn was sure he recognized Tommy Masucci's souped up bomb. And he knew exactly what Tommy and that girl were doing. He'd be doing the same thing himself in a couple of years when he got to junior high school.

Shawn turned to his sister. "Boy," he said, "are you dumb."

Chapter Thirty-seven

THE HUGE HOUSE was barely visible from the road through the tangled mass of wild trees and shrubs which had taken over the property. Its rambling, sagging mass of rounded bays and ruined dormers seemed ready to fall in upon themselves with the next heavy snowfall. Above the weather-beaten roof, crumbling gables peeked mindlessly at the gray sky. Still, dark trees scraped against the house's outside walls and few remaining windows.

A metal gate, tall and forbidding, sat heavily in a slowly deteriorating stone wall which ran around the entire immense structure of the house. What once were "No Trespassing" signs, now faded, hung unnecessarily along the wall. An awful, perpetual silence hung thick in the air around the shuttered house.

A lone figure, stooped from carrying its heavy burden, broke the silence as his boots crunched through the dry snow. He made his way past the rusting gate, across the front yard and entered the house from behind. Inside, his groping hand found a door latch. He lifted the latch and descended a dark, narrow set of stairs to the basement.

Chapter Thirty-eight

KATE WOKE FIRST and padded down the stairs in a pair of totally silly Donald Duck slippers which Downs had presented her with the evening before. It was quiet. She drifted into the kitchen to get the coffee going, spotted Allison's note on the table, and was immediately concerned.

Damn. She'd told her not to go out alone.

She woke Downs quickly, and five minutes later they were headed for the College Market.

"They probably weren't open when your eager beaver arrived and she's had to cool her heels for a while," Downs said.

But old Marty Bell, who'd been serving the campus since a couple of years before Downs had been born—and never ever forgot a customer's face, especially a young blonde's—did not remember anyone of that description coming in.

"Blonde? No sir, doctor." (Marty called every professor "doctor.") "Hell, I ain't so old that I can't at least remember what blondes used to do to me." The old man guffawed through a haze of foul smoke from a "rum soaked" Crook's cigar.

They quickly got back in the Mercedes and retraced the route to Kate's. They checked the house. Then carefully drove every campus road, then the main roads encircling Harding College. They questioned several Christmas strollers. They learned nothing. At a rise they stopped and saw the campus lying smothered in snow, roofs shining white beneath the gleaming sun. In the brilliance of the morning they found only desolation.

A frigid finger brushed Kate's heart, briefly beckoned, then slipped away. The snow all around her suddenly seemed oppressive; each flake so light and tiny as to be inconsequential, yet the mass of them together capable of smothering life beneath their cold weight.

They drove back to the house. Downs turned down the driveway, parked, and turned the engine off. Around them the wintry silence seemed profound, immutable. Encapsulating.

Then for Kate, like the march of jackboots, the dread came, carrying an awful premonition of horror. The fear quickly accumulated in her heart like snow on a window pane. She jumped from the car and ran quickly to the house. She entered the house and frantically called Allison's name. There was no answer.

When Downs reached the front porch he saw Kate staring intently at him through the shiny window of the storm door.

He saw his own reflection in the glass, overlapping Kate's, the images transparent, empty. Every nerve in his body suddenly tingled, as though an electric charge had run through him. And he knew, too, that something terrible had happened.

Chapter Thirty-nine

"I DON'T WANT to be crude, ma'am," said Sheriff Fredericks, "nor a disrespectful neighbor, but I myself seen the professor here with his car parked in your driveway most every night. Now you told me that your daughter didn't like Professor Palmer at first, but that then she changed her mind and liked him just fine. But then you also tell me that she had some troubles down in New York, and, hell, who wouldn't down in that sinkhole? Well, as far as I know, kids have a way of changing their minds—especially kids who may be upset anyway—and maybe that's just what your daughter went ahead and did."

The sheriff snapped his chewing gum thoughtfully a few times, then continued. "It certainly don't seem out of the range of possibility, at least to me anyways, that she resented your being . . . being friendly with the professor." The gum snapped twice before Glover's finale. "So she just up and took right off." The sheriff folded his arms triumphantly. "Probably headed for New York right now."

Kate sat stunned in an armchair across the room from the heavy set sheriff. It was 5:30 and completely dark outside and there was nothing to be hopeful about.

Downs battled to control his temper. "But Sherry Cahalan said she waved to her, even said she'd stop by later. That doesn't sound like a girl preparing to run away."

"Mrs. Cahalan's a fine woman but that don't mean that Mrs. Whitworth's daughter really intended to come back and see her."

"Allison!" Kate snapped. "Her name's Allison!"

"I know ma'am," Glover replied, "I got that." He began to read from a small spiral notebook. "Allison May Whitworth. Thirteen. Five feet two inches tall, one hunnert and twelve pounds. Blonde hair and blue eyes. And I got that pitcher you gave me right here." Glover held up a photograph of Allison and Kate began to sob.

"We'll find her, don't you worry," Glover said.

"What are you going to do?" Downs asked.

"I sent the girl's description to both the Onondaga and Oneida County Police and over the wire to the state boys as well. We notified the girl's father in New York and relayed the information to the city police, so they'll be lookin' out as best they can." The sheriff clearly felt their "best" would be completely fruitless. "Now another possibility could be a kidnapping, what with the family having money. Mrs. Whitworth, if you get any kind of note you let me know right away and then I'll contact the FBI boys outta Buffalo and it'll be their baby.

"I got my deputy and some boys from the county to help out too. We'll check with all the neighbors; asking about any strangers, strange cars, door-to-door salesmen, anything at all out of the ordinary. We'll check the buses outta Utica and some of the places where a kid might hang out for a while. If nothing happens, then we gotta wait. All we can do.

"She's a young girl, the weather's colder 'n hell; my guess is she'll be back home real soon."

Downs realized as Glover spoke that the man was not the fool he appeared. He chose his words carefully. Had probably baited them with his early comments to see how they'd both react. A violent reaction might have meant more trouble at home than they'd described.

"Anything you want, Mrs. Whitworth, you just call," said the sheriff. He walked across the room, suddenly ill at ease, and awkwardly put his big hand on Kate's shoulder. "We'll find that little girl of yours." He turned and walked quickly out of the house, nodding to Downs as he left.

Then they were alone in the silence.

* * *

When two days had passed with no word concerning Allison Whitworth's whereabouts, Sheriff Fredericks requested a computer read-out from Albany of all known sex offenders within a fifty-mile radius. He immediately relayed this information to the county and state police within that area. If a kidnap note is not received within forty-eight hours, he knew, there was only a very small chance of an abduction. By all accounts the girl had not fooled around with drugs, was a good student, had never been in any trouble—so it was unlikely that she'd disappeared into any of a dozen, sordid youth prostitution/drug subcultures which thrived in the state's larger cities.

The conclusion Glover came up with was disturbing: either she had tried and succeeded in killing herself—which was also kinda unlikely because most suicides don't run off; ugly as it sounded they wanted to be discovered—or someone had grabbed her for unknown reasons.

If that was true, things looked bad. Real bad.

On December 29th, four days after her disappearance, an all-points bulletin for Allison May Whitworth was issued throughout the northeastern United States. All state, county and city police departments received her description and photograph.

There were no responses.

December 30th, the fifth day. At 10:45 A.M. Glover Fredericks received a call from the Philadelphia PD; a young blonde-haired girl had been found murdered. "Have you found Allison Whitworth yet?" "No." "You'd better send someone down here."

11:55 A.M. Kate's phone rang with a loud shrillness. It was Glover Fredericks again. "Mrs. Whitworth, cancel your flight. The Philadelphia victim has been positively identified."

Oh God, stop this, please, please stop this.

Kate felt blank; her spirit like a precious liquid that had been siphoned from her body for five days. Only a terrible emptiness remained.

Chapter Forty

ALLISON AWAKENED and automatically moved her arm in a stretching motion only to have it jerk to a stop after five inches of movement. It was completely dark; she blinked repeatedly as if not believing what her senses told her.

The smell of mildew and cloying dampness were her next perceptions; then the fear, now an old companion.

She spoke out loud, "hello," her voice echoing through the enormous silence which engulfed her.

She lay on her back, bound naked to a metal frame bed. Vulnerable. Helpless. She'd heard stories about men who did . . . did bad things to girls. God knows her mother had warned her many times. But that had just been parent talk, like "look both ways," and "wear your raincoat," not talk about anything real or possible. Nothing to be afraid of. Not really. Now, faced with the possibility of an unspeakable perversion, an uncouth fear crawled maddeningly in her mind.

She was covered with thick paint; black and white horizontal stripes across her face, strange birds and thick-lipped, snarling dogs on her torso and legs, and a wide green snake which curled around her left thigh and whose head disappeared into the smooth skin of her pubis.

At first she had tried to think carefully, logically, but the silence and the darkness wrested rationality from her mind. Now, her inflamed imagination clamored shrilly for attention.

Lying face up she felt even more open to assault. It was his hands that she feared most; his fingertips had already touched her with with light teasing strokes, but there'd been nothing more. She could almost sense him ready to open the door, slowly pulling it back, then stalking in, stopping above her as he had done twice in the incomprehensibly long time she had been imprisoned, to stare down with his one hungry, inanimate eye. The eye a dark pool surrounded by a wide, yellow ring; a wolf's eye.

With this last ghastly vision her skin inflamed with revulsion and a shuddering terror again swept away any semblance of self control. Screams leapt from her throat again and again; finally, exhaustedly, winding down to a soft whimpering, like the plaintive call of a dying bird.

Chapter Forty-one

"I DON'T KNOW what this means, okay?" Will Barrett said, "but it means something. At its totally craziest—which makes no sense at all, I'm perfectly aware—it means that Austin Zellmer's alive."

"But even if that's true, what's that got to do with Allison?" Downs asked. Kate sat beside him on the living room couch, pale and thin and silent.

"Wait a minute, first things first." Will lit a Gaulois, picked a piece of tobacco from his lower lip, and sighed. God, he felt old.

"Will," Downs said, "start from the beginning." He sat balancing his forearms across his knees, head tilted slightly down, eyes up and staring intently at the dean. Downs' handsome boyish face was drawn, dark rings hung below his blue eyes like empty sacks.

"I guess I don't know where the beginning begins, that's the trouble. But I do know that the Aztec Collection in the Harding Science Building was burglarized by some pretty goddamn sophisticated thieves."

"What did they get?" asked Downs. He didn't understand. Where was this going?

"Three items worth a great deal of money. Items which were taken by Zellmer, with the collusion of our estimable college president, from the Cachton dig, mislabelled as practically worthless artifacts and then brought back to the States, to Harding.

"Now the artifacts are stolen, Ingrid Fox is dead, Collier's been implicated and obviously can't profit from their sale, and I'm wondering who else but Zellmer could be involved?" Will spoke quickly, anxious to keep going.

"All this is obviously not conclusive of anything; except perhaps that an old man can't ever drop his grudges, even against his deceased enemies. But there's more and I want both of you to listen carefully, then tell me if I sound as crazy as I feel." Will brushed ashes from his white shirt, rubbed his hand nervously over two days growth of gray beard, then continued.

"First we start with the premise that Zellmer was demonstrably mad. Then we observe that his madness was almost exclusively associated with the Aztecs. By exclusively I mean that he still wrote checks, lectured, attended academic symposiums: in short, he functioned."

Kate listened silently, her face expressionless, hearing the words but hearing her mother's haunting voice as well: *"He has risen. He wants your daughter."*

Will continued: "He wasn't just dedicated to the Aztecs, he was obsessed by them. As if they were mythic beings, gods that walked the earth. He revered the Aztecs. It's that simple."

A hum began in Kate's mind, droning like a winter fly behind a storm window. *Powerful, evil . . . secrets.*

"Imagine revering the Aztecs," Will said shaking his head in amazement. "That's the weirdest part. Obsessions I can understand. Hell, there's plenty of powerful, maybe even unhealthy obsessions running around campuses. Professors infatuated for chrissakes with *Tristram Shandy* or *Pamela,* who believe the twentieth century is a plot against "real" literature. Physicists so fascinated by black holes they forget to change their underwear. But the Aztecs, Jesus, the Aztecs were the most unrelievedly grim society mankind has ever seen. How do you attribute mythic qualities to a society that once put to death 147,000 people in a single three-day orgy of sacrifices? How can one begin to say that there was purpose, a goal, to that kind of slaughter? Sophistry, that's all it is, sophistry, pure and simple. With that kind of thinking anything can be justified. Idi Amin. Jim Jones' cyanide cocktails. But Zellmer believed in the Aztecs. Listen to this." Will jabbed his cigarette into an ashtray, lit another immediately, then pulled a piece of paper from his vest pocket and began to read.

> The Aztec priests were the psychics of their time, possessed of preternatural perceptive faculties. It is for this reason that our rational, logic-bound scholars cannot begin to fathom the depth and breadth of Aztec culture; a culture led by a class of priests dedicated to process, not goals; intensely aware of the flow of time, of history as a great continuum, rather than blindly faithful to whatever foolish, ethical standards were extant in their contemporary world. These priests were visionaries—and in one of the great tragedies of human history they were destroyed by the brutish ignorant power of the Spanish. Yet the power of their beliefs lives on, untapped, as palpable as the sun and the stars.

The hum in Kate's head was louder now, insinuating in its insistence. *He has powerful secrets, powerful, evil secrets.* Her mother's voice rasped across her mind like a fingernail raking a blackboard. Then Will's voice, reading from the piece of paper replaced it: "*the power of their beliefs lives on, untapped . . . as palpable as the sun and the stars.*" Then her mother's voice again, this time shrieking through the still, frigid air of the graveyard: "*He's alive, alive.*"

Kate stopped the voices. Madness. The rotting produce of a sick mind. Grasped only in desperation. Stop. Stop. Stop.

Will put the piece of paper down. "That's from a journal of Zellmer's I discovered."

"What are you saying?" Downs was thoroughly confused. What had any of this to do with Allison?

"Okay, I'm getting to that. Suppose a man believed that the Aztecs had real power?"

Downs couldn't hide his irritation. "But that doesn't make any sense!"

"Goddammit, I know it doesn't make any sense," Will snapped. He was suddenly aware that he was far more nervous than he had supposed; that the train of thought he had been following for a week had drained and rattled him. Again he felt old, tired and worn out. With a start he realized that must be the way one feels near death. Simply washed out. "I'm sorry," he said softly, "give me my head just a little longer, okay?"

Downs nodded wearily. "I'm sorry too." He was edgy, his sleep fitful since Allison's disappearance. There wasn't anything they could do, that was the worst part. Sitting, waiting, interminable day after interminable day. He was worried about Kate. The night before she'd said in a quiet, frightening voice that she wasn't sure how much more she could take. He'd taken her in his arms then, but her solemn, harrowing voice had echoed and re-echoed in his head. How much more? Where was the threshold of pain and grief beyond which a sane mind could not continue? When would the mind snap like a brittle rubber band? "Please keep going, Will," he said.

"Okay. This kind of thinking, attributing supernatural powers to the Aztecs, certainly isn't unheard of. Many academicians feel that Carlos Castenada's sorcerer, Don Juan, is completely legitimate; a man who has actual—and scientifically unexplainable—power over nature, even clairvoyant and telekinetic abilities. Don Juan is an Indian. The Aztecs were Indians too, primitive Indians who didn't even possess the wheel but who mapped out the celestial heavens with impossible accuracy and built temples whose huge dimensions required a technology they simply did not possess. We can't explain to this day how they did these things.

"So a leap from believing in Don Juan to believing in the supernatural power of the Aztecs is not so intellectually improbable as it would seem." Will paused and lit another cigarette. "Now suppose this man, a gifted scholar in his own right, began to lose his marbles; began to believe that the Aztecs' secret powers were accessible to modern man, accessible, perhaps, to a man who had devoted his life to the study of the Huactl cultures; a man, in short, who was worthy and capable of handling great strength. A man such as himself. Suppose this man, growing progressively sicker by the day, decided to seek access to the powers of the ancients: how would he do it?"

Downs shook his head. He still did not see where Will was going.

"Well, he might follow the rituals of the ancients. But he certainly couldn't do that publicly; after all, these ceremonies involve sacrifices and all manner of craziness which if discovered would get anyone, no matter how estimable, hauled off to the nearest institution. So he'd have to be completely free of the possibility of any interference whatsoever."

"So," Downs began slowly, "he would have himself declared dead."

"I think so, yes. And he'd do other things."

"Like?"

"Like obtaining implements necessary to certain Aztec ceremonies." Will lit another cigarette.

"The collection?"

"Yes. A ceremonial knife, an obsidian mirror, and an ancient scroll, or book as the Aztecs called it, were taken."

"What kind of ceremony were they used for?" Downs asked.

"I don't know. And neither does Judy Sjo-Gaber, our Archaeology Department chairman. But they are very rare, unusual implements not used in the normal Aztec ceremonies. That's why they're so fabulously valuable."

"Okay," Downs said, "let's theorize that Zellmer's alive, forgetting the fact that his body was supposedly at Cranston's Funeral Home . . ."

"Supposedly. I didn't see it. Did you?"

"Of course not. But I still don't get what this has got to do with Allison. Let him mumbo jumbo around, they'll get him eventually."

The droning in Kate's head had turned cold, sending icy metallic fingers slithering through the tender folds of her brain. *Powerful, evil* . . .

"His mumbo jumbo I believe has already killed two people." Will's face was grim, angry.

"What?"

"Don't you see?" Will said fiercely. "Harold Hogan and Ingrid Fox had their hearts torn out, like the victims in Aztec rituals."

Downs felt like he'd been slapped. "But Allison . . . what . . ."

Will glanced at Kate who remained impassive. He could not guess what she was feeling. He spoke softly. "She's a virgin. A blonde virgin. The most prized of all Aztec sacrificial victims."

Downs sat stunned and silent.

Secrets. He has powerful, evil secrets. The words rebounded mockingly again and again in Kate's cold mind. *He wants your daughter*. Finally her mind closed down, snapping like an overloaded circuit-breaker. She fell off the couch to the carpet, her dress rustling softly like the sound of a whispered, evil secret.

"I don't think we have much choice," Will said.

Kate and Downs nodded in agreement. Though pale, Kate was composed. At least now there would be something they could do.

A formal application to the county medical examiner for an exhumation would take at least a week. Even speeded up. And stood precious little goddamn chance of being approved. What reasons did they have for such a petition? A schizophrenic, hospitalized for thirteen years—and now deceased—had screamed that Austin Zellmer was not in his coffin. And three intelligent, well-educated adults shared a "feeling" that Zellmer wanted to pretend he was dead so he could practice Aztec sacrificial ceremonies.

Impossible. The more so because a signed death certificate existed, fully documented; pictures of the body, a horrible, self-inflicted wound plainly visible, were in the hands of the county medical examiner; a well respected mortician, Albert Cranston, had certified that Austin Zelmer was deceased. (When Will had asked Al Cranston about it, Cranston had given him an odd look; certainly it was the body of Austin Zellmer, who else?)

No, an order of exhumation did not seem in the least likely.

So, insane as it seemed, not to mention criminal, Downs and Kate and Will made a decision: they would exhume the body of Austin Zellmer themselves.

Chapter Forty-two

DEPUTY SHERIFF JOHNNY RUMSEY was tired. And highly irritated at his current assignment, guarding the Zellmer house throughout the night. Glover Fredericks was an asshole, he thought for the hundredth time that night.

The frustrating thing was he was an asshole who happened to be his boss.

What the Christ did Glover think was gonna happen in the middle of the fucking night? Other than that Whitworth broad sucking that English professor's cock. The lights downstairs had been out for half an hour; now only a dim light—a balling light his wife used to call it before she ran away with that faggot insurance man—was on upstairs.

Johnny opened a copy of *Sultry*, a third-rate porno magazine that specialized in plenty of pink. His right hand fell automatically into his lap as he gazed at the balloon-breasted, worn-out looking "models" staring vacuously out at him. Immediately his mood began changing for the better.

At precisely the instant Johnny was most enjoying himself, the back door of the Zellmer house he was keeping under strict surveillance swung open and Kate and Downs slipped out. They kneeled in the snow and strapped on the thin Bass touring skis which they'd waxed earlier. The graveyard was two miles away, and walking through the deep snow would be difficult; skiing over would be both silent and fast.

Drinking cup after cup of sweet, black coffee Kate, Will and Downs had waited impatiently for midnight, which they had decided would be the safest time to leave. Will implored them to "be careful." He would wait in the house; the graveyard was too far for a man with a bad leg and sixty-five years.

Downs leading, they slid through the backyard and down a slight incline. White moonlight reflected brilliantly off the snow, producing thousands of shining sparkles which blinked on and off around them like tiny Christmas bulbs. In this perfect niveous dream world they were both experiencing a pounding excitement; an excitement they gratefully embraced. At long last they were *doing something*. For the first time since Allison's disappearance Kate's eyes were bright, anticipatory, alive. She felt light, energized, her body again an efficient physical machine which she could depend on.

They slid past a row of campus houses, skirted the outer edge of the campus' main quadrangle, passing the theatre, and the old gymnasium, then went through a stand of tall spruces and onto the wide white expanse of the college's nine-hole golf course beyond which was the cemetery.

"Watch the sandtraps," Downs called softly as he turned just in time to avoid the lip of a steeply inclined hole.

"Yeah." Kate's voice, though a whisper, seemed loud to her in the stillness.

They moved across the golf course, the awkward-appearing yet effective lift-step-slide motion making them look like skittish sandpipers scooting across a beach.

Twenty-five minutes after they left the house they skied off the golf course and started to climb the long, easy incline to the Harding College cemetery which overlooked the campus.

On top of the hill they took off their skis and Downs walked to the cemetery's utility shed discreetly hidden behind heavy evergreen shrubbery. With one blow of the clawhammer he'd brought with him in his backpack, Downs snapped the shed's lock, then quickly located two pointed shovels. The ground would be frozen, but not packed solidly; Zellmer's funeral had been only ten days before.

They began digging, Downs at one end of the grave, Kate at the other. They discovered the ground was frozen only a few inches deep. For fifteen minutes they shovelled, a steady, unhurried pace designed for the long haul. It was then that the first blackbird landed on the empty branch of the massive, gnarled oak tree hanging over the grave. The bird was not just large, but huge, with two blood-red eyes which seemed to stare in primitive hatred at the two human figures digging in the dirt beneath it.

Moments after its arrival the bird was joined by two more blackbirds, both huge, both with the same blood-red eyes. They perched in a row on a branch and stared below them, their eyes like infrared lenses piercing the darkness.

Kate and Downs did not notice the silent birds. Steadily they worked, backs bent before the birds' malevolent eyes, slowly uncovering the buried brass coffin whose secrets they would soon violate.

Thirty minutes into their labors Downs said, "We're getting close."

Thank God, thought Kate, whose hands had blossomed

five nasty blisters, two of which had already popped. Her arms were heavy, her face a tight, frozen mask.

She stopped for a quick break. Downs kept digging, driving his hard compact body. Kate rejoined him and the double thud of their shovels filled the night.

"We're almost there," Downs said five minutes later. His back was killing him and his shoulder muscles felt like someone was carefully sticking tiny pins into them. With detached amusement he thought that whatever gravediggers were paid, it wasn't nearly enough.

Two minutes later Downs' shovel struck the top of the coffin with a metallic ring.

"All right," he said between heavy breaths. They dug with renewed energy, gradually exposing the ornate casket whose brass fixtures gleamed dully at them in the moon's light. When the casket was nearly completely uncovered Downs eased himself into the grave, brushed off the remaining dirt, then examined the hinges of the casket.

Kate bent down from above. "Sledge and crowbar do it?"

"Yeah," he sad.

"I'll get them." Kate walked to the shed.

Above her the old oak tree now swayed beneath the weight of hundreds of blackbirds crowded together on the tree's branches. Hundreds of fiery red eyes were trained hatefully on the clandestine gravediggers below. Like soldiers immediately before a battle the birds became increasingly nervous, shuffling on their perches, bumping one another, occasionally striking out, sometimes drawing blood. Yet there was never a squawk and their presence continued undetected.

Kate returned with the sledge and crowbar, her anticipation rising quickly. She handed the tools to Downs, then jumped lightly onto the coffin and a hollow, empty boom echoed eerily into the night.

"Hold the crowbar, I'll use the sledge," Downs said. "They oughta pop right open." They began at the foot of the coffin. The first hinge broke easily, and the second as well. The uppermost hinge proved more difficult, but the third blow from the sledge knocked it off cleanly.

Downs tied a rope to the handle of the casket lid, boosted Kate out of the grave, then struggled out behind her.

"Okay," he said tightly. His hands were shaking slightly. His pulse racing. He circled his strong hands around the rope and pulled with medium force. The casket lid quivered but did not open. He pulled much harder and the lid quivered and pried open ever so slightly at the foot.

"Give me a hand."

Kate gripped the rope directly behind Downs' hands. They pulled together and the lid quivered, the bottom corner opened, then with a metallic scream the lid sprung open sending them stumbling backward. They edged back to the grave. Downs took Kate's hand. They reached the lip of the hole and looked down.

The asphyxiated death mask of Timmy O'Roarke stared back up at them. His face, preserved perfectly by the cold, was twisted in agonized horror, as though only at the last instant did he truly understand his fate. His bound hands were frozen horizontally, palms up, as if he had impossibly tried to press out of his living tomb.

"My God," said Kate.

At that instant the shrieking began.

Downs and Kate snapped their heads up in time to see the oak tree above them explode in a monstrous rain of birds. Like squadrons of fighter planes the birds fell on them. The first wave struck Downs at the top of his shoulders and he wavered. A second assault hit him in the head and neck, a half dozen beaks drawing blood, and he pitched into the open grave. His forehead smashed against the edge of the coffin and a thin grey veil immediately blurred his vision. Dully he realized he was lying on the frozen corpse of Timmy O'Roarke. He felt a deathly cold steal up at him, and thought at first: I feel no pain, this is not unpleasant. Then he heard Kate scream.

Kate was hit in the head by the blackbirds, one beak taking a piece of skin from her forehead. Others simultaneously struck her knees and thighs. She swayed precariously above the grave, somehow regained her balance, then was dropped to a kneeling position by a blow in the center of her back.

Wildly she struck out at them as the birds beat their wings furiously around her. She screamed, but the shrieking of the birds overwhelmed her cry.

Then Downs was beside her, blood pouring in thick streams from his scalp. He pulled her to her feet. Supporting one another, flailing hysterically at the birds all around them, they frantically began stumbling through the deep snow to the utility shed twenty yards away.

"Put your hands over your eyes," Downs yelled. They ran with their fingers pressed tightly together covering as much of their faces as possible. Still the birds got through. Their shrieking seemed, impossibly, to get louder, an insane cacophony of horror. Blood was everywhere as the blackbirds increased the ferocity of their attack as Downs and Kate neared the shed. Five birds hit Downs on the top of his head and he fell to his knees. Kate reached down and he struggled to his feet.

Then they were at the shed. Kate beat two birds from her neck then screamed when a blackbird pierced her cheek with its beak. Downs yanked open the shed door and shoved Kate through. Frantically he fought off the birds with his left hand as he struggled to close the door against the weight of the animals' pounding bodies. Slowly the door began to swing closed. With a final burst of strength, Downs yanked at the door and it slammed shut with a crash.

Downs fell against the shed wall and slipped to a sitting position. He was quiet.

Kate's breaths came in painful, wrenching stabs. Her mind was blank and empty, incapable of comprehending what had just occurred. Slowly she calmed, her breathing smoothing out. We're safe. Safe. Nothing else mattered.

Then she felt the weight on her legs. Slowly, she looked down.

The decapitated head of a blackbird sat in her lap. Dark blood poured from its severed neck and ran over her thighs. Even in death its awful red eyes stared hatefully up at her.

Black terrifying words rose in her mind, stubbornly fighting to the surface: *Powerful, evil secrets*. A scream burst from her throat.

Chapter Forty-three

THE BLACKBIRDS DISAPPEARED as quickly and silently as they arrived. The wounds from their attack seemed immediately less painful. Kate's forehead, which had been deeply punctured, stopped bleeding; the gashes in Downs' neck and shoulders began to close. They did not, could not, begin to consider such impossible phenomena; the pain was subsiding, the agony apparently over—gratitude the only possible response.

After waiting fifteen minutes, assaulted now only by the bitter cold, they eased the door of the utility shed open. They were alone in the wintry stillness. Quickly they strapped on their touring skis and headed back across the campus. By the time they arrived at Kate's house neither of them had a visible wound. Kate looked at Downs, the expression on her face a mixture of confusion and dread. He could find nothing to say; there *was* nothing to say.

Will let them in the house. Downs ran to the phone and called Glover Fredericks' home. The telephone rang five, six interminable times before the sheriff picked up. His voice was not drowsy for long.

"What the hell? What? What do you mean you dug up Professor Zellmer's grave? Goddammit. Why in the . . . Jesus . . . all right . . . all right . . . I'm on my way. . . . I'll check the cemetery first. . . ." Glover Fredericks peremptorily hung up.

Kate first, then Downs took a hot shower. They each drank two fingers of brandy. While waiting for the sheriff they tried to describe what happened to Will. Verbalizing the events made them seem even more impossible. No, not impossible, insane. Crazy. Will listened silently, asking few questions, offering no opinion. What in God's name would I say? thought Downs.

Glover arrived thirty-five minutes after their phone call.

Downs opened the door. "Sheriff. . . ."

"Why make a fool outta me?" demanded the sheriff. His face was an angry mask. "What have I done to you?" Glover's hands were on his hips, his head thrust forward; a vein pulsed in his forehead.

Downs stepped back from the livid sheriff. He heard Will and Kate behind him.

"I don't understand, what's the . . ."

"Bullshit! What's the matter with you people?"

Will stepped past Kate and Downs, and said quietly: "Glove, why don't you close that door and come on in?"

"I ain't coming in, Mr. Barrett." Glover had known Will Barrett for over three decades and hadn't addressed him so formally in all that time. The dean had never seen the even-tempered sheriff even remotely as angry as he was right now. What in the world was going on?

"What's happened?" Will pleaded.

"Why don't you ask them," Glover jerked his thumb toward Kate and Downs, "they'd know best."

With a quizzical look Will turned toward Kate and Downs.

Kate's eyes were wide with confusion. Downs spread his hands not comprehending the sheriff's anger; at the same time a sick, nervous feeling settled in the pit of his stomach.

"What did you see up at the cemetery?" Glover demanded. "Come on, goddammit, tell me what you saw." His hoarse voice shook with rage.

"We found Timmy O'Roarke buried in Zellmer's coffin," said Downs. "It was horrible."

"You saw shit," Glover said venomously, "that grave ain't been touched." He took a threatening step toward Downs. "No dug up grave. No footprints. No Timmy!!"

"That's impossible," Downs began.

"You're either sick or crazy," thundered Glover, "but either way I ain't takin' it."

The sheriff abruptly turned and stalked away from the door, down the front walk to his patrol car. A moment later the big engine roared, and the car jerked down the driveway and was gone.

Chapter Forty-four

FIVE MINUTES AFTER Glover departed, Kate, Downs and Will left the house and drove to the cemetery. What Glover had reported was, of course, impossible. But how could he possibly have been mistaken? That was impossible too.

They reached Austin Zellmer's grave as the sun rose. A single set of footprints led from the road to the grave and back again. The snow over the grave was undisturbed. There was no blood. No decapitated blackbird in the utility shed which was securely locked.

Kate stared uncomprehendingly at the unblemished blanket of snow. She felt a tugging deep in her consciousness; a sweet beckoning which promised succor . . . relief . . . peace at last. She could not fight anymore. She could not go on.

They hadn't been here at all. That was obvious.

The conclusion was inescapable: madness. And that conclusion was oddly reassuring: at least there was a certainty in her life—though that certainty was the fact of her own insanity.

You were here. It all happened, just as you remember it!

But it couldn't have.

It couldn't have. But it did!

It's insane. It's impossible.

She fought her own mind; a silent, fierce struggle. Suddenly, the tugging abated and Kate became conscious of Downs beside her, and Will, and the cemetery, and the light of daybreak seeping over the horizon. A black curtain lifted from her eyes.

She turned to Will, her voice firm and determined. "We were here. We dug up the grave. We saw Timmy O'Roarke."

"I didn't say . . ." Will started.

Kate interrupted. "We are not insane." She reached out a small gloved hand and squeezed Downs' hand firmly.

A thought lodged in Will's mind: The mad can imitate the conditions of sanity with startling accuracy. He looked at Kate, then at Downs as they held one another.

No. He believed them; he did not know why. Nor would he ever. He simply believed.

But where in God's name did that leave them? He stared forlornly at the pristine snow. Small gray flakes began tumbling slowly from a dead, leaden sky. He turned and walked down the hill away from the cemetery. Kate and Downs followed.

Chapter Forty-five

"I DON'T SEE a lot of options," Will said slowly. "We've got only our own knowledge that Zellmer is not in his coffin. And that something has happened which could not happen. I think we have to assume he's alive. What else can we assume? So we have to find him. Where? I think the only possible answer to that question lies in Mexico. So I did a little checking. The doctor who signed his death certificate is "missing" according to the Mexico City police. The Mexican laborers who had worked for four months on the last dig were dismissed early in November. It's doubtful they would've been helpful anyway.

"There's one other person, according to a journal of Zellmer's that I discovered in his office, who might be of help. He visited the dig and he's an expert on Aztec civilizations. Apparently his presence at the excavation site was unknown; when I spoke to Judith Sjo-Gaber about it she was completely surprised."

"Who's that?" asked Downs.

"His name is Emanuel Belkonsky."

Downs stared at Will in surprise. "*The* Belkonsky?"

"The same."

"I thought he was dead."

"A lot of people do. But Judy assures me he's alive, if not well, in Mexico."

"Wait a minute," Kate interjected, "let me get this straight. You're talking about Belkonsky, the astronomer?"

"That's right," Will replied.

Downs face still registered surprise. "This is the same Belkonsky who had all those crackpot theories about the formation of the solar system?"

"The same fellow, except the theories weren't so crackpot."

"What do you mean?" Downs asked.

"Well, if you'll recall, his theories were based on the writings of an ancient Sumerian cult, a cult that almost all other scientists dismissed. Despite Albert Einstein's support, Belkonsky was practically driven from the scientific community in the early nineteen fifties. He couldn't get a teaching position for twenty years. Journals would not publish his articles. Publishers ignored his manuscripts. But in the late sixties an Apollo space probe confirmed a startlingly large number of his theories—and suddenly he was hailed as a man of courage and vision, a man unjustly persecuted for his brilliantly original thinking."

"But he's an astronomer. What was he doing with Zellmer in Mexico?" Kate asked.

"Belkonsky never accepted the apologies of those who condemned and ridiculed him all those years. He rejected all publicity, all awards, all interviews. He allowed his manuscripts to be published; so only his books speak for him. He moved to Mexico, announced he was going to devote the rest of his life to studying the great Huactl cultures, and disappeared."

"When was that?" Downs asked.

"Ten years ago. During that time, according to Judy, he has studied nothing but the Aztecs. He is supposedly an embittered, practically unapproachable man. Probably senile."

"What reason did you give Judy for asking about him?"

"Nothing that would prompt her to call the men in white suits. I simply told her that in order to establish the value of the artifacts stolen from the collection we'd have to discover exactly what they were used for. I mentioned that Belkonsky had been involved in the dig that they came from and was wondering if she had any information about him. She was very surprised, to say the least, to hear Belkonsky's name."

"Why such surprise?" Kate asked.

"First off, no one knew he was with Zellmer. Plus his reputation as an archaeologist is not widely respected; he has no degrees in the subject area. If the Harding Archaeology Foundation had heard of his presence on site, they probably would not have been pleased. According to Judy, Belkonsky has some "lunatic" ideas about the power of the Aztec societies."

"What sort of lunatic theories?"

"Well, she wasn't absolutely sure, nobody is since Belkonsky's been completely shut off from the outside world for a decade, but apparently he believes that true supernatural powers were exercised regularly within the Aztec culture. That these powers were controlled by the priestly class. There's even a rumor that Belkonsky believes himself to have some sort of power."

"How in the world is he going to be able to help?" Kate felt confused. Emanuel Belkonsky sounded crazy.

"Well I don't know if he can," Will replied, "but he's the only one we know who was at the dig. He's an expert on the Aztecs. He knew Zellmer. He might be able to suggest what Zellmer had on his mind in relationship to the artifacts. Maybe he knows the function of the stolen ceremonial artifacts. Christ, maybe he's involved in some way himself. There's just no way of knowing."

"Unless someone tracks him down," Downs said quietly.
"Right."
"That someone would be me. Correct?"
"Correct."
"And there aren't any other alternatives?" Kate asked.
"Not that I can see. If Zellmer's alive, if he has Allison, if he has the ceremonial artifacts and is planning on using them in some way, Belkonsky is probably the only man in the world who might know why."
"So," Downs said slowly, "if he's willing to see me, and if he's not senile or plum crazy, and if he's knowledgeable about the missing artifacts, he might be able to help?"
"Precisely," answered Will.
"Jesus."

At six fifteen that evening, New Year's Eve of 1982, Downs, who had flown from the Utica-Rome airport to New York's John F. Kennedy International Airport in the afternoon, was boarding Aeromexico's Flight 134 for Mexico City. From Mexico City he would make air connections to the State of Puebla, then rent a vehicle to the trip to the mountain village of Xococo where Emanuel Belkonsky lived.
Already that morning, when he stood in disbelief before Zellmer's undisturbed grave, seemed a distant memory.

Chapter Forty-six

State of Puebla, Mexico

"You have been a good daughter to me Elena," Belkonsky said in a soft voice.
"Please don't talk like that Father," she replied sharply.
"You who have believed in me for so long must not chastise me now. Please." Belkonsky gently took his daughter's hand.

"I am an old man but I am of sound mind. You know this too. But still I am afraid. And an old man should not have such fear.

"I've had a vision, Elena, a vision of apocalypse, which has haunted me nightly for nearly two weeks. I've kept silent, hoping that the dreams were only the product of deterioration; a first warning sign that my time is near."

"Father, you must not . . ."

"Yes!" the old man said with sudden vehemence, "I *must* Elena, that is exactly the point. My dreams will not go away. Instead they have crystallized. They warn that the power of the great civilization I have studied so long is alive. And that will mean great suffering."

Elena knew her father too well to argue further. He was the only truly great man that she had ever known. That she was his daughter was a privilege. Elena could imagine no better way to spend her life than in devotion to his genius. When the world had laughed at him her faith never wavered. No, she could not disagree with him now. No matter how improbable—and terrible—were his visions.

"I believe," Belkonsky went on, "there is a purpose to all life. A great purpose. And so did the civilization that dwelled on this plain. No civilization ever placed on this earth searched harder for true meaning in life than did the ancient Aztecs. In a thousand years of study they uncovered incredibly powerful forces in nature—and in the mind. But that power was lost when the Spaniards destroyed their society.

"Now I feel that power returning and here, Elena, is a great irony. Any power can be abused, that of man or of God. And I fear that the power of the ancients is in the hands of Satan—the greatest of abusers. After all my years of study, when finally I might prove to a disbelieving world that the ancients had true power over men, and over nature, I must instead fight to destroy that power."

"Can there be no other way?" A tear rolled down her cheek.

"No, Elena." Again Belkonsky took his daughter's hand. "Even now a man is coming to me. His story will confirm my fears. He will want me to help him. And I shall. But this man's faith in me, and most of all in himself, will be sorely tested. I must show him things of which he has never dreamed. Though today we call him Satan, it is the power of the ancients' Tezcatlipoca that is alive and growing. And to fight such a force one must first know him. And in that knowing there is great danger."

The old man's deeply lined face broke into a smile. "You must open a bottle of our best champagne, Elena. We will celebrate our friendship, and our love. It is my last New Year's Eve on this earth and with my daughter I will welcome it with the open heart of a child."

Elena sobbed, blindly stroking her father's wrinkled hand through her tears.

Belkonsky lifted his daughter's delicate chin with a gnarled index finger. "Do not deny me a final pleasure," he said quietly, "it is all that I have left." He smiled once more and kissed his daughter's soft lips. "Have I not always taught you that life is a great tragedy? Those who can still love life are truly the lucky ones. We have had such love."

Elena threw her arms around her father's once broad shoulders and they held one another in silent, intense adoration.

For those few moments Emanuel Belkonsky's happiness was as complete as it had ever been.

But when Elena left to go inside the house, the old man's joy fell away. He looked up at the spectacular vault of the wide Mexican sky, and his terrible dread began once again.

With quivering lips he silently prayed that he would have sufficient courage for his life's last battle.

Chapter Forty-seven

BECAUSE IT WAS New Year's Eve, Joanie Cahalan was being allowed to stay up late, really late, for the first time in her young life.

But her babysitters and older brothers, Shawn and Seth, were in the den watching a stupid old hockey game and wouldn't play with her at all, and Joanie was both disappointed and bored. She flopped down disconsolately on the living room couch, then twisted around on her knees and faced outside, her chubby arms resting on the back of the couch. She didn't understand why her brothers wouldn't play with her. Hockey was dumb. She wanted to have some fun.

Joanie stared out the window at the snow covered front yard, her big night now nothing but a big blah. As she stared forlornly through the glass her eyes caught something moving. She looked harder and saw a wounded blackbird lying in the snow in the corner of the yard by the driveway. One wing was extended out awkwardly and she could hear the bird's plaintive cries. The bird struggled up, hopped twice and fell into the snow. Got up again, hopped, and fell.

Joanie was immediately concerned. That birdie was hurt.

She jumped from the couch, opened the front door and stared through the storm door at the struggling bird. She knew she wasn't supposed to go out alone. It seemed she wasn't allowed to do *anything*, and her brothers, just because they were a little older, could do everything. It wasn't fair. The unfairness especially irritated her now because that birdie was hurt and her brothers were watching the hockey game and she *knew* they wouldn't come out and help. Besides, she didn't have anything to do. Joanie was sure her mommy would say it was okay to help the birdie if she were home.

Like a big girl, Joanie put on her outside jacket and her gloves and her rubber boots, then quietly opened the door and slipped outside, being careful not to let the storm door slam. She looked toward the driveway from the porch but couldn't see the black birdie anywhere. Then it emerged from behind a pile of snow next to the garage, hopped a couple of times and fell with a pathetic chirp into the snow.

"Birdie, I'm coming," Joanie called. She struggled determinedly through the nearly waist-deep snow, falling once but getting up quickly without crying and continuing on. As she approached the blackbird it stood up again and hopped a few feet away.

"Stop birdie!" Joanie called again. She knew the birdie was probably scared.

The bird hopped awkwardly around the corner of the garage.

Joanie knew it was dark on the side of the garage and she was a little scared herself. But that birdie was sick and she had to help it. "Here birdie," she called again. When it didn't appear Joanie plowed bravely around the corner of the garage into the dark.

But the birdie wasn't there. And it was *awfully* dark and suddenly very cold too. She didn't feel brave anymore. She was frightened.

Her eyes strained to see through the darkness but everything was much blacker than before and she couldn't see anything except dark, scary shapes. A breeze blew snow against her face. A fallen tree limb snapped sharply. Joanie began to cry.

There was another snap. And another. Then a heavy step crunched in the dry snow. She turned to run. It was too late.

At the instant of Joanie Cahalan's capture the crescent moon seemed to dim and the night become dark and fierce. A nocturnal hunter, standing in the snow, raised his great head to the sky in triumph, his eye gleaming with a red fire. Then he disappeared with his small burden into the night. As his heavy footsteps grew faint, the moon brightened in relief.

Chapter Forty-eight

Xipe placed the girl on a stone block and quickly removed her clothes: first the blue parka, which matched her eyes, then the pink jump suit, the tiny red panties, finally the small socks. The girl twitched and her eyes fluttered open. He removed a vial from his pocket, unscrewed its top, then squeezed the girl's nostrils shut. As her mouth opened to breathe he poured a fine white powder in. The girl coughed once, then swallowed. Immediately she was still.

Xipe looked at the naked body of his master lying on another stone block. The body was perfect: it had moved and breathed, then ceased altogether, just as had been written by the ancients. Now the master would rise. Together they would complete the rituals which would ensure his immortality.

He opened two jars and skillfully applied black and yellow paint in neat alternating horizontal stripes across the girl's face and body. He climbed onto the pedestal, knelt over the girl, and began to pray. As he prayed, the obsidian mirror next to him began glowing, alive with the feverous energy of the Great God of Darkness.

As the last words of his ancient incantation hung in the gloom the Indian seized the sacrificial knife and raised it slowly above his head. The girl moved then, but he had her body securely pinned between his thighs.

"Tezcatlipoca, Lord of the Night," he chanted, "be my guide."

His hand plunged down.

Xipe kneeled in awe before the dark man who now stood as tall and lean and strong as the mighty oak. The preliminary rituals were complete: first a beast, then a man, then a woman and finally a child. Xipe could feel the power of the ancients rippling through him like waves of adrenalin.

Now man must be set against man. Dissension spread. When twenty-seven lay dead it would be the golden virgin's time.

And the Dark Master would be forever free.

Chapter forty-nine

INSIDE THE Kirkton Country Club the New Year's Eve party was in full swing.

Outside the dark man stood alone, the power of blood seething in him, casting his hypnotic madness at the innocent revelers in the gaily lit building.

In minutes he, a lion among lambs, would begin to move the world to his design. He would open old wounds, stir old hatreds. Pit brother against brother, parent against child, husband against wife.

He would strip the most cherished beliefs from their lives. Friendship, love, faith, dependability—none of these foolish virtues would ever be trusted again. A torrent of cleansing violence would sweep across the land like a great tropical storm, bringing chaos to rich and poor, weak and powerful alike. Lamentations would wail in the air like sweet, futile music.

As if on command a wind rose from the south. He smiled lifelessly, then turned his soulless eye toward the twinkling lights. As he stared his eye became blanker still, devoid of the slightest humanity, like freshly washed window panes brilliantly reflecting the last rays of a dying crimson sun.

He held his pose for five minutes. Then he moved silently away, toward darkness and a terrible eternity.

BOOK FIVE
The Horror

Diseases desperate grown
By desperate appliance are relieved
Or, not at all.

SHAKESPEARE
Hamlet

Chapter Fifty

THE TWO ADJOINING ballrooms of the Kirkton Country Club were alive with the swelling music and the fragile giddiness that blossoms only on New Year's Eve. Soft, pastel-colored lights shone from the chandeliers overhead, highlighting the steady undercurrent of sensuousness which flowed perceptibly through the club's old high-ceilinged, oak-beamed rooms.

For Phyllis Morton everything since midnight had become a blur. Though she hadn't drunk that much, a suppressed, long-denied need now fully alive and stridently demanding, had burst free within her. She had always been faithful to George. In fact, she had never considered being otherwise.

When the clock had announced the new year she kissed him warmly. Then with increasing passion she found herself kissing John Nielson and Don Schiller and Dennis Holler. Every previous year she had disliked this ritual of kissing people she barely knew.

This year was different.

With each kiss her desire grew stronger; first her mouth relaxed and opened, then her body loosened and began pressing into the men she kissed, finally her hands grew bold. For the first time in her life Phyllis was overcome with an overwhelming need for a man other than her husband.

Now she danced with Tim Waibel, a college boy who spent summers teaching tennis at the club. Phyllis let the back of her hand graze the front of his pants and felt his immediate reaction. She continued to press into him and it was not long before people began to notice.

Phyllis Morton, however, did not—could not—care. On tip toes she reached an arm around Tim's wide neck and whispered, "I want you."

Tim Waibel couldn't believe what he'd heard. He felt like Dustin Hoffman in *The Graduate*. He liked the role. Until he saw George Morton striding across the room.

Phyllis turned vehemently on her husband. "Get away from me. Get away." Shock registered on Morton's face, then disbelief. Phyllis seemed like a total stranger to him, her face hard, implacable, her voice deeper and angry. He stood motionless as she moved Tim across the room.

Phyllis led Tim into the cloak room, stroked him again, then told him to get his car. She excused herself to enter the ladies' room. When Tim left the room Phyllis quickly walked toward the club's kitchen whose spotless metallic fixtures gleamed under harsh fluorescent lights.

She stood for a moment in the doorway and stared at the cleavers, paring blades, carving knives, and assorted other cutlery which seemed to hang expectantly from the kitchen walls. Phyllis picked a medium-sized blade and put it in her pocketbook.

George was waiting at the doorway of the country club.

"Phyllis, please," he said, his face a portrait of confusion and pain.

She slapped him hard, knocking him backwards, then turned and ran to Tim's waiting car. George Morton did not follow.

Twenty minutes later, at the Star Motel, Phyllis Morton was beneath the thrusting body of a terrifically energetic young lover. The intensity of their lovemaking made her delirious. As Tim's tempo continued unabated, she abandoned herself to raw pleasure, oblivious to everything but her own burning desire. An infinitessimal quickening of pace drove her higher. With a deep throaty cry, she slapped her hips at Tim and found the violent release she so desperately needed.

Minutes later Phyllis heard, as if from a great distance, Tim sigh, "My God." Immediately she wanted him again. She found his penis and curved her tongue in long strokes up and down its length while her captive groaned with pleasure. She needed this boy again, nothing else mattered.

She moved so that his mouth was underneath her and frantically pressed herself toward his face. As he exploded, Phyllis' frenzied climax shuddered through her body. Tim's orgasm seemed to drain every last drop of fluid from the center of his body. Slowly, he drifted off to sleep, a lazy smile on his lips.

George Morton sat alone in the darkness of his living room, their living room, his anger and fear now reduced to a dull, insistent ache. He had not even gone upstairs to check on the kids after saying goodnight to the babysitter. He couldn't bear to see their contented, soft faces. He had no idea what to do. No idea why this nightmare was happening. All he could manage to do was sit, blinking through the tears that kept welling in his eyes.

Phyllis crawled out of bed and lay for a long time with her face pressed to the dank motel carpet which smelled of mildew and stale, old dirt. Her body ached from the sex, but not in the pleasurable way it did after she and George finished loving. Now the ache was a thick discomfort. The scent of sex in the room was almost putrid, as though something had died and now lay slowly rotting in the corner.

A thick fog filled her eyes. Then a roaring began and quickly grew louder, rising and falling in a monstrous, mocking cadence. The cadence commanded her. She could not resist.

Blindly she groped for the kitchen knife in her pocketbook, tightly curling her fingers around its smooth handle.

Then she was above the boy. Phyllis lifted the knife slowly above her head, then hesitated as though somewhere deep within herself she still fought the force which controlled her so irrevocably. But she was too weak. Her mind emptied, and she obeyed her unseen master.

Like any small town, Kirkton had known its share of sin in the nearly three hundred years of its existence. There had been adultery, thievery, rape, even three murders. But never had it known the blind horror that rode the winter wind into the new year of 1983.

For the first time, the town of Kirkton knew evil.

Melissa Lutke sat in her living room, blankly watching the crowds on television celebrate the New Year. Her mind was occupied with the unhappy thoughts which had bothered her all evening. Her roommate, Becky, did not properly appreciate her. No, she didn't appreciate her at all.

Melissa's resentment gradually became anger, then her anger became rage. Becky was hateful, really hateful. Melissa did not think she could stand to see her face ever again.

As she continued to stare at the swaying Times Square revelers on the TV screen her eyes glazed over and her mind, suddenly drained of anger, became blank. Mechanically Melissa got up from her favorite chair and walked into the kitchen. She slid open a drawer, picked out a knife, and headed toward Becky's bedroom in the rear of the apartment.

Herbert Mahey had been married forty-three years and until this night he had always thought he'd been happy with Sylvia. Now, suddenly he realized with startling clarity that he had wasted his life with her. That he had been destined for big things had he not become entangled with her. What a fool! How could he have allowed himself to be dragged down? And now it was too late. His youth long since past. His future a short, shabby joke.

It had been her all these years, holding him back, urging him to be satisfied with the job at the dairy, making it impossible to follow his dreams.

Herbert finished oiling his double-barreled shotgun and admired his work. His rolling mind began to slow and he felt suddenly distant, somehow separated from himself. A soft roaring started in his left ear, spread to the right, then began building like wind whistling down a dark tunnel.

A moment later Herbert Mahey, gun crooked in his arm, was walking up the basement stairs. He saw and felt nothing.

George Morton jumped up from the couch when he heard a car pull in the driveway. It was five A.M. Finally she was home. His mind was a mixture of anger and relief. God, what would happen now?

But when he looked out the window he saw Kirkton's blue and white police chief's car. Then he saw Sheriff Fredericks push heavily from his seat and start slowly up the snowy path to the house. George moved mechanically to the door; he didn't want the doorbell to wake the kids. His heart thumped uncomfortably, forbodingly, in his chest.

Step by step his eyes recorded the big sheriff's footsteps coming up the walk. He heard snow slide off the rooftop and crash into the already heavily laden evergreens. The sheriff passed a six-foot-tall blue spruce. Phyllis had planted the tree five years ago. Her favorite.

George found his hand reaching for the door knob and observed that his wrist looked thin. That was odd. The door knob was cold to his touch and that was odd too. A slight electrical charge seemed to surge through his hand when he turned it.

He tried to smile at the sheriff as the door swung open but

it was no use. Something horrible had happened. He knew.

With the first sound of the sheriff's voice, George Morton's face collapsed like a pricked balloon, his facial muscles instantaneously incapable of holding his features in any arrangement other than total, abject horror.

With a whimper he fell to his knees.

Chapter Fifty-one

The Utica Dispatch

NINE DEAD IN SAVAGE MURDERS!
National Guard Called In

Killers, all Kirkton residents, catatonic;
Local, State Police Baffled

by George Cornell

KIRKTON——*January 1:* Nine Kirkton Village residents were brutally murdered between the hours of midnight and seven A.M. today in the worst episode of violence in New York State history.

Just last week the village was shocked by its first two murders in fifty years.

The victims were all relatives or close friends of the murderers. The killers, after committing the gruesome acts, were found near their victims in catatonic states. All the victims' bodies were mutilated.

The Governor ordered a state of martial law in Kirkton Village and surrounding Oneida County. The Governor also directed National Guard troops from nearby Griffiss Air Force Base to "protect the Village and its citizens."

New York State Attorney General Robert Abrams was at a loss to explain the tragedies. "We have no explanation for the murders at this time. There seems no possibility of a common motive for the killings; no link between the victims, except that they were all residents of Kirkton Village."

Unofficial speculation centers around the possibility of either sabotage of the Village water supply with an unknown drug, or the advent of a heretofore undiscovered virus or other contagious disease which affects the brain unpredictably.

State health officials have warned all residents of Oneida County to boil their water. A spokesman for the Disease Control Center in Atlanta confirmed that a team of their doctors will arrive in Kirkton today.

Experts searched vainly for modern parallels to the Kirkton tragedies. Professor Joseph J. Gadbaw, Jr., chairman of Harding College's history department, cited the case of a French village which in the nineteenth century experienced a wave of psychotic episodes which caused a number of suicides and murders. It was later discovered that a yeast used in the village's bakery had produced an LSD-like substance which was blamed for the incidents.

"But," Professor Gadbaw reported, "the cases are not all that similar. It is doubtful even a powerful hallucinogen would cause nine separate individuals to commit nine separate acts of murder. I know of nothing like it in documented history."

A shaken Mayor Joe Agresta has advised Kirkton's residents not to go out alone, to stay in groups of three or more, and to carefully look for the onset of catatonic symptoms which may presage further violence. (Catatonic symptoms include glassy eyes, dilation of pupils, slight tremors in the extremities, speech irregularities, and impaired reaction time.)

The victims were: Timothy W. Waibel, 20, of 17 Grove Street; Becky Forsano, 26, of 223 Clinton Corners Road; Sara Jane Shubert, 9, of 101 College Street; Sylvia Mahey, 64, ...

Chapter Fifty-two

THE TELEPHONE RANG and Kate raced across the living room to answer it on the second ring.

"Hello."

"Kate, are you all right?"

She sighed heavily. Again it wasn't Downs.

"Kate?" Joel Weltman repeated, "are you there?"

"Yes." At the sound of his familiar voice tears rose in her eyes.

"I just heard about it on the radio. Are you all right?"

Kate answered mechanically, "Yes."

"Look, you and Allison must get out of there now. Okay? Grab the next plane and stay with me down here. Right?"

"Allison's gone," Kate sobbed, and then she tearfully told him all that had happened.

Joel found himself breathing heavily into the phone, as though the air had been sucked from his office. He found nothing to say that could be even remotely consoling. Good Mother of God, how could what he'd just heard possibly have happened? How?

"I'm coming up."

"There's nothing you can do. We're waiting for Downs, that's all."

"I'm coming anyway. I'll hop the next plane."

Joel hung up quickly; he did not want to hear Kate's haunted, empty voice again.

Chapter Fifty-three

State of Puebla, Mexico
January 1, 1983

DURING THE NIGHT, a bank of damp air from the Gulf of Mexico had rolled swiftly across the broad coastal lowlands, collided with the cold air over the eastern edge of the vast ridge of mountains that rose abruptly from the Mexican plain, and then settled back to earth as heavy fog.

Now, at dawn, Downs could see the fog, his enemy throughout the night, enveloping the rocky peaks like a gray shroud. The land was barren and ugly. The few villages he had passed clung with solitary tenacity to the tops of steep ridges where sparse vegetation grew like tufts of lank hair. Now that he was finally close to the tiny village of Xococo, the loneliness he had felt through the night was replaced with anticipation. Belkonsky had to be there, he had to help.

Downs had arrived in Mexico City shortly before nine P.M. on New Year's Eve. It seemed the entire airport was busy celebrating and his flight to Puebla City, a town of 500,000, did not leave until eleven P.M., an hour late. By midnight he made Puebla, then quickly rented a Land Rover, with the aid of a twenty-five dollar bribe, and had left the city by 12:45. The trip east and south was frustratingly slow; the asphalt road disappeared five miles outside the city, replaced by a chuck-holed dirt path teeming with burros, wagons, sheep, cattle and a seemingly endless string of New Year's revelers drunkenly heading back to their villages. Twenty miles an hour was excellent time. Every four hours he swallowed a tiny red amphetamine capsule which his friend Dr. Healy had given him before he left; they kept him wide awake, but increasingly nervous.

As the sun brightened the horizon he snapped on the short

wave radio and heard a gruesome cavalcade of traffic atrocities that occurred the previous day on Mexico's deadly roads. He heard a weather report, in Spanish, then English, a morning prayer from a Mexican cardinal blessing the New Year, and general news, first national, then international.

Kirkton's tragedy was the lead international story.

First in disbelief, then in growing horror, Downs listened to the radio report about Kirkton's nightmare. Nine dead! Numbly he heard that the bodies had all been mutilated, the killers all catatonic. That the Governor had called in the National Guard. That no one had a clue as to the cause of the bizarre tragedy.

He heard it like a dream, a vivid, living nightmare, reality and unreality bumping heads in the dark. Then the radio announcer began listing the victims, and Downs sucked in his breath and held it, a picture of Kate filling his mind. Dear God, please.

"The dead are Herbert Effinger"—Downs knew him, a player on his softball team—"Becky Forsano," and the names rattled off, Lutke, Makowsky, Mahey, Petrella, Peters, the Shubert's girl, Melissa, then the W's . . . Wainscott . . . no, it wouldn't be, it couldn't . . . one more, just one more . . . When the voice announced the last victim, 'Steven Zabel' Downs did not know whether to cry or shout with joy.

He clung tightly to the wheel of the Land Rover and drove steadily on.

A little after eleven A.M. he reached Xococo, whose narrow dusty streets were completely empty. He weaved past squat, red-roofed white huts. An eerie gray light, barely capable of penetrating the thick combination of fog and cooking fire smoke that hung in the village, added to the sense of desolation. Only faint, muffled sounds told of human habitation: the crying of a baby; the steady clomping of a tethered burro; the dull, rhythmic pounding of corn being beaten into meal.

He stopped in a decaying, empty plaza, surrounded by crumbling concrete benches with a lichen-covered circular well at its center. No one was in sight. He waited a few interminable minutes. Still no one appeared. When he could no longer stand it, he leaned on the Land Rover's horn. Its blast into the silence was startlingly loud. After four noisy bursts an old man appeared like an apparition from behind a shattered wall and slowly limped toward the vehicle.

Yes, he did know the hacienda of Señor Belkonsky. Just outside the village to the east. A two-story hacienda, Xococo's finest building.

Chapter Fifty-four

"I HAVE BEEN expecting you." The frail old man held out his hand and Downs grasped it, surprised at the strength of the grip.

"But how did . . .?"

"I know you have great trouble." Belkonsky put his left hand over their handshake and Downs was curiously calmed. The old man's green eyes were bright and intense as though painted on a face burned dark by ten years work under the desert sun. His head was unusually large with a high forehead topped by a wild mane of white hair. "Come in, we will have some green tea. You have come a long way and must be tired." A resilient strength, the strength of a survivor, lived in the old man's face. Yet Downs saw something else, an immutable sadness, in Belkonsky's green eyes.

"You must have patience, there is much to learn." They sat at a round wooden table, a plain clay tea pot and two steaming mugs before them. "I know of the tragedy which has visited your town. And I also know, there will be more suffering."

"Then you know it's Austin Zellmer I've come to ask you about?" Downs asked.

"Of course," the old man answered quickly, then repeated more softly, "of course."

"What can you tell me about him and about the last dig he was on?" Downs asked quickly.

"I can tell you much, but I must do it in my own way. You cannot rush to battle the foe who is assaulting your town. His powers are already great and grow stronger daily. We must prepare carefully. You must see for youself the awesome splendor and the terrible power of the ancient Aztecs."

Downs felt confused and irritated at Belkonsky's parabolic way of speaking. "But what have the ancients to do with Kirkton?" he said, an edge in his voice.

"Everything." Belkonsky stared directly into Downs' eyes, the gaze unnerving in its intensity. "The powers of the ancients are alive. It is they you and I must fight." The old man's eyes were blazing bright, as though backlit by an orange fire.

Downs' irritation slipped away, replaced by an unsettled feeling, part unease, part fear. He suddenly did not want to ask any other questions, afraid of what the answers might hold.

A fire crackled and spit behind them like a cornered animal. The room seemed dark and small, confining, and Downs fought an irrational schoolboy impulse to bolt from his seat, to flee what he feared would come.

"I do not understand," he said fighting to control the quiver in his suddenly undependable voice.

"Of course not. But you shall. I will teach you." Again Downs had the feeling that the old man's eyes were burning into him, searing his soul. "The power of the ancients is more awesome than any earthly power. It is as constant as the night wind, as fierce as the jackal. This is a frightful enemy that we must fight."

Downs felt a thin shudder scuttle up his spine, like a cold electric current. He sensed that he was about to leave his familiar world of order and logic, the world he had always depended on and believed in. About to enter a world seemingly without rules or even common sense, a dimension ruled by forces whose derivation he could not even begin to guess at. And he was afraid.

Yet he could not forget the blackbirds, the death mask of Timmy O'Roarke, the pristine gravesite, the mass murders, the dog—and therefore could not help but believe that some monstrous, ineffable, impossible force was working in Kirkton. A force that he knew had taken Allison and shattered the woman he loved more than anything or anyone in his life. A force that he must pursue.

It was plain that the old man who sat quietly beside him, discussing concepts which two weeks ago Downs would have unhesitatingly labelled ridiculous and most probably insane, was the only hope he and Kate had left. Perhaps the only hope for Kirkton as well.

But the power of the ancients? What did that mean? How could he learn about such things?

"There's a question in your mind, my friend," Belkonsky said softly.

The old man's prescience startled Downs. He seemed able to read his thoughts.

"I know nothing of supernatural powers. A few days ago I believed there was no force on earth except that of man."

Belkonsky laughed. "No other force? You have much to learn."

"What do I have to learn?"

Belkonsky smiled, shaking his great head as though he'd heard something terribly humorous. But then the smile faded and again the green eyes bore into Downs. "About another world, a shadow world, that is as real, as knowable, as your own physical world."

"I. . . ."

* * *

"But mostly I will teach you about powei. True power."

A swift chill jumped from Downs' stomach into his chest.

Again Belkonsky seemed to read his mind. "Do not worry too much." The old man reached out both hands and gripped Downs' right forearm with surprising force. "We will go back to Kirkton together."

Belkonsky abruptly stood up. "Come. Let us begin."

"My God!" Downs exclaimed as the Land Rover slid to a halt at the base of an immense pyramid. His eyes followed stone steps that seemed to climb endlessly into a light blue sky bleached by the early evening sun.

He turned to Belkonsky, who was being helped from the vehicle by his daughter, Elena, and he was shocked at the old man's frailty. He spoke so forcefully, so vibrantly, that Downs had mistaken the voice's character as a sign of physical strength. Watching Belkonsky struggle out of the Land Rover, he realized the extent of the man's deterioration, another victim of indefatigable time.

"How high is it?" Downs asked craning his head up and back to stare in wonderment at the vast pyramid.

"Twenty stories. The perimeter of the base is over one half mile."

"I had no idea . . ."

"You had no idea a primitive race like the Aztecs could produce such a wonder?"

"I guess so." Downs felt vaguely uncomfortable, like a schoolboy caught unprepared.

"That's why I brought you here, so you can experience for yourself the greatness of this civilization." Belkonsky swept his hand across the sand-covered plaza choked with mesquite and sagebrush. "From the top of this pyramid one could gaze at an endless sea of temples and buildings covered with white stucco that glistened like ivory in the sun. Flat terrace roofs bloomed with flowers. Broad avenues opened into plazas ringed by brilliantly mosaic walls. No wonder Cortez, in a letter to the Spanish emperor, said this city "far surpassed in beauty and magnificence our own stunning Granada."

"Yet alongside such beauty existed incredible savagery." Belkonsky's voice was suddenly softer, sadder. "And that savagery you must also know, for the power that produced it is the same power which a dark warrior now employs."

Dark warrior? Again Downs felt irritated, ungrounded, as though Belkonsky's words somehow did not fit together, did not make sense even when listened to carefully. "But . . ."

Belkonsky waved his hand dismissively. "Later, you will understand. At the dedication of this pyramid, The Pyramid of the Sun, seventy thousand young men, captives of war, lined up for two miles to climb these steps," Belkonsky pointed before them, "to their deaths. Such was the power of the priests that these men did not resist, indeed lay without restraint on huge sacrificial tables while their still-beating hearts were torn from their chests."

As he listened, Downs' gaze caught, then held, two massive, hideous serpent heads with grimacing mouths filled with black obsidian teeth that flanked the pyramid's steep stairway. What horrors these blind stone heads had witnessed!

"Imagine the reaction of the Spanish Christians when they first arrived!" Belkonsky's voice seemed to force itself into Downs's mind, compelling his attention. "Marching past row upon row of heads impaled on stakes. Entering sacrificial rooms that reeked like charnel houses. Meeting priests whose robes and hair were clotted with blackened blood." Abruptly Belkonsky fell silent, and a glaze settled over his eyes. The animation dropped from his face, and his features settled slowly, the features of a worn out, no longer vital old man. Like a chameleon Belkonsky switched with startling speed from vigor to frailty. He murmured something softly, then repeated it, more to himself than to Downs or Elena. "Tezcatlipoca," he said more loudly. An uncomfortable thought lodged briefly in Downs' mind—he's insane—then flitted away. He could not afford not to believe in Belkonsky.

"Tezcatlipoca?" Downs asked, trying to break into the old man's reverie.

Belkonsky lifted his gaze to the top of the pyramid. He gave no sign of hearing. A minute passed, then another. Elena raised a finger, signaling that Downs should remain silent.

"Satan," the old man's strong voice was back again. "Tezcatlipoca to the Aztecs. Alive still."

"What do you mean alive? I don't . . ."

"Be patient. Later." For the first time the old man's voice was sharp. "Just a little patience," the voice soft once more. "I will explain everything." The old man smiled and there was a reassuring warmth in his eyes. "Trust me."

There was no choice. Downs nodded his head.

"Good, I will not let you down.

"There is more you must know about the Aztecs' greatness. Despite their barbarism the Aztecs truly searched for meaning in life. For eternal truths, and for power. They had advantages in this search. Their land was so fertile there wa little need to concentrate on mundane realities—like mechanization—which so consumed the time of other civilizations. The Aztecs had a huge priestly class, yet they had no iron, domesticated no animals, never even invented a plow. Instead they concentrated their total intellect on the heavens above.

"In a thousand years of study, they found incredibl powerful forces at work. In another thousand years, they ha learned to tap these forces. That was the purpose of th human sacrifices, my friend. They were a methodology, route to power and knowledge. Like today's meditation, c chanting, or the repetition of mantras. The gruesome sacr fices gave the Aztecs access to an immense power—a powe that western civilization is only now just beginning to explor and respect."

Downs felt confused, and suddenly doubtful.

"I know what you are thinking," Belkonsky said, agai reading Downs' thoughts. "It is what I thought at first, to

What any sane man would think at first. Utter craziness. But before my eyes I have seen men change shapes at will, transforming their spirit to that of the eagle or the hare. I have seen communication with intelligences that come from I know not where.

"I am convinced that mankind's refusal to accept such facts as I have witnessed is attributable to amnesia. Engulfed with the trivialities of everyday life, we have forgotten how much power we have within our grasp. The Aztecs, however, focused on those powers with an intensity that makes our passion for modern science seem dilatory."

While Belkonsky spoke the sun had begun to sink, now a shimmering yellow ball which danced on the jagged, mountainous horizon. In the half light of dusk the Aztec ruins seemed to expand, looming like prehistoric spectres emerging from the grave. A chill raced through Downs as the cool desert air sank from the sky. He felt hypnotized, under some powerful spell which had suddenly become a convincing reality.

Downs turned back to Belkonsky whose eyes blazed with fierce conviction. "Yet, my friend," the old man continued, "the Aztecs were mortal. For all their wisdom they made one tragic mistake. They believed the Spanish were gods. Before they could correct this mistake, Spanish steel had cut off a civilization in full bloom. The priests were put to death, temples torn down. The Spanish burned every book, every document, wiping out the knowledge of thousands of years. Only a few scattered rituals, folk knowledge you might call it, have survived, handed down from generation to generation in the remote reaches of the mountains. It is this primitive knowledge that I myself have seen.

"But the wise men, the shamans who possess the remnants of knowledge their Aztec forefathers once had, speak of greater power, long buried, but still alive, accessible if only it can be unearthed."

Another chill coursed through Downs as Belkonsky's voice changed quality, now deeper, almost reverent, filled with the kind of religious awe one usually hears only in the truly pious.

"It is that great, lost power which I fear is alive . . . and at the use of a man who is no longer a man."

"Zellmer," whispered Downs.

A single tear rolled down Belkonsky's lined cheek as the last rays of the sun fell from the desert and darkness reclaimed the earth.

Chapter Fifty-five

State of Puebla, Mexico
January 2, 1983

IT WAS PAST MIDNIGHT when they returned to Xococo but there would be no sleep for either of them. Belkonsky prepared a bitter-tasting liquid from the pulp of a cactus; they both drank. Almost immediately Downs felt his mind quicken, his perceptions sharpen; he was both energized and curiously confident.

Now he sat at a rough-hewn table, Belkonsky standing in front of him. A small fire burned behind him, fighting against the chill of the Mexican night.

"What you are about to read will explain much about the Aztecs' great, dark powers. When you finish, we will travel to the mountains, to a holy man, who will tell us what we mortals can do to fight Tezcatlipoca."

Belkonsky faced the fire which illuminated his face with an orange glow, as though he stood before the fires of hell.

"Is there time?" Downs asked.

"I do not know. First you must read. Then we will travel. It is not too far and I know the holy man will await us."

"How does he know we are coming?"

"He knows, my friend," Belkonsky said cryptically. "Please," he motioned to the papers before Downs.

As Downs turned to the manuscript before him, the quality of the light in the room became extraordinarily bright and vivid. Every object had a thin electric border, a neon fringe, surrounding it. The air was viscous like thick clouds, seemingly capable of supporting a man's weight. Downs waved his hand through the air feeling it pass like Jell-O between his fingers. After-images of his hand's movement trailed before his eyes, hung briefly in the room, then faded like sky writing. He was intensely aware of his beating heart, of his viscera suspended delicately in his body, of the mechanical bellowing of his lungs. He felt vulnerable, fragile, a human butterfly. He was afraid.

Downs twisted toward Belkonsky whose eyes glowed serenely, confidently down at him.

"It's all right," the old man said before Downs could speak, "you will need to see the world differently tonight. And you will need strength. My drink can only hurt you if you allow it to hurt you. Think of it as an ally, a guide, and she will be your friend."

Downs immediately relaxed. His mind seemed taut, like a perfectly conditioned athlete's body. He'd never felt more completely alive, more sensitive, more in tune with the world.

He looked up at Belkonsky once again. The old man smiled reassuringly and Downs smiled back, then put his head down and began to read.

A letter to His Holiness Juan Rodriquez Forneca, Bishop of Barcelona, Honored President of the Council of the Indies; from Fray Diego Portilla, pastor to the expedition force of the conqueror Hernando Cortez:

May Almighty God in His mercy guide my failing hand as I make this, my last report.

My strength has been sorely sapped by the struggle with the forces of darkness that rule this pagan land. I pray that I may find in His grace the peace denied me in this life of trial and pain.

Of the butchery of these savage Aztecs I have written much before. I report to you now, my excellency, what I have long feared: it is not ignorance and superstition we have fought here, but the forces of Satan himself. We must bring utter ruin to this kingdom of darkness, as the avenging angels of the Lord brought fire and brimstone to destroy wicked Sodom and Gomorrah in the days of Lot.

The seige of their unholy capital, Tenochtitlán, began in the latter days of May. By August, the defenders, wan and emaciated, supported themselves by devouring roots, the bark of trees, and the grass of the plain. Their men sickened and died in huge numbers, yet still they preferred to die than surrender. Famished wretches—men, women, even children—met our daily charges with unholy ferocity, until mounds of bodies taller than a man blocked the streets. We long wondered what power could make men—even these savages—fight on in such appalling conditions. To our horror we found it was no power of man.

Always behind their troops were the villainous high priest of their obscene religion. We often saw them in the distance their black robes flying in the breeze. Their mere presence seemed to send their troops forward with inhuman fury.

Cortez was convinced we must slay the priests to avoid further weeks of carnage. In darkness he sent a small band of men to reconnoiter the Aztecs' Great Temple. Once again the amazing ability of the Aztec priests to anticipate our move prevented the troops from penetrating their sanctuary. But youth, who wore the garb of an apprentice to the priestl class, was captured.

After hours of questioning the youth's lips remained sealed. Finally Cortez called upon me to give the blessing of the Lord before the youth was dispatched to a far bette world. Yet when I approached him he screamed and writhed away. His eyes were glued in fear upon my cross. I held th symbol of our Lord before me, and I swear upon a solem oath to the Blessed Virgin, that as the cross grazed his chee a welt instantly rose upon his flesh.

His fear of our Almighty God finally brought forth th following tale:

Centuries ago, the Aztecs were a small wandering band, pursued and preyed upon by more powerful, more civilized tribes who despised their savagery.

At their lowest ebb the Aztec leaders were visited by a god they called Tezcatlipoca. In truth he was no god, but the Prince of Darkness. With honeyed tongue, Satan offered the Aztec priests great power and wealth. In return, the Prince demanded that he be worshipped as their only god.

To this foul proposal the Aztecs readily acceded. Tezcatlipoca demanded that bloody sacrifices be made daily in his name. The Aztecs, with little regard for human life, quickly agreed. Finally Satan demanded that two high priests, shamans, pass through death in order to give up their eternal souls to his possession.

With a ceremonial dagger, the two most powerful shamans were slain. For five days sacrifices prescribed by Satan were made. The souls of the shamans returned from the foul fires of Hell to reanimate their bodies. As the prescribed rituals continued great powers accrued to these shamans—the power over the minds of others; the power to change shapes so they could run as a jackal or soar like an eagle; the power to conjure the future with the use of an obsidian mirror.

On the fifth day of unholy ceremonies, a blonde virgin was sacrificed; and the priests—now forever impervious to death and decay—gained the greatest of powers—the power to alter nature, to raise the seas, summon the wind, break the crust of the earth. As long as they took for their sustenance the hearts of human beings they would not yield to the relentless demands of time nor the ordinary weapons of man. They would not die.

Downs' mind reeled like a drunk through a lonely city street. Was Austin Zellmer alive and mad? Emulating an unholy religious ceremony believed by primitive Indians to give them "power?" Was Allison his blonde virgin? Did Zellmer actually believe this madness? Or could he be successfully replicating a ceremony that *actually* brought dead shamans back to life—imbued with supernatural power? How could that possibly be true? But how could it be ignored? How could a man—even a mad man—cause nine deaths in one night? What of the catatonia? There could be no rational explanation for that. Could there?

Reason seemed to have abandoned Downs' world, leaving only chaos and dread behind. His intellectual life had been dedicated to a belief in western concepts of reason. Linearity. Proportion. Causality. When he despaired of a world that produced napalm capable of sizzling flesh like a torch; or tolerated mass daily starvation of human beings with yellow, brown, black skin; or encouraged the deadly jingoism of nationality, Downs found solace in a fundamental, intrinsic belief that reason would prevail. A belief that irrationality—evil—must by definition ultimately fail.

Without reason what was there? His thoughts spun in cruel mocking elliptical swirls—and a cold metaphysical emptiness clutched at his heart.

His mind flashed on the book *Deliverance*, James Dickey's novel of senseless violence. Ordinary, decent men—men with education, good jobs, loving families—had been confronted with unreason, with evil, and had become evil themselves in response. It was Dickey's thesis that men respond this way—and Downs would always hate that idea. Now, for the first time, he understood the emotional truth—"they had no choice"—of Dickey's novel. And that truth revolted him.

What must I become? At what cost do I prevail?

Downs felt sick deep in his soul where his faith and hope now shivered like scared children. He felt Belkonsky's hand upon his shoulder—and again the old man's strength seemed to surge through him.

"You must continue," Belkonsky said.

"But I don't understand what I am reading."

"You understand, I think. But you are frightened. And you should be so. Yet there is no choice but to go on." Belkonsky reached down and grasped his hand. His eyes stared gentl at Downs. "You will not be alone. This I promise." Belkonsky offered more cactus beverage which Downs first declined. The old man insisted and again he drank the bitter liquid.

"I know that my drink can frighten, it has that side. But with understanding, it can produce great strength. And you will learn, that I now know. You have courage, though you are afraid. All brave men have fear. Those who conquer fear become stronger, braver men."

"Why are you so sure of me, when I'm not sure of myself?" Downs asked.

"I have watched you," Belkonsky chuckled, then cut himself short when he saw Downs' confusion.

"Do not worry, I am not mad," Belkonsky said with a smile. "I just thought of something my father once said to me when he was very old, even older than I am now. 'At my age, my son, I could not have helped but become at least half smart.' That is how I feel. I know, at least, some things. And one of these is that you are a good man. A man capable of understanding."

Belkonsky's vivid green eyes smiled brightly down at him once more. "Now read."

Downs bent his head and began again.

The fearful youth revealed that the two shamans who struck the pact with the Prince of Darkness lived at that moment in the sanctuary of the high temple. Each half century one was chosen from among the priests to join their heinous order. The undying now numbered seven and their arrogance grew daily as they feared no power of man.

As the youth fell silent each of us knew without speaking what must be done the next day. All our strength must be concentrated on cleaving through to the high temple to destroy its obscene occupants. Only then would these poor people be free from the centuries-old depravity to which they had been bound.

The youth's terror revealed a fateful weakness in the shaman's power. Tezcatlipoca had not told his minions of the greater power of Almighty God and of His Son, the savior

Jesus Christ. It was our crosses, not our swords, that could bring their deviltry to an end. Soon they would know the fear engendered by a wrathful God.

Before the next day's light we attacked, a party of two hundred plus Fray Hroitas, Fray Leon, and myself. Of the carnage we encountered on the way to that temple, I trust not myself to describe. At the base of the temple we met women and children, armed with nothing but sticks and stones. We offered them quarter, but as usual they refused, and we were forced, in God's name, to dispatch them to the Almighty's everlasting care. As we climbed and fought up eighty long steps nowhere did we step without encountering a body; around our feet ran rivers of blood.

At the top of the steps, in front of grotesque grinning idols, were the seven high priests. Clad in black robes covered with the insignia of the demon, unshorn locks matted thickly with the blood of their many victims, they stood before us with the arrogant power of Satan.

Then we attacked, and wave after wave of our brave warriors fell to their inhuman weapons. Finally, bronze cross in hand, I dragged my way over a mound of bodies and charged. At the sight of my cross, the priests retreated. One stumbled—the first sign of human weakness we had yet detected in this black coven—and I smote him a fierce blow with my cross. As his unholy wail rent the air, I doused his writhing frame with sacred water. Instantly the air was filled with thick, odious smoke. When it cleared—so help me God—only a contorted skeleton remained.

His six black brothers, seeing the power of the Lord, fled through a secret passage. Breathlessly, with faith that our true God would give us strength, we followed. Of those that had started out that morning, only we three priests, and a score of soldiers remained alive.

The passage led to the shore of a great lake. Before our astonished eyes, the six shamans threw themselves into the water and became great fish which swam rapidly toward the far shore.

We pursued in canoes but surely would have lost them but for their need to feed on human flesh. As darkness fell, we spotted smoke in the distance and after a torturous run of almost two leagues we interrupted their obscene feast. Two more fell to us, but at the cost of twelve of our men.

For two days and nights we pursued them continuously, hardly stopping for a bite of food or a sip of water. We lost two more to exhaustion and when the chase finally came to an end, we numbered but nine.

Night was falling when our quarry reached their sanctuary, an elaborate chamber deep within the earth, whose existence our captured youth had declared many hours before. It was at this very spot that Satan, three centuries before, had struck his bargain with the Aztecs. We soon found his awful power lingered there still.

We waited until morning for our final assault. From tree branches I fashioned rough wooden crosses for the six soldiers. I blessed them all and we three priests celebrated a last holy mass. At first light we attacked.

But the wooden crosses proved no match for the shamans' unholy power, shattering as our men's blood poured into the sand of this heathen place. Fray Leon stumbled, breaking his leg, and the monsters fell upon him. Fray Hroitas and I attacked and drove the hounds of hell back into their caves. We followed them deep into the earth down a long, precarious set of stone steps. The air was foul, filled with the stench of death. At the threshold of their unholy chamber we were forced to stop, our crosses burning like embers so we could scarcely hold them in our hands.

We retreated, unclear in our minds what to do with the little strength left us. Fray Hroitas's mind wandered in and out of this world as we prayed for hours not ten feet from the chamber's entrance. From the darkness we could see white eyes peering with awful malevolence at us, but in fear of the Lord's power they did not venture out. Finally the Savior came to me in a blinding flash and I knew what must be done.

I struggled to my feet, taking the three bronze crosses we carried, and reciting the Lord's Prayer as loudly and fervently as I could, marched to the entrance of the chamber. For a terrible moment I thought the beasts would pounce on me, but finally with inhuman cries they retreated further into the cave. I planted the bronze crosses at the entrance of the chamber; while we could not pass within, they could not pass without. Deprived of human flesh, they would surely yield to mortal decay, finally passing forever from the world of men.

When I returned to Fray Hroitas he had left this world. With great effort I struggled back toward Tenochtitlán until I was met by a search party sent for us by the conqueror Cortez. I learned with enormous relief that the capital had fallen, and that the one true church finally ruled this pagan land. At this news my failing heart rejoiced.

I now sit waiting for death as I write my last report. The ordeal upon both my body and soul has proved too great, but I shall meet my Maker with a peaceful soul. I have dispatched a crew of men to bury the entrance to that unholy chamber under tons of sand.

I can only pray for future generations that the evil knowledge that lies therein will remain untouched throughout eternity.

"Tell me what this means?" asked Downs. "What has happened?"

"You do not know? I think otherwise."

"Zellmer discovered this buried chamber?"

"Yes, of course," answered Belkonsky.

"And then what?"

"After the discovery I believe he entered the chamber and realized, whether through a scroll or writings on the wall I do not know, the awesome power of the now dead shamans. Where another man might have dismissed what he read as superstition or myth, Zellmer truly believed. Just as he believed in the literal truth of the document you have just read, though nearly everyone else dismissed it."

"Dismissed it?" asked Downs.

"Yes. Fra Diego Portilla was a religious fanatic whose

extreme bigotry and ignorance, recorded amply in his other writing, caused his last report to be universally ignored by church historians and archaeologists alike."

"Did you believe it as well?"

"Yes, from the very first."

"Why?"

"Because I believed that the Aztec civilization had some kind of preternatural power. Their monuments are too great, their astronomy too accurate, their scrolls too wise for them not to have had extraordinary power. It is simply a tragic mistake that they employed the Devil's sacrifices to attain that power."

"Why mistake?"

"There are many routes to power. It is only important that the route be a ritual which one believes can be effective. It is merely a means, and can be totally arbitrary. Like a transcendental meditation mantra. Or the elaborate rituals of the Indian sorcerer, Don Juan. The tragedy of the Aztecs is that an evil force, which some call Satan and others call Tezcatlipoca and still others feel no need to name, guided them toward power through horrible means. And those horrible means, of course, corrupted the power which resulted.

"The Aztecs had real, palpable power—this I believe with all my heart. They were surely the most advanced civilization in the history of mankind, save perhaps the ancient Hindus, in exploring what modern scientists now call "alternate modes of consciousness.' What a truly tragic thing it is that that search resulted in such barbarism."

Belkonsky's emerald eyes momentarily dimmed and Downs felt once more the deep sadness in the old man. The silence between them lengthened like the long, slow shadows growing in the evening. Finally Belkonsky spoke again.

"We have a long night ahead of us and our time is short. We must go to the mountains and find out what we must do to fight the risen priest of Tezcatlipoca."

"It is Zellmer himself then?" asked Downs.

"He is no longer Zellmer. He is a shaman of the darkness, the first of a new coven, and should he survive, the world will know great sorrow. Even now he is close to immortality."

"How do you know?"

"From what you have told me he has nearly completed his rituals. Twenty-seven will die in your town. The twenty-eighth will be a blonde virgin. At her death the Shaman will become immortal."

Horror surged into Downs' mind. With a quivering voice he asked: "When does the sacrifice of the blonde virgin take place?"

"Tomorrow. At sunset." Belkonsky stood and silently walked from the room.

Downs hesitated briefly, then followed the old man into the night. A blonde virgin. His mind would not let go of that terrible prophecy. A blonde virgin.

Chapter Fifty-six

GLOVER FREDERICKS was very much aware that nothing in his once safe, secure little world made any sense anymore.

He lit a cigarette, then picked up his third can of OB and took a long hard pull. His hand quivered. His nerves felt withered, as if physically deteriorating; after this hideous nightmare of a day he supposed, anything was possible.

The worst had been Phyllis Morton. It was impossible to imagine that pretty young woman doing anybody in—especially that way, sweet Jesus—but there simply wasn't any other possible explanation. That was the most terrible thing of all; there wasn't any getting around what happened. Glover remembered the Manson girls—pretty as pictures some of them were and they'd stabbed the shit out of all those people for no goddamned reason at all. But, Christ, they'd been sick shitheads right along, and Phyllis Morton was just as nice a person as there was in the world.

As if once more to confirm the reaity of the day's events, Glover picked up the *Utica Dispatch* which lay on his desk before him. Its headline: NINE DEAD! blared out at him obscenely. He felt the soft hair at the back of his neck stand on end like it did when one of those tinny, electric bull horns squawked with static. And he knew he was afraid.

The sheriff lifted his head from the paper, leaned forward and cradled his head in his arms. He felt reduced under the oppressive weight of the day's events. A weight he could not bear.

It was just past 5:30 P.M.—he'd been up for forty-one straight hours—and fatigue clotted him. Head in arms like a school child during rest period, he was asleep almost instantly.

At five minutes past six, a dark figure appeared beside Glover Fredericks' sleeping form.

"Sheriff," the voice called soothingly.

Immediately he was awake. "What the hell . . ."

"It will be alright, Sheriff, I promise you that."

The quality of the voice was so calm, so self-assured, that Glover could not bring himself to object to its owner's unannounced presence.

Glover looked up into the dark figure's moist, glowing eyes. His mind emptied. And soon after all pain, all doubt, all fear mercifully ceased for Sheriff Glover Fredericks.

Chapter Fifty-seven

Evening, January 1, 1983

AGAIN THE TOWN knew darkness. And fear.

That fear, now enormous, transformed shadow into bloodthirsty attacker, squeaking shutter into terrified cry, swaying tree limb into vengeful wraith.

Homes were abandoned, their owners fleeing to gather with friends and relatives so as not to be alone with wife, or husband, or child. Life's most intimate relationships could no longer be trusted.

In those homes still occupied, every electric light burned in useless defense against the newborn curse. Furtive eyes darted ceaselessly back and forth, searching the faces of neighbors and loved ones for a first sign: a blank gaze, the twitch of an eyelid, a quivering lip. In every soul a nervous energy lived, like an insistent itch. Few could sleep more than two or three hours uninterrupted. Many did not sleep at all.

The overwhelming majority of Kirkton's citizens chose to stay indoors. The night, if it ever had, did not belong to them.

Yet there were those few, who at least outwardly, would not give in to the inchoate dread; twelve people sat in lonely clusters at the Palace Theatre, Kirkton's aging movie house, and watched a rerun of *Superman;* a special evening church service presided over by a tremulous Reverend Wellborn drew nearly one hundred forty people, more than twice the average Sunday attendance; Harmony Hill, the local lover's lane, was occupied by five steamy cars; and the town's three bars, the Horseshoe, the Village Inn, and the Shamrock, were packed with young beer drinkers determinedly oozing bravado, and hard-drinking oldsters too wise to pretend they were not afraid.

At the "Shoe," Danny Herman had never seen business better. He wasn't a bit surprised. Like all bartenders, he saw people nakedly, defenses down. Tonight his customers were afraid, and when people were afraid they drank, to deaden nerves, to forget their fears—at least for a little while.

The last time he'd seen anything like this was four years

ago when there'd been rumors that the Oriskany Brewery would succumb to the economic pressures which afflicted local beer makers all across the country. The brewery employed nearly a quarter of Kirkton's men, and over half of Danny's regulars. During the week the bankruptcy rumors had been alive, Danny had brought in enough extra money to send him and Nancy to Acapulco for ten days.

But this was worse.

The drinking was ugly, almost desperate; everybody was on edge, waiting to be pushed off. Though it was only eight-thirty in the evening Danny had already broken up three fights, more than was usual in a month. The "Shoe" was neighborhood; people came in to get happily smashed, not kick ass.

Danny was worried things would get worse. He looked over at Hasty Malone, whose voice, high and artificially tight, was raised once again. The fear was really working in him.

"It's some kinda revenge plot," Hasty was saying. "And it's bein' done with drugs. Spikin' drinks, and food. With drugs."

"Bullshit," scoffed Al May, a young long-haired construction worker. "That don't make sense. Who in the hell wanted to get revenge on Sara Shubert? She's a nine-year-old kid, for chrissakes."

"Sense?" Hasty answered back angrily, "Who's talking about sense? Some psycho's loose. Got nothing to do with what's sensible and what's not."

"But even psychos got reasons for what they do. There's no plan here at all." May shook his head.

"Psychos don't have reasons, that's why they're psychos," said Hasty exasperatedly. "Jesus!"

"It's something a whole lot weirder than a psycho," the younger man said ominously, "a whole lot weirder."

"You're not gonna start this *Exorcist* shit again?" Hasty's eyes bulged with anger and Marge pulled at his arm.

"Come on Hasty, we oughta be going home," she said quietly.

"Wait a goddamn minute, Marge. Just wait a minute."

Hasty pulled his arm away from her. "I can't just let him say this shit. It'll scare people."

"It oughta scare 'em," Al May said stubbornly. "You didn't read the book, but I'll tell ya you'da been scared to death if you had. There's stuff going on in the world that nobody, absolutely nobody, understands—that's what the book's saying. And I think something like that's going on here. Some kinda evil force that gets into people's minds and makes 'em do things, sick things, that they wouldna been capable of before."

Hasty slammed his beer stein down on the bar top; it smashed in his hand and immediately he was bleeding.

"Hasty!" Marge cried.

Her husband ignored her, instead glaring at his adversary. "You're crazy!" he bellowed at May. "Sick!"

The bar was suddenly quiet, only a soft, sad Waylon Jennings tune playing in the background.

Al May stared back hard at Hasty, but said nothing.

"Come *on*," Marge said forcefully. Hasty stood up knocking his bar stool to the floor, glared once more, then turned and marched out of the "Shoe."

Marge turned to Al May. "He don't mean it," she said. "He don't; he ain't himself, that's all."

On Harmony Hill, in the back seat of his customized '57 Chevy, things were going better for Tommy Masucci. Donna Lave's blouse and bra were already off, had come off so fast, in fact, that he was amazed, and she was panting like a locomotive. The last time they'd been together he'd done something he'd never done before. And he was absolutely sure that she wanted him to do it again.

This time he was hoping she'd return the favor.

Tommy took a big hit from a joint of Colombian red he'd just bought and passed it to Donna.

She took a hit, then passed the joint back. He felt her hands on his belt buckle; soon both his pants and underwear were down at his ankles.

When she started caressing his naked thighs he quivered like a bow string. She moved up and Tommy groaned in delight. "Please," he said, "do me Donna."

She moved her head down and licked his stomach and Tommy felt like crying out loud. He put his hand under her skirt, found the elastic band of her pants, worked past it and slid a finger into her. She jumped with pleasure.

When her lips finally touched him he groaned so loud Donna pulled away. "You okay?"

"God yes! Do me."

And she did.

"What the hell is that?" Hasty said as he drove slowly past an empty field on Route 5. He was sure he'd seen some movement in the darkness.

"It wasn't anything," Marge said. She wanted only to go home.

"Yeah it was. I saw something." Hasty pulled the Impala off to the side of the road and stared into the darkness. A half moon, surrounded by a dim, cloudy circle, illuminated the snow covered field with an eerie light.

Marge was nervous. "We shouldn't be here," she said in a quivering, urgent voice. "Come on, let's go home."

Hasty was full of beer and embarrassment at backing down from the kid in the bar. "Hey, look!" he pointed toward a road sign which declared: Cozy Cabins—500 yards. Underneath the sign was a figure. As they stared the figure waved and Hasty saw that it was Glover Fredericks. The sheriff was leaning against the sign post, and looked like he was hurt.

Quickly Hasty was out of the car and wading through the snow toward the sheriff. Glover waved feebly, and Hasty knew for sure something was wrong.

But when he got up close, Hasty saw something else, a .38 caliber, police issue, in Glover's hand.

"Glove, what's going. . . ."

There wasn't time for Hasty to finish his question before a blast, like a fire cracker, shattered the night. Hasty fell straight back into the snow. He had one thought, a surprised thought: I'm dead.

Marge registered the sound of the shot. Then she saw her husband of thirty-four years fall. She saw the gun erupt again and her heart heaved in her chest. Marge shut her eyes. It couldn't be. A nightmare. Not real. She opened her eyes.

Glover Fredericks was walking slowly across the snow covered field toward the car. He was close.

Marge slid across the Impala's bench seat, sobbing in great hiccups, her heart beating a furious, chest-pounding rhythm. She twisted the ignition key and tromped the accelerator. The engine caught with a roar. Marge, in her desperation, kept her foot pressed to the floor a moment too long. The old carburator choked, then flooded. The engine died.

She yanked at the door handle, once, then a second time before it opened. She threw herself out the door. Then she was running down the salted, snowy street. Her legs were slow with fear. When she heard the gunblast it seemed far away, disconnected to her. She felt herself falling. The pain came when she slammed to the roadway. She tasted salt in her mouth. Then the fire cracker sound happened again. Margery Malone did not feel anything more.

Glover dragged Marge's body back to the car and placed her in the passenger's side of the Impala. He waded back to Hasty's body, laboriously hauled him through the field and put him behind the wheel. Then the sheriff climbed into the back, leaned his head against the seat and closed his eyes.

Fifteen minutes later his eyes popped open. They would never see again.

Donna was lying on her back, with Tommy's arms entwined around her neck, staring through the back window of the car up at the starry sky. She smiled at her boyfriend, gently tousled his curly dark hair. She'd never felt more satisfied. Doing him wasn't nearly as bad as she thought it would be. And when Tommy had done it for her again she could've cried. God but she loved it. Just thinking about it made her tingle. She smiled again.

At that moment a dark shape blocked out the stars overhead, casting a shadow across Tommy's naked back. Donna looked up and saw gleaming white eyes boring into her.

At first she wanted to scream. But the eyes were rivetting, insistent, somehow fascinating. She knew she should not look back at them. She could not stop herself. Then she did not want to scream any longer, or look away, or even wake Tommy.

Donna Lave fell gratefully into the cold depths of hell.

Chapter Fifty-eight

January 2, 1983

DAWN FOUND FIFTEEN additional Kirkton residents dead, among them Marge and Hasty Malone, and Tommy Masucci. Twelve presumed murderers were found in catatonic states.

Among the murderers was old Catfish Baker, Kirkton's only taxi driver, who had picked up a fare, Joel Weltman, a literary agent from New York, at the Utica-Rome Airport late in the afternoon on New Year's Day. Catfish's cab was found parked in the middle of the A&P parking lot, its passenger strangled, its immobile driver staring blankly, unseeing, through the windshield.

At 9:30 A.M. the Governor requested that Oneida County be declared a Federal Disaster Area; eligible for massive federal aid in the form of dollars, medical supplies, health investigators, specially trained FBI anti-terrorist squads and additional federal troops.

The President quickly agreed.

A nine P.M. curfew was imposed on Kirkton Village by Brigadier General Robert F. Leary, commanding officer of the New York State National Guard. Federal health officials, starting on Kirkton's north side, visited every house to take air and water samples. FBI agents, beginning on the south side of Kirkton, interviewed every man, woman and child.

Disease control officers from Atlanta concentrated on testing food, water and air samples in every public building in Kirkton.

National Guard troops patrolled every street, every corner, randomly stopping and spot-checking cars and pedestrians.

Volunteer medical officials from as far away as New York City and Boston began the grisly task of autopsying the twenty-seven people who had been killed in the first two days of the new year.

Volunteer psychiatrists conducted thorough tests on the twenty-one murderers, all of whom remained in deep catatonia.

The collective efforts of 3,115 soldiers, doctors, police officers, FBI agents, health investigators and other volunteers was futile.

They found nothing.

Chapter Fifty-nine

ALLISON woke and for the first time in days (weeks?) felt clear headed. Her first thought was that she had to do something, anything, to help herself.

She was still lying on her back, her hands, elbows, feet and knees bound to the metal table. Her skin was raw and bloodied where the rope had dug into her. Her muscles were so atrophied they felt like putty. Still for the first time in what seemed an impossibly long period the idea of escape flickered into her mind.

She had tried the ropes so many times before. The knots were taut and she had long ago accepted the futility of her efforts. But now she had lost so much weight there might be some slack.

Her left wrist was still tightly wrapped, but miraculously there was just the slightest freedom around her right wrist.

Slowly she rotated her right hand a quarter turn back and forth. The rope quickly raised a burn on her delicate skin which soon began to bleed. Concentrating her energy raised her body temperature and she began to sweat lightly. The perspiration and the blood formed a lubricant which allowed further movement. Now she could move her wrist almost 180 degrees. By alternately turning the wrist and pulling at the rope she thought the knot loosened just the tiniest bit.

Allison turned the wrist back and forth methodically and the blood and perspiration increased. All she needed was perhaps an inch of slack in the knot and she was sure her now emaciated wrist and hand would fit through.

A half hour into her struggle Allison pulled her wrist back as hard as she could. The knot slipped past her wrist but stuck at the foot of her hand and would go no further. The rope was slick with blood and she abandoned the back and forth motions to simply pull her hand straight back as hard as she could. The knot loosened and she felt her hand slip a bit further through. Then there was more slack, then a bit more, and finally her hand squeezed through, ripping skin off her knuckles as it came.

Allison sucked at the blood on her knuckles as she rested, pooling her strength, trying not to get too excited. She knew she was weak and there was much effort still to come. Be careful. Go slow.

She began working on the knot around her left wrist; five interminable minutes later it was off. With both hands she freed her ankles and knees. Quickly, suddenly, she was free.

She swiveled on the metal table and put her feet to the floor; she was so weak she wasn't sure she could walk. She stood, holding onto the table, then wobbled across the room and back. Gradually the tingling in her legs and arms receded. She could walk. She could escape.

The room was bare save for the table, which was bolted to the floor, and a toilet in the corner which he'd only let her use under his mirthful gaze. Up on the wall, perhaps seven feet high, was a grate. Allison walked under it, and jumped, but her body was so weakened she could barely get off the ground. The wall had no place for a foot to grip; even if she could get to the grate, she'd have to jam her fingers through its small square holes in order to hold on.

Allison stared at the wall a moment, then looked at the toilet and walked across the room. She put her hands on either side of the toilet seat and began working it back and forth with as powerful a jerking motion as she could muster. One side of screws let loose with a splintering crack and Allison stopped still. The sound seemed deafening in the room. How could he not hear?

She waited until she couldn't stand another moment, then gripped the toilet seat again and resumed her efforts. With another loud, splintering crack it came off in her hands.

Allison rested a moment, her breath coming in short, harsh gasps, fatigue pulling at her weakened body. Then she walked across the cell to the junction of the wall and floor directly beneath the grating. She set the toilet seat on its edge, leaning against the wall, curved side up. She took a deep breath, then another. With her right foot against the base of the toilet seat on the floor she lifted her left foot to the top of the curved seat. Carefully she put more weight on the top foot, spreading her hands against the damp concrete walls for support.

She was going to have to get that right foot off the floor with a fast jump, using her left foot on the tip of the toilet seat as an anchor, then make a grab for the grate. She had no idea whether it was possible.

Slowly she eased her weight upward. When the balance between her feet felt about equal, she pushed her right foot off the floor and jumped for the grate. The fingers of her right hand jammed into the grate, held for a moment as she frantically tried to grab with her left, then wrenched free. Allison fell painfully to the concrete floor, bloodying her naked back and buttocks.

But it could work!

Allison found a small plastic barrette which had fallen from her hair when they brought her in. She scraped the back of the barrette against the rough concrete of the wall, wincing at the loud sound, but stopping only when she tired. Three minutes of filing produced an edge on the back of the barrette the size of a broad screwdriver blade.

She went back to the wall, barrette in her teeth. Ten nerve-wracking minutes later Allison was hanging on the grate. Her "screwdriver" worked perfectly and in minutes she had the grate open. It led to a small, tight passageway; she wiggled in on hands and knees, then squeezed down the dank, narrow corridor, brushing cobwebs from her hair and eyes.

Perspiration poured from her body as she crawled. She saw dim light ahead of her. Inching forward she came to another grate. Without thinking about noise she kicked viciously at it with both feet. A second kick and the grate flew out and crashed into the darkness below. Allison hung on the concrete wall, feet dangling above the blackness, then dropped. She landed on her feet after a short fall. She was in another part of the basement. There was a set of stairs leading upwards. At the top was a heavy storm door and through a crack came a small stream of cold air. Hanging on a hook by the door was a pair of overalls and two old-fashioned rubber boots. She put on the overalls and boots.

A moment later she had pushed through the storm door into the night, walking then running through the deep snow away from the forboding house, her freedom an untrusted dream.

She saw a faint glimmer to her left, walked through a thin stand of pines and spotted a dim light perhaps a quarter of a mile away. Her eyes, accustomed to nothing but total darkness for over a week, felt weak and sensitive; even the moonlight reflecting off the snow seemed painfully bright.

She struggled through the deep snow toward the light, each step wooden, exhausting; her legs felt as they used to after a particularly tough workout with the school swim team: rubbery and weak. A thousand years ago. She crossed a road, continuing toward the light. As she got closer she saw that the light was overhanging a large shed. She got closer and the shed became a refreshment stand. On the side of the stand was a coinless telephone.

She punched "O", and waited. Endless silence. Finally: "Mrs. Jordache. May I help you?" Breathlessly she gave the operator her mother's number.

She heard the phone ring on the other end of the line. Once. Twice.

"Hello." Her mother's voice.

A branch snapped behind her.

Chapter Sixty

State of Puebla, Mexico
January 3, 1983

THEY LEFT Xococo at three A.M. heading north toward the Sierra Madre Oriental Mountain range and Citlaltepetl, Mexico's highest peak at 18,855 feet. After crossing the Ayoyac River on a frail metal bridge that looked to Downs as old as the desolate land around them, they started climbing steadily.

Silence enveloped them. The headlights of the vehicle seemed feeble, pitifully weak against the enormity of the vast, dark land. Downs assumed from the quiet that Belkonsky had fallen asleep, but when he glanced over, the vivid green eyes seemed to glow luminescently back at him through the Land Rover.

An hour and a half into the trip they passed the last pueblo village and their dirt road became a path. The landscape was dazzlingly austere. In the brightening dawn Downs noticed shadows occupying canyons and arroyos like primitive, patient enemies charting their every movement. From layers of softer red sandstone and pale white limestone, huge croppings of basalt towered into the sky as though in defiant challenge to the harsh, unyielding climate.

Downs felt his familiar world—the civilized world—as a barely memorable dream. An insubstantial, perhaps imaginary reality; a reality on which he could no longer depend.

Just after dawn, with the sky streaked mauve and light red but the ground still dark, Belkonsky ordered him to stop. Downs sought a level place on the steep mountain path to pull over. When he swung toward a likely spot the left side of the Land Rover dropped sickeningly as a lip of rocky trail crumbled beneath them. For a terrible, interminable moment they tilted precariously over a steep, deep ravine. The Land Rover's three grounded wheels spun futilely in the loose earth of the path, spitting gravel and loose stones. Downs gripped the vibrating steering wheel desperately. He looked down to his left and saw 2,000 feet of dark ravine below him; he did not look again. Then with a powerful thrust, as though someone had yanked them forward, the Land Rover leapt back onto the path.

Thirty feet further up the mountain Downs found a level spot of rocky ground and the big engine fell silent. He wiped his perspiring forehead and tried to slow his breathing. God, that had been close.

They waited in the Land Rover for perhaps five minutes. Then a silent campesino appeared out of the gray gloom leading three tethered burros toward them. Ten feet away he stopped and bowed to Belkonsky who smiled warmly in return. Without a word the campesino moved to Belkonsky's side and helped the old man onto the smallest burro, gestured Downs toward a second burro, then mounted the third. With a light tap at his burro's flank the campesino led them up the mountain through a narrow, dark arroyo.

Despite the cool mountain air Downs sweated continually. Where were they going? Belkonsky's silence increased his apprehension.

A coyote cried a lonely song in the distance. Somewhere above them a nighthawk screeched a protest at their intrusion. Twice Downs heard the light whoosh of rapidly beating wings—and dark shapes flashed by him down the mountain; the high cries of the bats fleeing the dawn further unnerved him.

He looked up, past the next rim of mountainous rock and saw the first blue of dawn easing into the sky. With a tight smile he greeted the light.

Belkonsky, with typical prescience, turned toward him with a reassuring smile. "Soon," he said, "very soon." He smiled again, and resumed his silence.

Slowly, awkwardly in the unsure footing, the burros continued steadily up the mountain.

An hour later they arrived in front of a small adobe hut sitting in an almost perfectly flat shelf of rock perhaps fifty yards square. The shelf looked as though it had been dug from the side of the mountain by a huge steam shovel. The flat ground was devoid of any vegetation or machinery. It reminded Downs of a monk's retreat—completely austere.

Above them the morning sky was a deepening sea blue, promising a warm, dry January day.

A tiny, wizened old man stepped from the adobe hut. He was barely five feet tall. His face was chocolate brown, covered with a profusion of deep wrinkles which ran wildly across his features like perverse tattoos. His ageless black eyes seemed without pupils, small dark ovals which revealed nothing of their owner's emotions. Despite the chill of the morning, the old man wore only a leather quilt around his midsection. Small, stringy muscles hung from his body like drooping necklaces, obedient now only to the demands of gravity. He seemed older than life itself, like an ancient hill imperceptibly eroding year after year, continually diminished, yet never conquered.

The old man beckoned them in. He bowed silently to Belkonsky who returned the greeting. Inside the adobe hut the old man seated himself cross-legged on the hard dirt floor. He was lithe and graceful despite his years.

Without speaking he picked up a three foot long red clay pipe, poured a grey-white powder into the bowl from a pouch which he closed and placed in another pouch. He lit the pipe and inhaled deeply, then handed it to Belkonsky who received it carefully, slowly brought it to his lips and also inhaled deeply. Belkonsky passed the pipe to Downs who accepted it and tentatively drew a small amount of the thick smoke into his lungs. It was hot and bitter but Downs fought down his cough. Belkonsky nodded approvingly.

Silently they repeated the process a second and third time. Suddenly a thousand little bubbles of light bloomed before Downs' eyes. The air in the room seemed to hang like drapery, and Downs felt his heart jump into his chest, though the sensation seemed far off, detached from his own body, not uncomfortable but rather a curious phenomenon to be noted. His mouth was cottony dry and he looked around the hut for water but found none.

For the first time the old man recognized his presence, holding out his hand in which a pebble rested. Downs stared at the pebble uncomprehendingly.

"Put it in your mouth," Belkonsky said. His voice seemed to come from a great distance.

With extravagant caution, as if he were handling fine bone china, Downs picked the pebble from the old man's hand. He placed the pebble on his tongue and magically his thirst diminished. Downs fought down the urge to laugh; instead he smiled and felt, though he did not actually see, the old man's eyes twinkle back at him.

Moments later the sensations from the smoke changed and Downs' smile disappeared. Blood pounded in his ears, and his pulse quickened uncomfortably. Downs closed his eyes and brilliant purple shapes outlined in vibrant orange danced before his eyelids. He snapped his eyes open and jerked around toward Belkonsky.

"You have smoked datura; it will give you fear but also strength," Belkonsky answered his unspoken question.

Downs tried to speak but could only manage a stutter.

"It will diminish, and as it eases you will be invigorated. The datura is our host's ally, his friend, and to speak with him we must share his ally. Don Carlos is a brujo, a man of knowledge."

For the first time the old man spoke. His English was simple yet evocative, spoken in a soft lilting accent.

"Fear is natural," he said, "everyone must experience her. There is nothing we can do about it. But it is far more frightening to think of a man without knowledge. How then does he combat his fears?" Don Carlos' eyes glowed into Downs, the gaze consoling, almost physically warming.

"I know you have great trouble," Don Carlos intoned softly. "I will help you to understand this trouble."

"How?" Downs managed to ask.

"Knowledge is power. Learning is the most difficult task a man can undergo. But I think you have learned much from my friend. He is one of few white men who understands."

Downs fought back his anxiety and concentrated all his faculties on listening. He felt sharper, and less afraid.

Don Carlos raised his hands above his head, then slowly let them drift down to his sides. Eyes closed, he began chanting in a rhythmic cadence. Downs felt a pleasant lassitude in his arms and legs as the melodic voice washed over him. As quickly as his fear had come, it left. Don Carlos' voice rose and fell, never breaking its perfect, beguiling rhythm. Downs felt calm and placid. When the chanting stopped Downs slowly, languorously opened his eyes; the small adobe hut was now imbued with a warm yellow haze, the effect quiet and comforting.

The silence in the room remained unbroken for five minutes. Then Belkonsky spoke.

"Is what I fear true?" he asked. "Has the great Tezcatlipoca risen?"

"You know it is so," said the brujo without rebuke, "that is why you have come to me."

"Don Carlos, we need your help. We are white men and we need your blessing to fight the dark one." Belkonsky's voice was filled with respect.

"He too is white," answered Don Carlos, "and that is very odd. It is not what I had expected."

"How must we fight him?" asked Belkonsky.

"Hatred burns inside this man who no longer is a man." Don Carlos' voice was suddenly deeper, uncracked with age, filled with passion. "Like a white-hot fire he is pure in his beliefs. A man of power. His god is the dark spirit, and that makes him as fearsome as the ocelot of the plain, as unsparing as the vulture.

"There is but one way to fight him. He is a great evil now. The power of man can oppose him no longer. But there is hope. His time has not yet fully come."

Suddenly the ancient brujo's eyes snapped wide, like the gummed eyes of a corpse springing open in the grave. Downs jerked in startled surprise.

"You are a Christian?" the brujo asked.

"Yes," answered Belkonsky.

"And you?"

"Yes," replied Downs.

"That is good. Even Tezcatlipoca fears the Christian God, though why this is I do not know." Don Carlos closed his eyes again, and his head dropped to his chest.

The brujo broke the silence only twice in the course of the next half hour, each time to chant with head raised to the sky as though importuning a great god for instruction.

Finally he opened his eyes again.

Despite his flat emotionless voice, Downs felt an enormous apprehension . . . even fear in Don Carlos.

"I will prepare you. The god Quetzalcoatl will bless you."

"Tezcatlipoca's greatest enemy in Aztec mythology," Belkonsky whispered to Downs.

"My own ally—the datura smoke—and the cross of your God will allow you to approach the risen prince. But these things cannot defeat him. Only the ancient knife of the Huactl gods can penetrate his heart and thus his immortality. Such a knife I will give you."

The brujo struggled to his feet, this time without his former grace. He tottered briefly, caught himself on a wooden table, then left the hut. Suddenly his age seemed to weigh heavily on him.

"He is giving us an Aztec ceremonial knife," Belkonsky explained, "which is over six hundred years old. I have seen it only once myself. Indian mythology says it was used to slay a Moctezuma—an Aztec king—who sullied his throne by misusing the power of the gods. Today it is a symbol of vitality for Don Carlos' tribe—it is by far his most prized possession. It is incredible that he would allow it to leave his care; and more incredible that he would allow a white man to carry it away."

Don Carlos reentered the hut carrying two pouches and a thick leather sheath.

"Hold out your arms," he ordered.

Still sitting cross-legged both Downs and Belkonsky stretched out their arms, palms up as Don Carlos indicated. The old man took a vial of red sand from one of the pouches and poured it over a thorn. He pricked the left, then the right forearms of both men. Blood ran down their arms in thin rivulets; the old man studied the pattern of the blood, then grunted in satisfaction.

"Quetzalcoatl," he intoned sonorously, "bless thy messengers in their hour of peril. Bless thy sword."

The old man, standing stiffly upright, carefully drew a stone knife out of the leather sheath, held it above his head, and chanted once more.

He turned his back to Downs and Belkonsky, the knife still raised above his head. Then in one terribly quick motion he jerked the knife down, and plunged it into his abdomen.

Downs gasped. A groan escaped Belkonsky's lips and he quickly got to his feet. The brujo turned and angrily gestured him back down. Once more with his former grace, Don Carlos settled into a cross-legged position before them.

When he spoke again there was no pain in his voice or his face. His hands, entwined around the handle of the knife, were the only recognition of its presence in the center of his body.

"It is the only way. Do not be afraid. I am an old man and now I must die. But this knife is now of my spirit." The brujo lifted one blood-speckled hand from the knife's handle and waved it impatiently as if to dismiss a forthcoming question. "There is no other way!" he said emphatically. "Datura is in one pouch," he said, "two sacred amulets in the other. Bring them to me."

Downs quickly retrieved the pouches and placed them before the brujo.

Don Carlos removed two small, blood-red stone dogs from the first pouch. Each had an odd, open-mouthed snarl, tiny white teeth, and thick negroid lips. He kissed one idol then leaned forward and looped its leather thong around Belkonsky's neck. His breath now coming in painful gasps, he repeated the process with Downs.

"You must go quickly, there is little time." Don Carlos' voice was weakening. He motioned to Belkonsky. "You must take the knife from me, my friend," his voice barely a whisper, "do not be afraid." The brujo managed a smile.

His face a grim mask, Belkonsky reached over and with two shaking hands slowly drew the knife from Don Carlos' stomach. A whisper of air escaped the ancient brujo's lips as the blade left his body.

"It is done," his voice faint, dying.

"How much time do we have?" Belkonsky asked softly, his face just a few inches from Don Carlos'.

"He rises with tonight's moon," whispered the brujo. "The virgin will be sacrificed then. If so, it will be too late."

Belkonsky reached out to grasp Don Carlos' shoulder, but the old man shook his head impatiently. "Go now. Go quickly!!"

Don Carlos laboriously stretched his legs out in front of him, then slowly lay back on the dirt floor. As his head reached the ground, a thin, dry rattle sounded in the back of his throat.

Belkonsky kneeled beside the dead brujo's body and grasped his right hand. Downs kneeled and held the left.

"Thank you, my friend," Belkonsky said softly.

They held their position for a minute, then rose and hurried from the adobe hut.

Chapter Sixty-one

BLACK, phantasmagoric shapes swooped down to skim the top of her head, sometimes brushing her breasts or thighs, then disappearing into the gloom. Fingers adorned with long, twisted yellow nails grasped angrily out at her. She could not move. She could not escape.

The phone rang. Kate woke up in a cold perspiring panic. It was 2:15 A.M. She picked up the telephone on the third ring.

"Mom," Kate's mind rejected what her ears heard. (No, it's just another nightmare. It's not her. It can't be.)

The voice spoke again, "Mom," and Kate managed to say her daughter's name. She heard a sob of joy in the background.

Then the scream came. Kate listened helplessly. A bang told her the phone had fallen from Allison's hand. She heard what sounded like snapping twigs or branches and a kind of crackling noise. She heard a soft whistle like the wind. Then a faint cry. And finally . . . silence.

Kate held onto the phone as though it were a child who had just died.

She looked up to see Will, in a bathrobe, standing in the doorway.

"I heard you . . ." he began.

"It was her," Kate whispered, "her."

"What?"

"Allison. It was Allison," she whispered again.

Chapter Sixty-two

"WE'VE HAD twenty-seven murders in this town in the last three days. I simply can't start combing every inch of Oneida County looking for your daughter. We don't even know if she's in the county at all."

Brigadier General Bob Leary was a beefy, florid-faced man with a relentlessly sunny disposition under normal conditions. But for the past three days he had been in the middle of a nightmare. He had barely slept at all during that time. The fact that this phone call from a Mrs. Whitworth came at 2:35 A.M. and had awakened him played no part in his negative reaction. There just wasn't anything he could do. Sheriff Fredericks, before he'd . . . he'd gotten sick, had told him the girl had probably been a runaway in any case.

"I know. I know that too." Leary listened patiently to the distraught woman, and thought sadly how desperate she sounded. He had a daughter himself, grown up now, and he could imagine how awful this Mrs. Whitworth must feel. "I'm sorry," he said sincerely, "I really am. But if I'd responded to every phone call I've received in the past three days I woulda needed the entire United States Army up here. I'm sorry." Leary hung up the phone. He almost wished he'd voiced his last thought: he hoped to God her daughter was a runaway, that she wasn't anywhere near this dying, God-forsaken town.

* * *

"Exactly what did you hear?" Will asked. "Let's go through it as slowly and carefully as we can."

"Okay," answered Kate. They sat at the kitchen table, steaming mugs of black coffee before them. Through the kitchen window a faint light was lifting the eastern sky. It was 3:20 A.M.

Kate concentrated her energy on Allison's phone call, trying to recreate it perfectly. There was so little to remember. The contact so brief it was as though it hadn't occurred at all.

"Could the roaring sound have been traffic?" asked Will. "That would probably mean the Thruway, the only highway in the area that might have traffic in the middle of the night."

"No, I don't think so, it was kind of steady, not like passing cars."

"How about the sound of machinery?"

"No, it wasn't mechanical at all." Kate turned to Will. "I think it was wind. The wind blowing really hard." Suddenly she was excited, she was sure it was wind she'd heard.

"Okay," said Will thoughtfully, "that probably means she was in a phone booth or at an unprotected telephone somewhere. What else did you hear?" He lit a cigarette and pulled on it hard, coughed, then pulled again.

"Something snapping. Like wood."

"Anything else?" asked Will.

"Yeah. A crackling kind of sound. Like when you're ice skating on weak ice."

"Let's make an assumption," Will said, "which we must do even if it's wrong. Let's assume that this phone call came from inside Kirkton's town limits. If it didn't we couldn't possibly check all the outside phones in Oneida County anyway. Of course, the call could've come from further away than that."

"I just feel like she was close."

"Okay, let's assume that we might be able to check out all of Kirkton's outside phones."

"How many do you think there are?" asked Kate.

"No idea, but couldn't be all that many. Especially since the phone company turns off plenty of the phones which aren't used during the winter. Like out at the golf course. And by the lake."

"And," Kate said excitedly, "we could eliminate some of the ones which are working if we could find out where they're located. I mean I know there's a phone booth on Main Street but where would the sound of snapping wood come from on Main?"

"Yeah, good point." Will dragged on his cigarette. "And I think I know where we can find out the phone booth locations."

"Where?"

"I have a close friend, college roommate in fact, who's with New York Telephone over in Syracuse." Will quickly dialed his friend.

Five minutes later he hung up. Mike Seitzinger would be at the office when it opened at nine A.M. He was sure he could get the information. He'd call immediately.

Mike Seitzinger's call came in at 9:35 A.M. There were twenty-six outdoor pay phones in Kirkton Village. Eleven were out of service for the winter. Seitzinger gave the locations of the remaining fifteen. By 9:50 Kate and Will were in Kate's Saab heading for the first phone on the list near a Getty gas station on the north side of town.

They were back at 2:15 P.M. They had found nothing.

Kate's expectations had risen so quickly that it was difficult for her to once more confront the reality of her situation; she was totally powerless again, unable to find anything further to do to help find her daughter.

Will poured a shot of Irish whiskey for them both, but the warmth of the liquid did nothing to fight the deep chill they both felt. Checking the phone booths had not only been futile thought Kate, it also was foolish. It was stupid of them to have even considered the possibility of hope.

Now the waiting would be unendurable. Impossible.

The phone rang. It was Mike Seitzinger again. Suddenly there was hope. Three more telephones; they should have been turned off, but weren't. One right outside the new county tennis courts just put in last summer. A second by the boathouse on Thrush Pond. A third on the wall of the refreshment stand next to the Little League field.

"Thanks, Seitz," said Will quickly. "Yes, we'll call you immediately." Then they were out the door.

There were no footprints anywhere near the county tennis courts.

The boathouse phone on Thrush Pond was a mass of tracked snow. Skating parties were popular among Kirkton's teens; beer bottles littered the area, but there was no wood anywhere around. What could have caused the snapping sound? There was no ice near the phone; and the snow, trampled everywhere, had no crust. What could have caused the cracking sound?

They drove to the Little League field; adrenalin shot into Kate's system like a powerful drug. She clenched her fingers around the steering wheel and drove fast.

When they reached the field, she pulled the car three quarters of the way off the narrowed road. They got out of the car and saw the tracks immediately: two sets headed toward the field, one set returning. Kate's heart pounded hard in her chest.

They waded through the deep snow to the phone. The receiver was hanging off the hook. The snow around the telephone had been disturbed. In the hollow of a footprint Will saw dark droplets shining brightly against the whiteness. He leaned down and Kate moved next to him and looked over his shoulder. The droplets were red.

Kate turned and followed the footsteps which headed

toward the road. Will was right behind her. When they reached the road he stopped her.

Will opened the trunk of the car and removed two white towels. He unwrapped one and produced a small, steel-gray pistol.

"Take this," he said.

Kate gripped the grainy butt of the gun. It was slightly oily, like she'd always imagined snake skin would be, and it felt ominous, even repulsive. She hefted the gun; it was heavy, adding to its ugliness.

"Is it loaded?" she asked.

"Yes. Eight shots."

Kate looked down at the gun like she might at an alien being.

"It's a Smith and Wesson, .32 caliber and it can kill," Will said. "You can use it, right?"

She looked at the gun once, then said to Will, "Let's go."

Will nodded and unwrapped his weapon, an old .38 caliber army issue that next to the sleek Smith and Wesson looked like a short elephant gun.

They crossed the road, picked up the single set of tracks, and continued walking. When they passed through a stand of thick spruce and pine they stopped simultaneously. A dozen droplets of blood were sprinkled in the snow before them.

Kate looked up and suddenly realized where they were. King House was in the distance.

Kate remembered being enthralled by the stories of King House which used to circulate regularly through school. The tales were always the same. A young man—a big, shambling hulk of a fellow, reputed to be a genius—had married in his teens, produced three children, and had bought the house in 1905. Seth King and his family had lived—according to all reports—seven happy, even idyllic years in the house. Then one balmy May evening Seth King butchered his lovely young wife Sarah and their three children with an axe. After he was done with the family he had drawn himself a bath, opened an artery in his leg, and bled quietly to death.

No one had ever lived in the house again. Generations of Kirkton school children drew a delicious fear from the endless stories of King House; stories which always ended with the ghost of Seth King marching resolutely through the house, beckoning children inside with sweet, seductive promises.

Kate looked through the still woods at the King House with trepidation. The house's decaying wood was a lifeless and rotting gray, the grayness seemingly transmitted to the snow and even the sky around it, giving the entire portrait an overwhelmingly sinister, evil look.

With shock Kate saw that the sun was setting. Shadows stretched across the snow and she could feel the darkness gathering quickly. A chilly winter evening wind picked up around them.

Will touched her shoulder. She nearly screamed.

"Come on," he said. "We've got to use what light we have."

Kate reached out and grasped Will's hand tightly. Together they walked toward the glowering hulk of King House.

Chapter Sixty-three

DOWNS AND BELKONSKY started back down the mountain at 6:30 A.M.; the descent was quick and they made the Land Rover by 6:55. By 7:25 they were off the mountain and back on dirt road, heading directly west from Citlaltepetl to Puebla City.

Downs drove wildly; they made the thirty-seven-mile trip to the airport in forty-three minutes. Eight minutes later a plane left for Mexico City. Downs and Belkonsky were on it.

They landed in Mexico City at 8:45. Again luck was with them. They boarded Aero Mexico flight 322 non-stop to New York's JFK airport and were in the air at 9:03.

They landed in New York at 4:02 P.M., eastern standard ime, and quickly connected to Allegheny's flight 101 for the Jtica-Rome airport.

At 4:46 they arrived at Utica-Rome Airport. They rented a ar and began the frantic twenty-five-minute drive to Kirkton.

The winter moon would rise at 6:14 P.M.

Chapter Sixty-four

HE DARK MAN stood over Allison like a pagan idol towering bove a frightened tribesman. His cold pitiless eyes were as feless as the winter night; they revealed nothing of his dead oul's monstrous secrets.

He had stopped his infernal chanting. His eyes poured into er like white molten heat, exploring her nakedness with the ad lust of a slobbering rapist. Strength now gathered in him ke a great storm rising from the ocean, building to an wesome power before finally descending on the hapless, agile land.

Soon the ultimate tribute to the Lord of Dark Waters, to e great destroyer, would be made. With that offering ould come his own immortality.

He began to prepare the girl.

The golden girl's screams were like sweet music to the aman as he ran long, cold fingers across her face, over her uivering, budding breasts, over her smooth flat stomach to er lightly downed pubis, his stroke like death itself.

The Shaman smiled down at her and his fetid breath ashed over her like raw sewage. Then his face was next to ers and she could not close her eyes, could not avoid turning his blank, deadly gaze. She felt herself sinking into m. A feeling of warmth began to subtly replace her terror. lison fought back, knowing that his black eyes meant death. e dug her fingernails into her palm, cutting his hypnotic spell with pain. As her blood flowed her resistance stiffened

But when he spoke, his voice was cool and soft, inexplica-bly inviting.

Then her fear dissipated. She welcomed this new, tende voice. Next her sense of vulnerability slid away, transforme into a sensuous desire for this awesome, steaming, desirabl man who now so lovingly pursued her.

"Soon, pretty one, very soon," he whispered, "you shal have me." His voice hung in the air like silver thread an Allison embraced its promise with all her soul.

Chapter Sixty-five

DOWNS PULLED his Mercedes into the driveway of the ol colonial house as the sun went down. It was 5:12; the moo would rise in sixty-two minutes.

The house was dark and Kate's car wasn't in the driveway Downs let himself into the house. Belkonsky stayed in th still running car. No one responded to his calls so Dowr quickly dialed Will Barrett's house. No answer. Downs fe panic pound feverishly at him. What in God's name coul they do now? He ran out of the house and back to the car.

"No one's here," he said breathlessly.

"I know." Belkonsky had been silent for hours, his fac placid, as though he were completely detached from the ma series of events that had rushed into his life. Now Belkonsky face was transformed, the eyes narrowed, lips drawn tigh the skin stretched taut over the high cheekbones and stro jaw.

"There is no time," the old man said.

"I know, but where . . ."

"Be quiet." Belkonsky's voice rung with authority. "Y must do everything I say. Get in the car!"

Downs slid into his seat. "Where are we going?" he aske

He felt bewildered and panicky; desperation gathered in his stomach.

"I know where to go," Belkonsky said grimly. "He will be there."

"But . . ."

"Go to a place called King House." Belkonsky reached out and grabbed Downs' shoulder like a claw. "Now!!"

Downs thought of King House and a shiver crawled up his spine.

He wheeled the car into the street, then pushed hard on the accelerator. The car fishtailed once, then spitting snow sped down the road.

In fifty-five minutes the winter moon would rise.

Chapter Sixty-six

ENVELOPED BY the evening's gray desolation, Kate and Will stood before the great house. Shadows, like fingers, grasped out at them from the structure. Leafless boughs scraped and moaned in the burgeoning darkness.

Powerful, evil secrets.

Kate squeezed Will's hand tightly. "God help me, I'm scared." The world seemed smothered by the snow lying silently around her, muffling all sound, all light, all life itself. Only the deep, uncertain thudding of her own heart argued against the unreality of this alien place.

She looked at Will and saw an old man; tired, exhausted, scared, but still capable of fighting.

"I love you," she said.

"And I you," Will answered softly.

They walked up the broad, rotting steps onto the wide, old porch of King House.

"Watch it," Kate cried softly, pointing to a gaping hole in the porch's planking directly in front of Will. Despite the lack of light, she was surprised he hadn't seen the gap.

He nodded mutely, stepped back, then followed Kate's tracks across the porch. The doorknob of the massive, carved oak was rusty and stained, but without dust. Will turned it slowly until he heard a click, then pulled. Locked.

They moved around the porch past the shattered remains of a swing to a set of narrow doors which led into a room that was once a study. The doors were locked but the panes of glass had long since been knocked out by those few school-boys brave enough to get within a stone's throw of the house.

Kate thought she could fit through a frame. She carefully removed shards of glass from the bottom window frame, then lay down and inched her head, then shoulders through the space. Pushing with her feet she squeezed forward, stuck briefly at the hips, then was free and in the house.

She opened the study door and Will was beside her.

The smell of King House was more than the sum of sixty years of animal droppings, mold, rotting wood, and damp plaster. Much more. A malevolent fecundity was alive in the structure, oozing pungent juices and sharp, stale sweat, as though the house was pregnant with evil, on the verge of giving foul birth.

They knew they were not alone; the feeling so palpable it was unnecessary to verbalize.

Will beamed a big four-battery flashlight around the musty room. The walls seemed to absorb the light, reflecting nothing, sucking up the bright yellow beams like a sponge.

"Over there," Kate pointed. They walked through doorway into a huge living room filled with Victorian furniture, collapsed and rotting. Faint sounds scratched at Kate's consciousness, like dim memories of childhood nightmares. A high, jagged screech . . . a brief scuttle of clawed animal feet . . . the rasping scrape of a tree limb.

She spun quickly and peered down a long, dark hallway that led into the silent depths of the house. Her heart thudded uncomfortably. When she turned back into the room Will wasn't there. Panic grabbed at her.

"Will!"

"Here," he said softly. The flashlight beamed at her from the other side of the huge room, shining a safe path for her through the heirlooms of a dead family. She walked through bright motes caught in the flashlight's beam.

Something moved behind Will. A long shadow stretched above him into the air, then plummeted down with terrible swiftness.

The shadow, a huge arm, flashed through the half light and crashed like a giant scythe into the juncture of Will's neck and shoulder. He fell like an axed tree, his scream echoing in the dark. The flashlight flew from his hand and landed on the floor.

In a swift motion Kate raised her gun and pulled the trigger. Its blast was incredibly loud and the gun kicked back at her hand like a squirming animal. The huge shadow leaped across the room at her. She fired again and heard a bestial grunt.

Then a single yellow eye was before her and a blow, sharp like an electric charge, struck her high on the chest. She was lifted off the floor and slammed backwards over a low table. She crashed to the floor and felt ribs snap like kindling wood in her chest.

Kate scrambled frantically on her hands and knees away from the figure. A savage kick smashed into her abdomen. She felt something burst deep inside her. Her fight was over.

Secrets, powerful, evil secrets. Alive.

Lying on her back she stared through the gathering shadows of unconsciousness and saw a monstrous figure above her, its red mouth agape. Warm spittle fell on her face as the giant stepped over her, his feet planted tightly on either side of her waist. Though bleeding from the neck the thing's yellow malefic eye still glinted with evil life.

The monster descended slowly, his knees on either side of her pelvis, his twisted, impossibly ugly face now a gruesome parody of desire. She screamed and the thing stuck three fingers in her mouth, twisted them around her lower teeth and jerked viciously down. Huge psychedelic flowers blossomed before her eyes and then there was nothing but white, blinding pain. The back of her head cracked against the floor.

The gun scope of her diminishing vision registered the thing straddling her, then changed focus and caught the weaving figure of Will Barrett behind the monster's shoulder. Will seemed a great distance away. To her amazement he was moving closer, then closer still. He wavered, but kept coming. His arm came into her view and she looked down the enormous barrel of a gun which bobbed like a drunken fighter.

Then there was a dazzling shatter of light and a deafening thunderclap. A huge weight was lifted from her and was thrown aside.

"Can you hear me?" Will's voice was as unreal as a distant memory. She blinked, struggling to comprehend what the voice wanted, finally understood, and raised a shaking hand which was immediately clasped.

The giant lay still beside her. She wanted to talk but her ruined jaw hung loose and useless. Weakly she motioned to Will who bent close and put his ear to her lips. Her pain was terrible, impossible, a searing that assaulted every thought forcing her into herself, leaving no room except for suffering. Darkness elbowed in at her from all sides, like a crowd pressing in closer and closer to a grisly automobile accident.

She realized that the darkness was death and fought it onslaught.

Some instinct drove a sliver of consciousness through her pain. She tried to form words with her wrecked mouth but could produce no sound. She tried again, and managed croak. It was enough.

"Allison," she said.

Will squeezed her hand and Kate felt him put his heavy winter parka over her and his mittens under her head.

"I'll find her," she heard him say.

Then his footsteps receded into the house. Then her visio

dimmed further and she could make out nothing through the quickening darkness.

Kate closed her useless eyes and a veil descended slowly in her mind, like a movie curtain after a late, last show.

Chapter Sixty-seven

THE CAR SKIDDED wildly on the snow-covered road as Downs drove frantically against the 6:14 deadline. It had begun to snow and small flakes shot through the headlights and struck the windshield like thousands of tiny machine gun bullets.

Downs peered intently into the swirling snow. Sweat beaded on his forehead. His body reacted purely on instinct; every jerk of the wheel, every stab on the accelerator pedal perfectly precise.

5:51. Kate's Saab appeared out of the half light. Downs fishtailed the car to a stop, shooting a wave of snow across the road. The hulk of King House loomed through the darkening woods. He stared at the house as if it were alive, hiding in the black night, ready to spring out and devour them in one voracious gulp.

When Belkonsky saw the house the first sharp pains flashed up his left arm. His head and upper body quivered at the pain. Stubbornly he withstood it. His heart shook dangerously, once, twice, then calmed. Only a few more minutes, that's all he wanted. He prayed for just a little more time.

Suddenly a light shone in King House, flashed wildly about, then with chilling abruptness went out. A gunshot burst out. Then another.

"Hold on," Downs shouted. He spun the Mercedes perpendicularly across the road so it was facing King House. Then he slammed down on the accelerator and they barrelled through an open space in the trees. The heavy old vehicle blasted through the deep snow like a tank, knocking down saplings, bouncing off larger trees, slowing in the deep drifts, then surging on. The engine screamed protestingly against the cloying snow which pushed back at the car; still it moved forward.

Two hundred yards from the house Downs swerved wildly to avoid a big tree. Suddenly they were plummeting down a ravine, which fell in front of them like a perfectly placed trap. Downs jammed the car into first gear in a desperate attempt to slow their fall. It did no good. The engine howled like a bloodied, terrified animal. King House disappeared when they neared the floor of the narrow, steeply walled ravine. A granite boulder loomed out of the night like a deadly, submerged iceberg. Downs ripped the wheel to the left. The Mercedes smashed sideways into the rock and flipped onto its back with a ripping crash of metal.

For a moment there was total silence in the woods, then a lick of flame, like a serpent's tongue, crackled from the car's underside, then another followed, and another, slithering and snapping like orange demons.

Belkonsky groaned. Downs worked his way over to him and helped him turn so that his rump was on the roof of the flipped car.

"Are you all right?"

Belkonsky shook his head slowly and Downs saw tears in his friend's eyes. The old man held a clenched fist over his heart and his breath came in short, labored gasps.

"Pill," he stuttered and motioned toward his satchel which had been thrown in the crash to the back seat.

Downs felt the heat of the growing fire. "We've got to get out of the car."

Belkonsky shook his head. "Pill," he rasped painfully.

Downs ignored him. They had to get out immediately. He smashed his boot through the driver's side window, then pulled Belkonsky into that side of the car. Downs let himself out of the broken window, slashing his forehead on a jagged ıard. He reached back through the window, grabbed elkonsky under the arms and pulled his frail body out of the ır. He strugged to his feet, hoisted Belkonsky into his arms ıd waded awkwardly up the steep ravine away from the car. t the lip of the incline twenty-five yards from the car and an qual distance from King House he set his friend down, ırned and half fell, half slid back down the slope to the car.

The fire was roaring above the vehicle now, flames ngeing the bare branches of a few small trees, then jumping to the lowest branches of a big spruce. Quickly the dry ne needles caught fire, and flame jumped hungrily up the ee. Downs crawled back into the car, grabbed the satchel ıd squeezed back toward the smashed window. The odor of ısoline filled the car. A drop of flame fell on his neck and he reamed. The gas tank, he knew, would go any moment.

Downs dove through the window, his neck burning ıinfully, and plunged up the hill away from the flaming car. ıen an enormous explosion shattered the night and liquid e rained around him, burning his scalp and setting his cket aflame. The blast knocked him down and he rolled ıntically in the snow to kill the flames on his body and othing. Then he was scrambling up the steep hill.

He reached Belkonsky who was groaning in agony. Downs ınd the nitroglycerin pills in the satchel and placed two of e small blue capsules in Belkonsky's open mouth.

Belkonsky's pain subsided quickly. "Time?" he asked rough clenched teeth.

"6:06."

Belkonsky knew he was dying. He wanted only a few more ınutes.

"Get the amulets," he said, "and the knife."

Downs put an amulet around his friend's neck, then other around his own. He found the small crosses, held em before Belkonsky who nodded emphatically, and put em around their necks as well.

"The powder."

Downs produced the pouch. Belkonsky reached into the

datura with a finger, drew it out carefully, then made the sig
of the cross with the powder on Downs' forehead. He mac
another cross on his own forehead.

"Cut my palm, then yours," Belkonsky said in his weake
ing voice. "Mix the blood, then cover the amulet and cro
with it."

Downs sliced his own palm, then Belkonsky's. He press
their palms together and the cuts blossomed blood whi
quickly ran together. Belkonsky gripped the cross and t
dog amulet in his palm. When he removed his hand bo
were glowing with a strange, purple iridescence.

6:10.

"I have no time," Belkonsky gasped. "If the moon has ris
before you reach the Shaman, the black ceremony will ha
begun. It will do no good to kill him then. You must use t
knife to tear his heart from his chest, then burn it. Do y
understand?"

"I understand," Downs said grimly.

"Help me up."

Together, Downs' arm firmly around Belkonsky's sho
ders, they waded desperately through the snow, climbed t
steps, and entered the terrible darkness of King House.

Chapter Sixty-eight

WILL INCHED DOWN the narrow wooden stairs wincing
every creak. Cobwebs grabbed at his hair and face w
mindless tenacity. A sticky dryness rose in the back of
throat and oozed uncomfortably into his mouth.

He swung the flashlight back and forth in short arcs hop
not to be surprised. At the bottom of the stairs he reache
dank, uneven concrete floor which spread out around h
like a vast, silent sea. He swung the flashlight through
basement, uncovering mounds of decaying furniture, he

f moldy books and newspapers, miles of cobwebs glinting
rightly in the flashlight's yellow beam hundreds of small
iles of animal feces—and a door at the far end of the
avernous basement. Small, shining eyes challenged him
ullenly from dark corners. He walked slowly toward the
oor.

He thought he heard a remote, muffled sound. Will
vaited. Nothing more. He kept moving through the dust to
he door.

A tiny, but distinct squeak sounded in the darkness and
Vill stopped. His flashlight trembled in his hand, sending a
haking beam against the door now in front of him.

It creaked and swung open.

Through the opening he saw flickering candles eerily
ghting a small square stone chamber. The candles abruptly
topped dancing and the chamber brightened. Then he saw
er.

Allison was lying naked on her back upon a metal table.
Her body was covered with grotesque painted designs. She
id not move. He called her name. She did not respond. Gun
rawn, Will moved forward. Suddenly the light spilling from
ne room was blocked out. A figure of a man magically
ppeared before him. The figure seemed to have emerged
om the spot on the concrete floor where he now stood.

The figure moved toward him. Will raised his gun and
red, then fired again and again, each retort louder and
narper as the sound ricocheted off the basement's stone
alls.

The dark figure drew back its head and laughed hideously,
sound of hellish nightmares and interminable suffering.

Then silence reclaimed the basement, broken only by
Vill's gasping, frantic breathing. He knew he couldn't have
nissed.

And suddenly Will knew it was Zellmer, though the figure
efore him was bigger and younger, rippling with glistening
usculature and a terrible, vital power. Zellmer oozed an
human putrescence which filled the air with a dead, rotten

smell. In a now distant lifetime, what stood before Wil
Barrett had been a man. No longer.

The lurid laughing rang again then quickly ceased, sur
prisingly replaced by silky words which slid smoothly fron
the figure's lips. "You have walked into the valley of death,
it began, "yet you shall fear no evil. I am thy staff, th
protector, with me you shall have eternal life."

The words continued in an unabated, seductive flow bu
their content seemed irrelevant, unimportant. Meanin
slipped further away. Now Will heard nothing but flui
cadences and soft caresses. His eyes felt comfortably heav
His body, betraying the terrible strain of the past weeks, wa
fatigued; the feeling not unpleasant, but rather loose an
relaxed as though Will had just finished making love.

He thought—or felt—for just a flash of a second th
something was wrong. That he shouldn't listen to the coo
soothing words. But it was too late; the spell too beguilin
too tempting.

Will Barrett slipped painlessly from the world of the sa
into a region of sweet unconsciousness; a land ruled by t
thirsty ravenings of an alluring God of Death.

Chapter Sixty-nine

ON THE PORCH Downs turned and looked at the fir
shimmering glow of the moon peeking through the nake
trees. It was 6:14. He gazed at the moon for a moment, the
arm around Belkonsky's waist, he entered King House.

They stood in the gloom waiting for their eyes to adjust
the dark. When Downs first heard a whimpering sound h
thought it might be a cat meowing. A second whimper and h
knew it was not.

He left Belkonsky and hurried through a doorway towa

he cry. She was on her back, unmoving, bloodied, as pale as
body in rigor mortis.

He knelt beside her, tears flooding his eyes. He put his
hand on her brow, "Kate," he said softly. Her eyelids
lickered open, struggled briefly, then closed again. He put
his hand over her heart and found only a dim, erratic
pumping.

"Downs," her voice a faint whisper. He put his ear to her
ips, and heard one word: "Downstairs." She said nothing
more.

At that moment a stair creaked behind him. A shudder
umped through his body. Another creak sounded, then
another. Downs rose to his feet, his hand gripped tightly
around Don Carlos' stone dagger.

Downs peered into the dark, saw nothing at first, then
movement. A figure formed out of the gloom and he tensed.
The figure moved toward him.

"Stop!" Downs shouted harshly, successfully controlling
his jumpy voice.

The figure moved forward.

"Stop, I said." Every nerve, every muscle tight, expectant.

Ten feet away the figure became recognizable. A thin
whistle of relief escaped Downs' lips when he saw Will
Barrett. Thank God.

The dean walked toward him in an odd, stiff-legged gait as
hough he'd been hurt. His eyes were glassy.

"Are you all right?" Downs asked quickly.

Will continued walking toward him. He did not respond. A
un hung listlessly in his hand and suddenly a realization
ashed in Downs' mind.

At that instant, in a startlingly swift motion, Will lifted the
un and fired. The bullet tore into Downs' right shoulder,
hattering the end of his clavicle. He was lifted off his feet
nd thrown backwards. He felt his head crack against the
oor, the sound sharp and close, yet the pain curiously
emote. The gun exploded again and wood splintered next to
is head.

Downs rolled to one side and a bullet smashed into th wall directly behind him. Ponderous footsteps headed towar him. Desperately he looked for escape but he was pushe into a corner, trapped. He slid behind a chair. His right ar hung loose and useless from his shattered shoulder. But h had to attack. There was no choice. He got to his feet in crouch, the footsteps now upon him. He took one shor breath then threw the chair forward into Will's feet and leap after it.

As Downs crashed into Will's knees, the gun explode over his head, the bullet whistling harmlessly past. Will wen down and the gun clattered from his hand. He scramble after it and quickly had it again. Downs picked up the ston dagger. Behind the gun he saw Will's impassive face, th eyes heavy-lidded, half open like a snake's. Downs leap toward Will, toward the gun, toward death. He heard a lou click as the firing pin hit an empty chamber. Then h plunged the stone knife into Will Barrett's chest.

The dean fell onto his back. His hand, holding the pisto wavered in the air, then dropped its burden. The empt hand remained upright for a moment, clenched once as trying to choke the air, then fell, the knuckles crackin sharply against the wooden floor.

Downs stared at the body of his friend, his breath comin in pained, ragged spurts. A thousand memories of the ma Will Barrett had been flashed in mind.

Downs struggled to his feet. He looked at his watch. 6:1 God, don't let it be over.

Then Belkonsky was at his side. "Quickly," the old ma said fiercely. They moved across the room and down th basement stairs, Downs supporting Belkonsky with his goo left arm.

At the bottom of the stairs they stopped and listene Guttural chanting poured from the walls, engulfing the da basement with a hideous cacophony of sound. Downs flash the light around the basement until it hit a door across th room. They moved toward it, supporting one another

Downs' strength ebbed with the blood flowing from his shoulder. As they approached the door, the chanting got louder. Now it was a rising scream, Baal calling forth the legions of hell.

"It's begun," cried Belkonsky. "My God, I can feel it." The old man shuddered and for the first time Downs saw fear in his eyes. Belkonsky held his arms close to his sides, fists tightened, summoning all his courage.

Behind the door the chanting had reached a feverish pitch, a deluge of inhuman shrieks that seemed to shake the entire foundation of the house with their power.

Unhesitatingly, Downs threw himself against the door, slamming his good shoulder three, four, five times against the oak beams. The door frame split on his sixth hit. He kicked viciously at the frame and it broke, the door falling forward into a chamber lit by wildly flickering candles.

A hideously painted giant of a man, knife raised above him, was poised over Allison's still body. The man jerked swiftly around to face them. He opened his mouth, revealing bloody, wolfish teeth. A venomous hiss escaped his lips. He threw his arms up, fingers spread wide, extended toward Downs and Belkonsky. A bolt of lightning flashed through the dark chamber and crashed into the wall next to Belkonsky.

The old man, eyes gleaming with hate, advanced toward the Shaman, holding the glowing amulet and the cross extended in his hand.

The Shaman howled and retreated from Allison, toward the far wall of the chamber. His red eyes burned and his jaws snapped open and shut like a cornered snake's. Still he retreated.

Belkonsky marched toward him, Downs directly behind. Their crosses and amulets glowed a brighter and brighter purple. The Shaman continued his retreat until his back was against the far wall.

"Get the girl," said Belkonsky, his eyes never leaving the Shaman.

Downs picked up Allison. Her pitifully light, almost fleshless body, was covered with a profusion of obscene designs. She was unconscious but her heart was still beating. Downs warily backed from the chamber.

As he reached the door, a huge thunderclap cracked in the room. Belkonsky wavered before the Shaman, whose arms were spread wide, fingers again extended. Downs remembered Don Carlos' last description of the Shaman: "He is a great evil now, and the power of man can no longer oppose him." Downs' fear was sudden and powerful, riveting him in the awful chamber. A second thunderclap crashed through the room and a blast of wind struck Downs in the chest like a stream of water from a fire hose. He was slammed against the near wall but kept his feet. Belkonsky was thrown to the floor.

The Shaman threw back his head and howled triumphantly. He pointed at Belkonsky and a streak of lightning flashed across the room. Belkonsky screamed in agony as hi left arm was severed at the shoulder. Blood burst from th gaping wound. Belkonsky stared at the arm lying beside him Then—impossibly—he was crawling across the chambe toward the Shaman. Downs saw fear flicker across th Shaman's inhuman face. Belkonsky brandished the do amulet and the cross before him. The glow from the object seemed to reach out and the Shaman recoiled backwards.

Then Belkonsky was on his feet. The two men faced on another in silence, like ancient enemies who had battled on another through the millenia. Then Belkonsky charge forward, stabbing the dog amulet and the cross he hel clenched in his right fist into his opponent's chest.

The Shaman shrieked, the sound unlike any Downs ha ever heard, a shriek of horror and recognition from a long dead century. Belkonsky slammed the talismen against th Shaman's face and smoke billowed around the demon as h collapsed to his knees. Wail after awful wail filled the room The stench of burning flesh rose in the air.

As Belkonsky stood over the Shaman, arm raised to delive

another blow, a violent shudder shook his body from head to foot. A look of terrible, mortal pain shot across his face, twisting his features grotesquely. Belkonsky's fingers loosened and the powerful talismen fell from his hand. The old man's head snapped back, the tendons in his neck stretched taut. He swung unsteadily on his feet but did not fall.

The Shaman jumped up and struck Belkonsky high on his forehead. He went down as though he'd been shot.

Downs threw himself at the Shaman. Halfway across the room a bolt of lightning exploding from the Shaman's fingertip like a bullet knocked him to the floor. An exultant shout followed Downs as he fell. Lying on the uneven concrete, Downs felt no pain and was surprised. He looked disinterestedly at a bone that pushed through the skin from his broken right wrist. Almost bemusedly he realized he was going to die.

The Shaman turned back to Belkonsky.

Instantly Downs realized he had been presented with his last and only chance of survival. He had to get up now. He did not know whether that was possible. Using all his fading strength, he gathered his legs slowly beneath him. He pushed his broken body to its knees. Tiny dots of white light swam before his eyes. His pain came in great waves. He closed his eyes and fought it off. He rose to his feet and knew that he had just done the most difficult thing of his life.

Downs dragged himself across the chamber to the entangled figures on the floor. He fiercely gripped the stone dagger. The Shaman's back was to him. Downs raised the ancient stone dagger with his only good arm. The pain attacked him again, bringing a moment of blackness. Then he was conscious again, standing above the Shaman. He viciously plunged the knife deep into the broad back before him.

The Shaman shrieked. Flames burst from the wound and burned Downs' hand. He pulled the knife out and struck again. Then again. Blood and flame spurted from the monster. The Shaman somehow managed to turn over. His breath was like raw sewage. He spat hot bile which scalded Downs' forearm. Downs raised the knife again. He did not look at the Shaman's face. He plunged the knife into the monster's neck and twisted it savagely until the body went still.

Downs pulled the smoking body away from Belkonsky who lay in a pool of blood. Miraculously the old man was still alive. He pulled Downs to him.

"His heart," whispered Belkonsky. "His heart or he will rise." The old man's head fell to his chest. His eyes were wide open but they would not see again. Downs looked away from his dead friend and stared at the bloodied figure at his feet.

The demon's legs trembled. Downs stared in horror as the Shaman's fingers quivered. His eyes snapped open. Downs saw a terrible power in the hellish depths of the red eyes. A smile split across the Shaman's face and, impossibly, a soft voice poured from his butchered throat.

"I am so misunderstood, my friend," the voice said sadly. "So terribly misunderstood."

Dumbly Downs shook his head no. His mind reeled. He knew he could not look again into the dark eyes. Yet he was not sure he could fight their fatal attraction.

"If only you would listen for a moment or two," the Shaman continued softly, "that is all I ask. There is great clarity in the universe if one is only willing to listen."

Downs closed his eyes and shook his head. He felt his mind clouding. The voice began again, smoothly insinuating, but Downs knew he could not listen to another word.

Downs raised the knife above him.

"My friend," the voice said beguilingly, "do not forsake me."

Downs lunged down and rammed the dagger into the Shaman's chest. Like a madman, again and again he slammed the knife into the heaving chest.

The sweet voice ceased.

Downs opened his eyes and saw a bloody mass before him. He fought back the vomit rising in his throat. He was not finished. Not yet.

Using the dagger he cut into the chest, the sharp blade cutting muscle, cartilage, and finally muscle again. Frantically he worked completely around the blackening heart, then reached into the chest with his bare hands and gripped the bloody pulp. With a great jerk he ripped the heart from its cavity, then stood with the dripping organ in his hands.

His mind was blank and empty. He saw nothing, felt nothing, heard nothing. Slowly he struggled toward the door, holding the heart in his hands, ignorant of the roaring blaze around him. By the time he reached the doorway, the chamber behind him was a wall of flame. He stood in the doorway for a second, fatigue and fire mesmerizing him. Then with a primitive cry of agony and triumph he pitched the heart into the center of the towering flames.

Downs picked up Allison and carried her up the stairs, through the house, and onto the porch. Unhesitatingly he went back into the blazing cauldron of King House; back for Kate, back for his life.

Epilogue

THE BLUE Volkswagen camper was headed west on US Route 80. It was a beautiful early June day in the Colorado mountains. Though an old Lovin' Spoonful tune boomed happily out of the tape deck, the dachshund puppy sleeping peacefully in the back of the van never stirred.

Downs looked over at Kate who smiled back at him. He noticed that the deep wrinkles in the corners of her eyes had started to recede. She was tan and had let her dark hair go naturally curly. Her shapely legs were stretched out in front of her, resting on the top of the dashboard.

"You're a foxy lady. You aware of that?" Downs asked.

"Yes, I am aware of that," she answered with a twinkle.

"I figured you knew."

"Pretty obvious, right?" Kate said with a laugh.

"Listen, I have an idea," he said.

"I won't eat another bowl of chili. Forget it," she answered.

"Why don't we get married?"

She smiled full at him. "When?"

"Oh, today, let's say."

"Okay," Kate said. "Good idea."

The blue Volkswagen pulled onto the shoulder of Route 80 in a swirling cloud of dust. Downs slid across the bench seat and kissed Kate long and thirstily.

"You guys are gonna corrupt me," Allison sang from the back seat. "I *mean* it now. No fooling around." She skipped through the camper to the front seat and put her arms around Kate and Downs.

The three of them held each other for a long time.

And it was good.

Author's Note

I LIVED with *The Shaman* for two years (at the end his breath was rank and he'd been hitting the Mezcal) and during much of that period there seemed ample cause for concern over the state of my mental health. To paraphrase Woody Allen, I often felt at a terrible crossroads: one path leading to despair and utter hopelessness, the other to total extinction.

The following people provided succor of various sorts during *The Shaman's* gestation time, thus allowing the battle between the novel and myself to be waged for yet another day. In addition to helping me, they also tolerated me. It couldn't have been easy.

Most of all I wish to thank my literary agent, Jay Acton, for his confidence in me, his kind words in time of crisis, his oft opened wallet, and his deft editorial judgment. Jay torpedoed *The Shaman* when I originally thought it had reached port. I hated him for it, and planned fiendishly clever revenge against him and his loved ones. When I sobered up I realized he was right. Thank goodness.

I'd also like to thank Tom Biracree, with whom this book was born and conceptualized, for his editorial suggestions and his friendship.

When I reached a crucial impasse in *The Shaman's* evolution (Or should I say devolution? Reader you be the judge.) Rodman Philbrick buried deep into the manuscript and pointed the way home. His editorial contributions are deeply appreciated. Tom Nassisi read the final manuscript and spent hours correcting all manner of error, to him my sincere thanks. And thanks also to Rich Nassisi for his typing of the manuscript.

My long-time friends Ted Baker and John Palmer provided valuable support in times of need—thanks sincerely to you both.

And finally I'd like to thank my mother, Marion MacRury Coffey, for her unstinting love.